STILTSKIN

Andrew Buckley

A Division of **Whampa, LLC**
P.O. Box 2540
Dulles, VA 20101
Tel/Fax: 800-998-2509
http://curiosityquills.com

© 2013 Andrew Buckley
http://www.planetkibi.com

ISBN 978-1-62007-394-0 (ebook)
ISBN 978-1-62007-395-7 (paperback)
ISBN 978-1-62007-396-4 (hardcover)

WHAT CELEBRITIES ARE SAYING
ABOUT *STILTSKIN*!

"An epic fantasy tale that tickled my nether regions and warmed my heart."
—Academy Award Winning Actor, Sir Anthony Hopkins

"This book changed my life, I may never lick another sledgehammer again. Who am I kidding? Of course I will!"
—Recording Artist, Miley Cyrus

"What are you doing here? Get out of my house! I'm calling the police!"
—Award winning novelist and screenwriter of 'The Princess Bride',
William Goldman

"Much better than that boy wizard stuff that I wrote a few years back."
—Author of the Harry Potter Series, J. K. Rowling

"Now that Breaking Bad is over I look forward to playing Rumpelstiltskin in the movie adaptation of Stiltskin."
—Emmy Award Winning Actor, Bryan Cranston

"Buckley takes fairy tales and throws them in a blender, the result is tasty."
—Indie Film Director, Kevin Smith

"I took time away from adopting children and making movies to read Stiltskin by Andrew Buckley. It was a delight!"
—Academy Award Winning Actress, Angelina Jolie

"As a rockstar I found it easy to relate to Stiltskin as I too live in a fantastical world full of strange and unusual characters."
—Recording Artist and Lead Singer of Maroon 5, Adam Levine

"In 40 years someone will release a book called Stiltskin. It'll be mildly amusing but nowhere near as good as Lord of the Rings."
—Quoted in 1973 by Author, J. R. R. Tolkien

*Note from the Author: While all above reviews are completely fictional, I'm completely comfortable if you choose to believe they're real —AB

TABLE OF CONTENTS

For anyone who loves a good classic fairy tale…
this book probably isn't for you.

THE WORLD OF THISLE

PROLOGUE

Darkness lay restlessly across the land, crept up the walls of the tall Tower, and sneaked through the cold, shadow-clad cells of the inmates. Mist swirled down from the distant hills and settled upon the surrounding water.

The tall Tower prison that held so many guests loomed against a rain-swept sky. Lightning flashed. The moon glanced from behind dark clouds as Jack made his way across the stone bridge, which spanned the vast moat around the tower, with long purposeful strides. He ignored the shrill scream from somewhere high above; after all, this wasn't his first trip to this land or this prison. No surprises waited for him here, or so he told himself. No one remembered the real name of the prison or even who built it; the inhabitants and all who knew and feared it referred to it simply as *the Tower*.

The Tower consisted of a large, perfectly square building with tiny, rectangular, barred windows, and a high tower protruding from the top. The stone bridge spanned the length of the moat for almost a mile, and was the only way in or out of the Tower.

Jack stopped for a moment, lost in thought, then approached the side of the bridge. The rain bounced off the cobblestones and soaked him to the skin. His black suit and tie, which looked out of place in such a medieval setting, clung to his muscular body.

Jack's reason for looking into the lake was the ripples in the water. The creatures that lived beneath the dark surface were restless. The underwater guardians normally slept unless a prisoner stepped on the bridge, but tonight, the creatures stirred regardless. The unease Jack felt at being summoned here showed in his bright blue eyes.

Another half-hour passed before Jack reached the Tower side of the long bridge and stood before the one and only prison guard.

The three-foot-nothing Troll with speckled, dirt-brown skin, a shiny bald head, beaked nose, and black, dull eyes stared up at Jack and drooled on himself with an exemplary amount of skill.

"Troll," nodded Jack.

"Glarrblleeft," drooled the Troll.

"I understand one of the prisoners has some information. I don't like being here so let's get this over with, shall we?"

The Troll's voice sounded like someone had wrapped him in sandpaper and rolled him across wet gravel. Tiny rows of sharp teeth infested the inside of the crescent-shaped mouth when he spoke.

"He wants ta speak ta you pacifically." The Troll's drawl and accent had always irritated Jack, almost as much as the stubby little creature's appearance.

"Well, I'm here, aren't I? Let's go," said Jack as he stepped around the Troll and through the Tower's iron gates.

The Tower held the worst of the criminals from Thiside. Originally, guards were posted throughout the Tower; however, as the inmates were never allowed to leave their cells, and any that escaped the Tower would be killed by the moat creatures, guards became pointless. They became bored; most took up playing cards, which quickly turned to gambling, which turned into fighting, and finally, a great deal of head chopping. The guards were disbanded, those who still had heads, and one inmate in particular, a particularly small and ugly looking troll, who had constantly demonstrated good behavior, was placed in charge of guarding the Tower. His job was to make sure no inmates ever left their cells, and that they received a plate of greenish brown substance to eat every day. Theoretically, he was still a prisoner and any attempt to cross the bridge would be met with the utmost joy by the moat creatures.

Jack hurried through the courtyard within the Tower grounds; he didn't want to stay here any longer than he had to. The Troll shuffled along, his butt dragging lithely along the ground.

"Did he say what kind of information he has?" asked Jack.

"Dunno, screamed un shouted but ah dint tek no notice fer a while. Screamin ain't not usual ere. Aftur a week sorta figured he wuz serias."

They passed through another large gate that placed them directly under the Tower itself. A seemingly endless spiral staircase started its ascent to the left. Ahead and to the right were long stone corridors lit by hanging torches hung intermittently and with little care. Thick, dark wooden doors lined the corridor walls. Small barred windows were cut into each of the doors. Screams and shouts, growls and snarls bounced around the corridors. The same shrill scream resounded high above from the tower.

"Ome sweat ome," drooled the Troll.

"I hate this place," said Jack.

They headed down the right-hand corridor. Sunken eyes stared out through the tiny windows. Some shouted, some spit, and some whistled: female and male voices and in some cases, animal. Obscenities flew like seagulls over a garbage dump.

"They jus appy ta see ya, Jack," chortled the Troll.

The pair stopped at the last door. A pale, skeleton-skinny face with deep, sunken eyes of the lightest brown stared out of the tiny window. The man's lips were thin and blood red. His brown hair hung in greasy strands across his face, and he grinned the grin of a man who should be locked in a cell. The irony of the situation wasn't lost on anyone.

The Troll walked back up and down the corridor telling the inmates to *shrrup* and *knock er off* until what could only be described as semi-silence drifted through the Tower.

Jack leaned against the stone doorframe. The pale man's tiny pupils followed Jack's eyes. Jack steeled his nerves against such stares; it was what he was used to. He looked around the corridor at nothing in particular. Some things had to be played carefully.

"Nice night tonight, isn't it, Hatter?" said Jack as he turned to meet the man's eyes.

Lightning was generally an atmospheric discharge of electricity that typically occurred during a storm. In the world that Jack currently occupied, lightning occurred whenever it damn well felt like it, especially during ominous moments such as now.

Lightning flashed across the sky.

The Mad Hatter stared at Jack and grinned a maniacal grin.

"I want my hat, Jack, my head's cold without it. Do me a favor and run and get my hat, Jack." The Hatter's sing-songy voice rang around the corridor like a deranged children's storyteller.

"You called me here, Hatter. You said you had information. Important, life-threatening information. Now, are you going to waste my time with games or do you want to get to the point?"

"The point, ahh yess, the point, the point of the pen or the sword. They're both mighty, you know. You never come to my tea parties anymore, Jack, why is that?"

Jack turned to leave.

"Wait! The Dwarf is afoot!" The Hatter's pale spindly fingers gripped the small bars with such ferocity and he pushed his mouth as far through the little opening as possible.

Jack turned back. "You're going to have to be more specific than that," said Jack, "I can think of seven I know well. Which dwarf?"

"The evil one, which one would I be talking about you idiot? The evil one! The magic one, the biting, spitting, treacherous one, the tricky one. You know, you know!"

"If we're both talking about the same evil Dwarf, then we both know that you're lying because he's a resident here in the East wing. Which means you dragged me here to this cursed place for no good bloody reason!"

"You don't believe, Jack, that's your problem. Too much time in the Othaside is rotting your brain. Check the cell! Check the cell and then bring me my hat, dammit! I miss the mouse, I really do. That damn cat."

Jack eyed Hatter up and down for just a moment. He'd known the Hatter for centuries and his fall into madness had gone on for what seemed like an eternity. He was mad, no doubt, and Jack had been there when the madness turned psychotic. Once, he was amusingly mad and had entertained in the finest courts for royalty and the highest of society. And then it all fell apart. Jack didn't like the Hatter. But he knew something else about him, too. The Hatter didn't lie.

"Check the cell," Jack barked at the Troll.

"Ee's not gone anywhere. I woulda noticed."

"Check the damn cell!"

The Troll padded off down the corridor with a waddle that would make a goose blush. Jack turned back to the Hatter.

"Do you remember why I put you here Hatter? All those years ago?"

The Hatter grinned and tipped his head to the side. "You ruined my tea party."

"Try again."

"You let that infernal cat eat the mouse."

"Do you remember the woman?"

"I remember, you took my hat. The rabbit ran, the mouse was eaten, and you brought me here."

"I did. But I often wonder if you remember why," said Jack.

The same shrill scream that Jack heard earlier sounded again from above. Hatter looked up at the ceiling and frowned.

"The witch is restless. She knows."

"C'mon, Hatter, you remember, I know you do."

"Why is what, and when is where. If only I had my hat. We could have a tea party again, Jack." Sincerity and calm crept into the Hatter's voice. "But I suspect you're going to be far too busy from here on out."

"Eee's gone! The Dwarf, eee's nor in is cell," yelled the Troll as he ran back down the hallway. This wasn't entirely inaccurate as Trolls never ran; the legs moved, there was breathing and drooling and they made it from one place to another just a little quicker than when they were walking.

"That's impossible. No one gets in or out; the moat creatures would've taken him."

"His cell's still locked up n solid, no oles I can see, nothing. E jus vanished."

Jack thrust an arm through the narrow opening of the Hatter's cell door and grabbed a handful of his grubby shirt and pulled him against the door.

"How the hell did you know he got out? Where did he go? How did he do it?"

The Hatter scrabbled skinny limbs against the door, to no avail.

"Questions, so many questions, my dear Jack." The madness so apparent in his voice before was now gone. Instead, in its place, a smooth, cold, void of a voice remained, dark and menacing.

Jack pulled the Hatter's shirt and slammed him against the interior of the door. "No games, Hatter. What's going on?"

"Let go of me, fetch me my hat, and let's talk."

Jack's answer was simple. He slammed him into the door again.

"All right, all right," said the Hatter, "or we could talk now. The Dwarf got out; he's gone looking for something. He's looking to cross over to Othaside. He wants only to finish what he started."

"He can't cross over, he doesn't…"

"He has the power to do so if he has reason to use it. He doesn't even need the White Rabbit's help."

"Who would give him reason?" Jack breathed hard.

The Hatter glanced over his own shoulder at the wall behind him. "We share a wall."

The grin that cracked the Hatter's face was worse than maniacal; it was satisfied. Jack slammed him into the door twice. Blood began to trickle down the Hatter's face.

"Time's short, Jack, he'll be over by now, it wouldn't take long, so you'd best run. If I tell you where he's going, you might stop him in time. But of course, what do I know? I'm mad."

"Where is he going?"

The Hatter laughed a cold laugh. "To pay a visit to my blood."

Jack dropped the Hatter in a heap in his cell and turned to the Troll. "Search the Dwarf's cell; I want to know how they've been talking."

Jack stalked off down the hallway ignoring the shouts and screams as the inmates broke into a frenzy.

"The Dwarf's free!"

"What happened? Someone got out?"

"The Dwarf, the Dwarf!"

"*Rowr!*"

"He owes me money!"

"Where's your cow now, Jack?"

"Guess his name, guess his name!"

"Run, Jack, run!" screamed the Hatter.

The voices faded behind him as Jack crossed the courtyard and all but ran through the gate back into the rain. He pulled out a small black rock the size of a golf ball, held it to his lips, and whispered the word, "Veszico."

The rock became fluid and unfolded itself; tiny black wings unwrapped and shook themselves as the Fairy got to its feet. The miniature shape of a woman with dark hair and eyes of pure black blinked at Jack.

Jack spoke to the little creature with urgency. "Veszico, I need you to find Lily and the others. Tell them the Dwarf has got out and he's going for the Mad Hatter's son. We don't have a reason yet. It's going to take me a while to find a door. Tell Lily to find the son and tell everyone else that the Dwarf, Rumpelstiltskin, has escaped! Go now."

Veszico gave a little nod, twitched her wings, and a bright blue light emanated from her as she rose from Jack's hand. The faster her wings beat, the brighter she shone until she was a floating ball of light. She took off like a bullet in the direction of the bridge and was soon lost from sight.

Jack broke into a run across the long bridge away from the Tower. The rain blew against him, somewhere high above a scream was lost on the wind, and on either side of him the moat creatures stirred and writhed beneath the tempestuous waters.

In his cell, the Hatter sat leaning against the wall licking the blood that dripped from his forehead to his lips. The Hatter giggled, then laughed, then chortled, then guffawed; he tittered, he snickered, and he chuckled, and then screamed at nothing. High above the Tower, lightning splintered across the sky.

CHAPTER ONE

ROBERT DARKLY

Robert Darkly was miserable. And not just miserable; he was really miserable. His right pant leg was soaked up to his crotch, which was fast becoming uncomfortable and this only added to his miserable state. The rain poured in London's East End, which caused puddles that large vehicles simply couldn't resist driving through, hence the soggy pant leg. Some would ask what the problem was as Robert had already walked three blocks in the rain without an umbrella and was already suitably soaked.

The reason Robert had no umbrella was because he had left it at work. The main problem there was that Robert no longer had a job due to a recent incident that involved Robert and his boss and a stern firing. His umbrella, which had been given to him by his adoptive mother as a twenty-seventh birthday gift, was one of the things he'd forgotten to grab on his way out as his brain grappled with what had just happened.

"Come in here, please, Robert," his boss had asked and Robert had obeyed.

"Yes, sir?"

"Sit down, Robert," said his boss and Robert obeyed.

"You're fired."

"Sorry?"

"No use apologizing now, what's done is done."

"I'm fired?"

"Reiterating the fact is going to do nothing for you. Clean out your desk and get out."

"But this is so sudden. The company is doing well; I thought my work was excellent. Well, not excellent but not that bad, anyway," explained Robert.

"Don't get me wrong, Robert, we think the world of you, you're a top notch accountant, excellent with numbers. Time for you to go, though, I'm afraid."

"I don't understand."

His boss laughed. "You and me both, my friend, makes no sense to me either."

"Then why am I being fired?"

"It was the strangest thing. We had our usual managers meeting this morning and your name came up. We all thought you were doing a fantastic job and we were all impressed at how you handled that Jenkins file."

"I'm so confused."

"We had our coffee and then we made the unanimous decision to let you go."

"Unanimous?"

"Unanimous! Strangest thing, like I said. But we hope you'll be very happy with whatever it is you end up doing."

And with that the phone rang, the boss answered it and waved Robert, who was still fairly dazed, out of his office.

Robert staggered out into the sea of cubicles that constituted the accounting monolith of Chikum Finance. Several heads peered up over their cubicles and stared at Robert, who was replaying the conversation over in his mind.

"All right there, Robby?" said Martin.

Martin was one of the few people at Chikum Finance that Robert could actually stand. Or at least tolerate for small amounts of time. This was despite the fact that Martin's eyes were situated far too closely together.

"Yeah," replied Robert.

"Oh. They told you, eh? Thought they might've waited 'til later in the week."

"You knew?"

"Well, yeah, mate. It was a big secret, ya know, so obviously everyone around here knew about it."

Robert glanced at the sea of cubicles and most of the heads bobbed back down below their fabric-encased walls. "Well, that's just great, isn't it?"

"Uh… is it?"

"No, it's bloody not," said Robert and stalked off out of the building, completely forgetting to take his umbrella with him. An hour later, he found himself standing on the corner of a street he didn't recognize soaked to his skin and getting constantly wetter. Every few minutes, a bus would drive through one of the various, well placed puddles and splash him. He didn't care. He was miserable.

He decided to head west. He lived in the West End of the city in a small leaky apartment with ancient fixtures and high rent. His landlady was a turbulent old bat named Gertrude who never removed the rollers from her hair because she believed it would ruin the curl. Robert didn't feel like seeing Gertrude right now, but he did feel like going home and taking a bath.

Baths always relaxed him; as far back as he could remember it was his favorite thing to do, and if anything had even the remotest chance of curbing his misery it was a nice hot, relaxing bath. The one thing Robert's apartment had going for it, and the primary reason that he took the place, was the antique bathtub. It was beautiful white porcelain with a high hanging shower head, clawed feet, and a set of taps that would make members of the *Antiques Road Show* wet themselves. Yes. A bath would be a good idea.

A double decker whooshed by and drenched Robert.

Miserable.

He turned and headed west, nearly knocking over a pretty young girl with auburn hair and the kind of face that wasn't pretty, wasn't ugly, but lived in that special place in between the two. By the simple act of almost bumping into her and noticing her hair colour, he was immediately made even more miserable. Sarah had auburn hair. Sarah didn't live in that special place in between pretty and ugly, she lived very much to the North of pretty, over the mountains and far away. She was gorgeous. And up until last night, she had been Robert's on again, off again girlfriend. This time it was off for good. In the past, they had fallen out for whatever reason, usually ridiculous stuff. Robert would forget to take out the trash and Sarah would get angry. That easy mistake would turn into World War Three and they would break up, only to get back together again the following day realizing they were just fighting over something petty. This time, she had no good reason. The breakup was over nothing. She'd just called it quits. Robert spent the day heartbroken. Sarah had gone to Paris to shop for the day. The two of them had never really balanced in the way a healthy couple should.

Sarah was petite, with long, flowing, auburn hair and greenish-grey eyes. Robert was tall, almost lanky, with messy brown hair and an awkwardly chiselled face. Sarah had graduated from Oxford and majored in Psychology. Robert had attended the University of Manchester where he barely scraped together enough credits to graduate with a degree in accounting. Sarah liked animals and had always kept a cat as a pet. Robert was allergic to cats; they brought him out in a rash. Sarah was funny and social and captured the attention of everyone in any room she walked into. Robert was ignored in a corner like a stained piece of carpet that's hidden by placing the TV stand over it. Sarah had a family that could be traced back generations without the slightest hint of divorce. Robert's adoptive parents separated when he was six years old, and he had tried several times unsuccessfully to find his real parents who apparently didn't exist anywhere in the entire world. Sarah exercised. Robert didn't. Up until last night, Robert had truly believed that opposites attract. Now he believed that it was all a matter of perspective.

Sarah had come over to his apartment and stood in his doorway looking beautiful. Robert thought that the doorway probably felt very lucky to have someone so beautiful standing in it. She had looked Robert in the eye with barely any emotion and told him point-blank, "Robert, I'm leaving you." Her voice was silken smooth and had the ability to make penguins melt.

"What?" asked Robert from his recliner. Robert's voice made penguins tilt their heads in a questioning motion.

"I'm leaving you, Robert. I have to, I'm afraid. I'm so sorry," she said.

"But why?" asked Robert and dropped his potato chips.

"To be honest, I'm not sure. It's just something that has to be done. I'm sure one day it'll make sense to both of us." And with that, she walked out of his life.

Stupidly annoying nonsensical things like this had happened to Robert all his life. At the age of ten, they had irritated him but now he was thirty-three it just seemed common. When he turned five, every single toy in his room had vanished. His adoptive parents were furious but at the same time couldn't figure out how a five-year-old could make all those toys disappear. Robert didn't know either, he'd just woken up and they were gone.

When he was thirteen, an overdeveloped twelve-year-old girl had bullied Robert to the point where he was on the edge of insanity. One day while bullying him, for no reason at all, her hair fell out. Robert had been accused of shaving her head and promptly punished. At sixteen, he had passed his graduating math exam with flying colours. Later that same day, he was expelled for no apparent reason. At the ages of three, seven, twelve, eighteen, twenty-two, twenty-six, and thirty-one, he had fallen asleep only to wake up somewhere else entirely. One time he woke up and found he was locked in the Tower of London. Another time he woke up at Stonehenge. And another time he'd woken up in his elementary school teacher's flower garden. While attending university in Manchester he had maintained a three-hour conversation with a friendly German Shepherd who had told him why dogs sniffed each other's rear ends. None of it made sense. And what had worried Robert the most was that it never scared him, never seemed strange to him, and worst of all it had since stopped concerning him to the point where he just accepted it.

Robert hailed a cab and finally got out of the rain. After spending thirty minutes in the hell that was London traffic he entered the front door of his apartment building and squelched his way up the ancient staircase, leaving sopping wet footprints as he went.

"Darkly!" screeched Gertrude, whose voice sounded like a nasally version of nails on a chalkboard. Gertrude stood at the top of the stairs wearing a flowery nightgown over faded jeans. The rollers in her hair looked like they could be removed only by utilizing some serious power tools. "Look what you're doing to my floors with your dampness, why you're dripping wet, what are you dripping wet for, Darkly?"

"Hello, Gertrude. Sorry about that. Having a bad day."

"You think you're having a bad day? The damn TV service isn't working, I've missed three shows already this morning. And now I find you making a mess in my hallway."

"Sorry, Gertrude. I just want to get upstairs. It's been a really bad day."

"I hope you know the rent is due tomorrow, Darkly? You were two days late last month. You should borrow some money from that lady friend of yours if you're coming up short. Nice girl, that, very pretty. Not sure what she wants with the likes of you but there you go."

The sound of a game show drifted from Gertrude's open door.

"Oh, the telly's back on!" she exclaimed and shuffled back into her room, slamming the door behind her.

Robert had never put much stock in game shows but today he thanked his lucky stars that at the very least, one thing had gone right today. He continued upstairs and unlocked his door.

He checked for messages on the answering machine and discovered that exactly what he expected was true. No one wanted to talk to him. He walked into his once white bathroom, which over time had started turning a funny yellow color, and turned on his bath. He turned the taps to get the temperature just right and stuck in the plug. He took off his soggy clothes and dumped them in his laundry basket. He wandered, naked, into his kitchen and turned on the kettle. *There's nothing like a good cup of tea after a hot bath.* He looked through a stack of smutty literature sitting on his coffee table and finally selected one of Sarah's old celebrity gossip magazines. He heard a *sploosh* somewhere close by and figured he must have water in his ears from all the rain.

He looked at the cover of the magazine to see a couple of pretty actors had just adopted their seventh child from a poor country, making them the nicest people alive. He pushed open the bathroom door and then a variety of things happened which would change Robert's life forever.

First of all, there was a fully clothed Dwarf holding a large knife sitting in the over-flowing bathtub. Secondly, Robert realized he himself was naked. And thirdly, the Dwarf was looking at him with a pair of the darkest eyes he'd ever seen. Chills ran laps up and down his spine.

"You must be Robert Darkly," said the Dwarf.

Robert promptly screamed like a girl and slammed the bathroom door.

CHAPTER TWO

10 MINUTES AGO...

Rumpelstiltskin cackled incessantly as he ran along the riverbank putting further miles between himself and the Tower. He couldn't help himself. Sixty years to the day he'd been trapped in the Tower, and finally he was free. Free to do exactly what he wanted. Free to trick and cheat and cause trouble. And more importantly, he could finish what he started. Getting out of the Tower was the easy part; the deal he'd struck with the Mad Hatter guaranteed he'd get past the lake guards and through any doorway to Othaside. All he had to do was find one. He remembered it being easier; he remembered doors being everywhere. That was sixty years ago and a lot of things can change in sixty years.

The Dwarf stopped and looked over at the edge of the river. In the water's reflection, he could see clearly that he'd aged in those years. He counted the wrinkles around his eyes and could see that there was definitely one more than was present sixty years ago. Dwarves in Thiside aged at a literal snail's pace.

Rumpelstiltskin was a typical Dwarf, standing a little under four feet tall with a crooked oversized Goblin-like nose, small, black, beady eyes, and scruffy grey hair. He still wore the rags that he wore in the Tower and a peaked hat that drooped down his back.

He pulled the knife out of his belt and watched as the rising sun reflected off the metal. The boy who was fishing never heard Rumpelstiltskin, never saw the evil little man sneak up behind him, and was completely ignorant about what the hell was going on when the Dwarf strangled the boy with his own fishing line. He just wanted the boy's knife.

Rumpelstiltskin snickered. He had a plan and it was about damn time he put it into action. He had to deliver the message he promised and fulfil his end of the deal with the Hatter. Then he had other things to do, other people to find. All he had to do was find a door and, in line with the terms of his deal, it would take him exactly where he needed to be.

The little Dwarf danced in a circle, gleeful at his own maniacal brilliance. Order and peace had been kept for so long in Thiside and Othaside and it was about time that order was upset. Those damn do-gooders were going to pay for locking him up. The Hatter could do whatever he wanted but Rumpelstiltskin had his own agenda, and as much as he wanted to revel in his freedom, he had to get moving.

He took off at a run down the riverbank, keeping a lookout for what he needed. And then it caught his eye; off to his left in the middle of some dense shrubbery. The light in the middle of the shrubbery was fractured, as if there was a small tear in the very fabric of reality. The gash wasn't very big but the distortion was crystal clear. Doors healed themselves and never appeared in the same spot twice. This particular gash in the reality of Thiside was only two feet in length, meaning it was almost closed. Soon it would vanish, and somewhere else another door would open.

Rumpelstiltskin gripped his knife tightly and stepped up to the door. Anyone could climb through a door, good or evil, big or small. Doors always went somewhere; most of the time they went to another door in Thiside unless the traveller had secured a passport from the White Rabbit allowing said traveller to pass from the world of Thiside to the world of Othaside. Rumpelstiltskin had no such passport but it didn't matter. The wish that the Hatter had made bypassed that rule. He had wished that Rumpelstiltskin would deliver a message to his son. It was as simple as that. All Rumpelstiltskin had to do now was climb through and he'd be in Othaside.

He grabbed the inside edge of the door with one hand and hauled himself up. His feet dangled for a second as he pulled himself through. The light glow from within flashed once and the door closed up, leaving no indication that there ever was any door or any deranged evil Dwarf anywhere in the vicinity.

Travelling through a door felt like someone sticking a large hand up the traveller's rear end and tickling the intestines. It was awkward and uncomfortable. Climbing into a doorway was easy. Coming out on the other end was always difficult as the traveller could never tell where it came out or where the door was positioned at that exact moment. In the case of the door that Rumpelstiltskin exited, it was placed perfectly over the top of an antique bathtub located in the apartment of Robert Darkly in London's West End. Rumpelstiltskin fell unceremoniously out of the doorway and splashed into a very full and warm bathtub. He gripped his knife and seethed quietly at his misfortune and waited patiently for the annoying tingling sensation in his stomach to subside.

Several seconds later, a naked man came through the bathroom door and froze, looking surprised and slightly scared to see a Dwarf sitting in his bathtub.

Rumpelstiltskin looked into the man's eyes and recognized exactly who the man was.

"You must be Robert Darkly," said Rumpelstiltskin.

Robert Darkly promptly screamed like a girl and slammed the door.

Rumpelstiltskin snickered and hauled himself out of the bathtub.

In the Northern Territories of Thiside, in the quiet countryside just East of the Beast's Castle, as the sun crested the mountain peaks and the shadows fled for cover, a world-shaking occurrence suddenly occurred.

The tiny dirt road that everyone knew as Drury Lane had been in existence since before the Castle was built, before the Beast took residency, or even before the Northern Territories had been named. The lane had always played host to one small cottage, and well before the sun decided it was time to rise, a small plume of smoke could be seen billowing from its chimney. The Muffin Man awoke at 3:00 a.m. every day to begin his work. He shaved, showered, dressed, kissed his sleeping wife, and fired up the ovens. It had been this way for over three hundred years and wasn't likely to change anytime soon. The Muffin Man provided baked goods all over the Northern Territories. People would travel from as far as the City of Oz to sample his vanilla iced bread fingers.

Today was no different from yesterday and yesterday struck a startling resemblance to the day before that. At 7:00 a.m., the Muffin Man pulled out his last batch of dinner rolls and left them to cool. The sunlight now streamed in through an open window and a light breeze rustled the leaves on the oak tree in the garden. He looked at the old clock on the wall; another half hour would bring his delivery men and women to pick up the bundles of baked goods that would be taken away over the hills and far, far away.

The Muffin Man looked out over the landscape and felt thankful for the life he was leading; a simple baker without a care in the world. It was at that exact moment that reality turned itself inside out. Everything happened in a split second, which was much like a regular second, only shorter: the mountains that could be seen through the Muffin Man's window volcanically erupted one by one, spraying molten lava high into the sky; clouds appeared from nothingness high in the sky; and the worst ever unrecorded snowstorm in history flashed into existence, blowing sleet and rain through the cottage's open window. The Muffin Man shielded himself with a cookie tray. The snowstorm froze the molten lava in mid-eruption, the result of which formed giant statues of ducks performing ballet at the peak of each mountaintop. The sun spontaneously fell out of the sky, throwing the world into immediate darkness.

It was moments like these that the normal human reaction was to run for cover. The Muffin Man couldn't help but watch from his now snow-covered kitchen. The moon flew up from behind the mountains and exploded in a shower of sparks that threw fluorescent light, much like the annoying kind found in hospitals, across the landscape and briefly silhouetted a perfectly-normal-yet-not-at-all creature off in the distance. The Muffin Man squinted at the creature but was instantly distracted as the mountains with the duck statues flipped themselves upside down while the snow-covered trees sprouted legs and ran around in circles, the Earth shook, and fire shot across the sky. A nine-thousand-pound rhinoceros blinked into existence and raced across the landscape, unaware of his real purpose in life but running felt good so he figured that was a start. Lightning cracked across the ground and it began to rain upward; gravity realigned itself and the Muffin Man found himself stuck to his ceiling. His head felt like it was about to split open as the pressure of the universe centered itself across the valley he called home, and with a small squeak, it all stopped.

The Muffin Man fell to the floor as gravity returned to its normal state; the sun reappeared exactly where it was supposed to be. The duck statues were gone, the mountains were the right way up, the snow had vanished, the trees were rooted once again, and even his kitchen was exactly as it had been. The only telltale sign of the last few moments was the nine-thousand-pound rhino that was happily charging up the valley away from the Muffin Man's house.

The simple baker knew the silhouette of the creature he'd seen momentarily during the cataclysm. He also knew of only one creature in existence that could have caused what just happened but it was impossible. Everyone in Thiside knew that the Cat was dead.

CHAPTER THREE

LILY

airies came in all shapes and sizes. Well, not really sizes; they were all basically the same size, around about six inches in height. In Thiside, Fairies fell into three different classes: the Good, the Bad, and the Simplistics. The Simplistic ones lived in the Northern Territory Forests and kept to themselves. They stuck to simple life principles, which included eating, sleeping, and sex. It should be noted that Fairy sex was not like regular sex but involved a lot of wing flapping, humming, and high kicking. It was actually quite disturbing to witness, so much so that a self-help group was formed in the Eastern quarter of the City of Oz to help explain just what witnesses of such an event had actually seen.

The Simplistics spent most of their lives living out the three prime principles and stayed hidden away in the forests because it was safer. When any Simplistics ventured into the cities, they often died, not because of any murderess intentions against Fairies but rather from the simple fact that they lacked the brainpower to avoid glass windows and many ended up flying into especially clean windows and breaking their neck. Hence the rarely used phrase, "As dumb as a Simplistic Fairy in a city."

The Bad Fairies lived in the Grimm Mountains in the East and spent their days fighting with each other, forming small gangs, and stealing from anyone who dared follow the mountain paths.

The Good Fairies lived in the Southeast quarter of the City of Oz and worked with the Wizards of Oz to herd magic in the right direction.

Veszico was an outcast Fairy. She was the result of a very unusual meeting between a member of the Good Fairies and a member of the Bad Fairies. It should probably be pointed out at this time that Fairies lacked gender in much the same way that a brick lacks a sense of humour. They were either male or female, but tended to be both or neither. The different sects of Fairies never socialized but back in the days before the Agents, before the Tower was built, and when only one wizard occupied Oz, a meeting referred to as a Sumthin was held every year in the Emerald City. The purpose of the meeting was to find out how everyone was getting on with their lives, an update on the situation with the doors, to ask questions like *is the Beast still angry?* and *what happened to the dragons?* or *where the hell do all the Gnomes keep vanishing to?* The meeting consisted of various races ranging from Fairies, Humanimals, and Goblins, to Giants, talking animals, Dwarves, and, of course, humans. It was at this meeting that a Good Fairy who had partaken in one too many thimblefuls of beer fell victim to the libido of a Bad Fairy.

Veszico was the product of that one night, and due to her mixed blood, she was an outcast. The shame of being an outcast had given Veszico an anger management problem and some violent tendencies, which almost landed her in the Tower. One day she'd thrown an Inquisitor of the third order into the River Ozmus but not before stripping him naked and painting him blue. Just as she was about to be sentenced, the Agency interceded and hired her, which is why she now found herself sitting in Lily's pocket as she knocked on an apartment door in Othaside.

Robert blocked the bathroom door closed with a golf club. It had occurred to him at the time that it was strange he even owned a golf club as he couldn't play golf, had never tried playing the game, and anytime he saw it on TV it made him want to kick himself in the groin in order to get away from the boredom that the game conveyed. However, he was happy that he owned one, as it secured the bathroom door rather effectively, trapping the evil-looking Dwarf inside.

There was a knock at his apartment door. Robert looked from his bathroom door to his front door and back again, and then he looked at his right hand where he was brandishing a frying pan as a weapon, and then noticed in the mirror that he was still naked. Answering the front door didn't really seem to be at the top of his to-do list at the moment.

"Open the door, Darkly," said the voice from behind the bathroom door.

"Er… w-what are you doing in my bathtub?" stammered Robert, tightening his grip on his non-stick frying pan.

There was another knock at the front door, but this time it carried a hint of urgency, and more than a touch of impatience.

"Why don't you open the door and we can talk about it," said the Dwarf and snickered.

"Like hell I'm opening the door, you've got a knife!"

"I can put it down if you like?" answered the Dwarf.

Robert thought about this for a moment. *Nope, he's not going to put it down.*

"Forget it!" he shouted, a little louder than he intended.

Another knock at the front door, this time with a dramatically increased sense of urgency and a boatload of impatience splashed with a smidgen of *open the bloody door!* And then a female voice followed the knock; it was smooth yet strong and independent.

"Robert Darkly, my name is Lily, I'm from the Agency. It'd be best if you opened the door."

Robert was getting close to losing his grip, and not just on the frying pan. The weight of the day's events coupled with his brooding over Sarah and then finding an evil-looking Dwarf in his bathtub, well, it was all too much.

"What Agency? What are you talking about?"

Robert was almost certain that he heard a sigh from behind the front door that spoke volumes. If those volumes could be turned into words, it would have sounded very much like, "I wish this idiot would open the door so I can get on with my day and why the heck does he sound like he's naked?"

"Look, if you just open the door I can explain everything," said Lily.

"Don't listen to her," said the Dwarf, "if you just open this door I'll—err," and the Dwarf hesitated, "explain everything. I'll even put the knife down, can't get a better deal than that."

"Uhh," said Robert, "okay, you outside the front door, do you have a knife and are you a Dwarf?"

There was that sigh again.

"No, I'm not a Dwarf and not carrying a knife," said Lily.

"Will you please stop sighing, it's not making me feel any calmer," said Robert and then to the Dwarf, "Forget it, Dwarf, she doesn't have a knife, therefore she sounds a hell of a lot safer than you."

Rumpelstiltskin was drying himself with a towel. He hadn't expected the Agency to catch up so quickly. *What the hell is the Mad Hatter up to?* This made things very difficult. The Dwarf tried opening the door again but to no avail.

"I have a message for you, Darkly; it's from your father, your real father. He says he would like to see you. There you go, that's it, that's all I'm here for. Simple, eh?"

Images of the Tower loomed at him from corners of his memory. *I need a way out! I've got bigger fish to fry.*

"My... my father?" said Robert, "How do you know my father?"

Rumpelstiltskin's tricky little mind worked feverishly and then the answer hit him like a wet herring. "I bet you've always wished to see your parents, haven't you, Darkly? I bet you've wished for a lot of things; you should wish for something now, maybe it'll come true."

Robert was unnerved; any talk of his real parents had always unnerved him and he'd never really understood why.

"Who are you talking to?" asked Lily.

"There's an evil Dwarf in my bathroom," said Robert with resignation and then to the Dwarf, "I just wish you weren't in my bathroom."

"Granted," said the Dwarf as Robert's front door was kicked open and a beautiful young woman with dark-coloured eyes, jet-black hair, and dressed in a black pants suit walked through his door. Robert was suddenly acutely aware that he was standing naked in his living room holding a frying pan as if he intended to do some sort of damage with it.

Lily rolled her eyes. Male stupidity was just as apparent in Othaside as it was in Thiside and probably everywhere else in the universe.

"Get the door, Veszico," said Lily.

Veszico floated up out of her pocket and flew like a bullet at the bathroom door, blowing it into a million shards of wood upon contact.

Rumpelstiltskin was gone.

"Damn it!" exclaimed Lily. "Put the frying pan down, you idiot."

"Not a chance, lady."

"And put some pants on, that's entirely more skin than anyone has a right to see upon a first meeting," said Lily as Veszico buzzed around Robert's head.

Robert mustered that tiny part of his soul that bore the closest resemblance to courage and swung the frying pan at Veszico. Had Robert known anything about Veszico, this simple act of attempted violence never would have crossed his mind.

The Fairy's normal blue glow turned a fierce and vibrant red; she snatched the frying pan out of his hand and swung it full circle to smash into the side of his head.

Robert's head was not conditioned to being hit with hard objects and his brain decided that this was a good time to become unconscious. He fell backward into his coffee table, smashing it into several small pieces.

"Nice swing, but not really why we came here. Find Jack and tell him I've found Darkly but the Dwarf is gone. He'll still be here in Othaside, probably looking for a passport so he can get back. Tell Jack I'll meet him at the Exchange and tell him I'm bringing Robert Darkly with me."

Veszico shook her head and pointed angrily at the unconscious naked man.

"I know, Veszico, but he's involved somehow and we need to know how."

Veszico *hmphed*, turned a light greyish kind of color, and flew out of the window, instantly blending in with the dark clouds.

"All right, Robert Darkly, son of a madman, time to wake up."

Sad irony existed throughout the Universe. Ironically, the fact that it was sad didn't stop it from being amusing to outside observers. This was the case with the North London Association of Khuzdophobia Sufferers. Khuzdophobia was a term made popular firstly by the online gaming community and secondly by the North London Association of

Khuzdophobia Sufferers. Khuzdophobia was the completely non-medical, non-sanctioned, un-technical term that described someone who had a fear of Dwarves.

As with any popular term that isn't completely real, it immediately garnered a great many followers, hence the formation of the North London Association of Khuzdophobia Sufferers, otherwise known as N-LAKS. Its two hundred and seventy-one international members crossed every demographic known to man. Only twelve of the members actually lived in North London and those individuals met on a sort of weekly basis for group therapy, which consisted of lots of group hugging, stories of close encounters of the Dwarf kind, how to embrace your fear of short people, and so on and so forth. The group rented an assembly hall at a local elementary school that smelled like dust and the sweat of seven-year-olds.

At about the same time that Robert made his wish, Jasper Clementine, the self-appointed lead therapist, was standing in the middle of the group encouraging everyone to admit their fears and discuss their phobia openly.

"All right, everyone, let's come to order," said Jasper enthusiastically, and then as an afterthought, "let's try and leave the tea and cookies until the end of the session, shall we?"

The group shuffled their chairs closer into the circle around Jasper. Jonathan, who was about to help himself to a chocolate chip cookie, backed away from the refreshments and quickly took his seat as Jasper continued.

"I realize it's been a few weeks since we all met together and I know we all have stories to share, but I'd like to start with Doris. She had quite the ordeal last week while up visiting her sister. Doris?"

Doris was four hundred pounds wearing a strapless, flower-print dress and uncomfortable shoes. That is not to say that the shoes were uncomfortable for her to wear, but rather, the shoes felt uncomfortable having a four-hundred-pound woman standing on them. She leaned forward on the folding chair, which complained to no one in particular.

"Well, I went to see my sister ya see, up in Birmingham, nice place is Birmingham, not really known for its short folk. Anyway, my sister, Alice is her name, says she has a surprise for me and that I should get dressed up, and I don't really like to get dressed up because I prefer to be comfortable, but as it's my sister and we don't see each other much, I thought it'd be nice. Anyway, she ended up taking me to the circus."

31

Shocked gasps arose from the group and one twitchy gentleman named Ralph who never said a word and emanated the smell of six-week-old dirty socks shuddered ever so slightly.

Doris nodded in unspoken agreement.

"Well, she didn't know, did she?" said Doris.

"People should know better," piped up Jerry, a thirty-something grocery store clerk who moonlighted as a completely ineffective contract killer.

Ralph shuddered in agreement.

"Now, now," said Jasper, "It's not for us to judge people who don't understand our affliction. Please continue, Doris."

"Well, I didn't want to insult my sister, she'd got us very nice seats down by the elephants and there's always the chance that there wouldn't be any small people. Everything was going fine, the strong man was very impressive, huge muscles, very tight clothing, got me quite flustered for a while. I like tight clothing on a man, you know, and my Barry, well he's not much to look at, skinny as a rake actually and—"

"Let's try and stick to the point, Doris," reminded Jasper.

"Oh, yes, sorry. Anyway, everything was going fine until the clowns came on and there they were; three of them dressed up as miniature lion tamers. Midgets. I couldn't help myself, I let out a scream that upset the elephants and they took off charging across the circus tent. I bolted from the circus screaming."

Bolted may not have been the correct term as Doris was unable actually to bolt anywhere. What really happened involved Doris ploughing through the crowd in much the same way a large ice-breaking ship ploughs through ice. Children scattered in her wake, adults trampled other adults underfoot, and one small dog named Bitsy was forever mentally and emotionally scarred for life.

"I couldn't leave my bedroom for three days!" finished Doris with a flourish, followed by a sad pout.

"Aww," said the group.

Ralph shuddered.

"That is quite the situation," said Jasper, shaking his head. "Now there are a couple of different ways to look at this. Should Doris have reacted so strongly knowing she was indeed at a circus, which we all know is the second most common place to find a small person? We all saw the news and we know that several people had to be taken to the hospital after the incident, and then there was that poor little dog that's probably scarred for life. We must learn to deal with these encounters in a calm and collected man—"

Time momentarily froze. The molecules of Rumpelstiltskin swirled into immediate existence and reformed themselves into the evil little Dwarf holding a large knife. When Robert made his wish, Rumpelstiltskin was able to grant it and therefore immediately vanished from the bathroom, and of course once something disappeared, it must reappear. Rumpelstiltskin knew it was risky, as he could have ended up anywhere, in Robert's living room, for example, or back in Thiside, or in Bermuda. But, as it turned out, the Universe was not without a cruel sense of humour.

Time un-froze.

"—ner," finished Jasper. The group gasped a horrified gasp. Jasper looked down to see an evil-looking Dwarf staring up at him. The Dwarf was dressed in medieval clothing and held a large knife in one hand. The Dwarf snickered an evil snicker. Jasper screamed with an intensity that had only been achieved once before by an Italian opera singer who, during a standing room only performance, had hit such a high note it shattered the spleen of an elderly man sitting in the front row.

As a whole, the entire group fled the building ahead of Doris who was making her best attempt to bolt.

CHAPTER FOUR

THE EXCHANGE

The electrical impulses to Robert's brain began firing again, all the while spurred on by the not so gentle slaps to the face by the female standing over him. His ears also switched from blurred noise to, "C'mon, wake up! You're still naked and it's starting to disturb me."

Robert pulled himself up into a sitting position.

"You can stop slapping me now, I'm awake."

"Oh, right," said Lily.

Robert pulled a blue fluffy blanket from the couch and covered himself appropriately.

"You need to get dressed," said Lily. "We really have to get moving before he gets too far away."

"Look, it's been a really weird and disappointing day and all I want is a bath and several hours' sleep. If there's any chance of you just leaving and taking your glowing insect with you, that'd be great."

"Don't you care that a Dwarf randomly appeared in your bathtub talking about your father about whom you have absolutely no knowledge?"

"I'm used to weird things happening to me, really, it's nothing new. If he comes back, I can call you."

"Or how about the fact you just got knocked out by a Fairy?"

"Well, yes, that was strange," admitted Robert, "but honestly, I just want to be left alone."

Lily's anger was starting to get the better of her, the heat rising to her face as she spoke. "It's a hard thing to explain all in one shot so I'm not even going to try but you have to come with me. Dwarves don't show up in people's bathtubs just for the hell of it so you need to get some clothes on and come with me."

"Thanks but I'll pass."

"I can start slapping you again, if you like?"

Robert's shoulders sagged dejectedly. "I'll go get dressed."

Against its better judgment, the rain had become a light drizzle and the sky grew darker as Robert Darkly, dressed in jeans and a sweater, stepped out of his apartment building with Lily close behind.

"So where are you taking me?" asked Robert.

"We need to go to the Exchange. It's the first place the Dwarf will head, and maybe we'll get lucky and arrive there before he does. We'll need to get you a passport while we're there, too."

"Ya know, it's bizarre but I understood maybe ten percent of what you just said," replied Robert.

"You're an accountant, aren't you?"

"Well, yes, but…"

"Only accountants speak in percentages."

"In my defence, I'm not a very good accountant."

Lily crossed the street and Robert obediently followed.

"We're going to need a cab."

"Why don't we just take your car?" asked Robert.

"Don't know how to drive." Lily stopped at the corner and whistled for a cab parked across the street.

Robert looked at Lily, really for the first time since he put on some clothes. *It's amazing, the way perception shifts from when you're wearing clothes as opposed to being stark naked and getting hit with your own frying pan.* When Lily had kicked open his door she had been, well, beautiful. Now as she stood in the pouring rain she looked like the most beautiful and strange thing he'd ever seen. Her hair had seemed black at first but now he could see streaks of auburn, and her eyes had been dark brown but in the natural light outside they seemed almost amber and twinkled ominously. She was at least a foot shorter than Robert was, but if someone was to look at the pair they would instantly recognize who was in charge, and it wasn't Robert.

Possibly the strangest thing about Lily was the way that the rain didn't seem to touch her. Robert's sweater was already covered with a thin sheen of classic London rain. London rain was the sort of water that even if someone found themselves stranded in the middle of the Sahara Desert on the hottest day of the year with no clothes and a sunburn with their camel lying dead next to them, even then they wouldn't even consider drinking it for fear of illness and instantaneous diarrhea.

Lily was almost completely dry. It wasn't that the rain wasn't falling on her but rather it chose to ignore her completely.

"Stop staring at me, it's creepy," said Lily suddenly and fixed him with those amber eyes.

Yes, definitely amber. "Sorry, it's just… how come you aren't wet?"

The cab pulled up and Lily opened the door.

"Your world doesn't believe I exist," she said with such a matter of fact tone as if to convey her answer should explain everything.

"Right, then," said Robert agreeably and got into the cab.

The Royal Exchange had existed in one form or another since the mid-sixteenth century and was still considered to be the hub of London commerce, although where once it was used for trading, it now stood as more of a mall for rich people. The current Royal Exchange building was built in 1844 and sported some lovely columns that gave it a somewhat Roman feel, as if an escaped lion from the Coliseum could suddenly pounce from its doors at any moment.

In 2001, it was remodelled to accommodate the sale of some of the finest and most prestigious brands in the world, including Gucci and Tiffany, not to mention a restaurant and a coffee shop.

Patrons of the Exchange, located on the corner of Cornhill and Threadneedle Streets, didn't notice as a small figure dressed in a long waxed jacket, recently stolen from a now emotionally and mentally incapacitated member of the North London Association of Khuzdophobia Sufferers, made his way past the entrance and headed down the side of the building on Cornhill Street. He walked around the right-hand back corner of the Exchange and stopped in front of a large, old, wooden door that had been painted red.

The door didn't look like it should have been a part of the Exchange, and at closer inspection, the doorway itself looked like it had been carved away by hundreds of rabbits scratching at it. This was, of course, entirely inaccurate as there had been only ninety-three rabbits.

He knocked on the door three times and stepped back. The sound of ancient bolts being unbolted could be heard, followed by rusted hinges protesting as the large door swung open to reveal a crudely carved staircase. Only ninety-two rabbits had the opportunity to work on the stairway, as Floopsie, as he had been affectionately known by his friends, had been crushed in a tragic accident earlier in the day. Thankfully, Thiside Rabbits were notoriously unemotional and the accident didn't halt construction in the slightest.

It appeared that the door had opened of its own accord. The staircase was lit by light bulbs hanging from the ceiling with bits of chain. Rumpelstiltskin entered and began down the stairs as the door swung itself shut behind him.

Unbeknownst to the tourists and London residents milling around the Exchange, the lower regions of the building were untouched by time, ignored by everyone for hundreds of years. The last resident of Othaside to fall upon the Lower Exchange was Sir Thomas Gresham in 1565, the original architect of the building.

After the Royal Exchange was complete, Sir Thomas spent many hours inspecting every facet of the structure. During the last several months of construction the doorway was built, the red door moved into place, and the Lower Exchange had been excavated. Thiside magic ensured the doorway would never be noticed by any Othaside resident, but as it turned out, Sir Thomas happened upon the door before the magic could fully take effect.

He couldn't open the door, as it only opened for the right people, with the right knock. He'd berated the construction council for the eyesore and horrible workmanship that had been put into the door and questioned why it had been built in the first place, as it could not be found anywhere in the plans. He dragged the lead foreman at the time around the back to show him the door, by which time the magic was in full effect and Sir Thomas was told he'd been working too hard and should go home, have a nice bath, and maybe a strong nightcap.

As Rumpelstiltskin descended, he went over his plan that was nestled in the tiny inner workings of his devious little mind. It all stemmed from his frustration, of course: limitless power within his little Dwarf body but a complete inability to do anything with it unless someone made a wish. His original plan was reaching the pinnacle when those damn Agents threw him in the Tower. But now he'd have his revenge; all he needed was the key. He cackled and the noise bounced around the stairwell as the dim light from the bulbs skittered shadows hither and thither.

He reached the bottom of the stairs that opened up into an antechamber. The little room contained nothing but a small table with a thick, black, leather-bound book and a writing quill. The wall directly facing the stairs didn't have the same look as the rest of the tunnel. Rather than looking like the antechamber, which definitely looked as if it had been tunnelled out by ninety-two rabbits, the adjacent wall looked smooth, with a silvery quality to it so that when looked at from the right angle it seemed to shimmer slightly, and at a second glance, it just looked like a regular wall.

The Dwarf flipped open the leather-bound book and took up the quill. He jabbed the point of the quill into his hand, drawing blood, and then, with the utmost calligraphic skill, wrote his name in the book. The name faded away into the page as if it had never been written.

The shimmer in the wall rippled, giving it a liquid-like quality. Rumpelstiltskin licked his bleeding hand and cast off his disguise. He walked up to the wall and placed the palm of his hand up against it. There was a sucking sound, much like a five-year-old makes when he's trying to get the last bit of milkshake through a straw. And with that, the Dwarf was sucked into the wall. For a while there was nothing but silence, but there then followed a screeching sound that only rabbits can make when they're extremely excited or extremely distressed. The reason for the screeching in this instance was the latter.

Rupert was the name of the taxi driver who was haphazardly driving Lily and Robert in the general direction of the Royal Exchange building. The taxi smelled faintly of hotel soap which, as Rupert enjoyed explaining at length, was due to his hobby of collecting different kinds of soap that he stole from hotels around England. Rupert's interjection was making normal conversation difficult but the day was hardly turning out normal.

"Back there at your apartment you seemed not to care what was going on. Doesn't it bother you that there was a Dwarf in your bathtub? That a Fairy knocked you unconscious? Aren't you even curious about where we're going?" asked Lily impatiently.

"Of course I'm curious but weird things have always happened to me; I suppose they just don't make the same impact that they used to," explained Robert.

"You see, it's not just the smell of the soap that's appealing, there's also texture, the amount of oil they contain, the class of hotel, there's a lot of things to take into consideration," explained Rupert.

"Look," said Lily, "for argument's sake can you at least appear to be concerned?"

"Fair enough. How about you start with telling me who you are?"

"No," said Lily.

"Okay then, how about explaining what that Dwarf said about my father?"

"No."

"How about you just tell me what you'd like me to ask you? It might speed up the conversation."

"The funny thing about hotel soaps," explained Rupert, "is that a lot of them are switching to that liquid stuff. I don't stand for that kind of thing myself."

Lily sighed. "You can ask me about the Agency."

"All right, what's this Agency all about?"

"The Agency was formed hundreds of years ago for the sole purpose of policing the border between Thiside and Othaside."

Robert's right eyebrow rose of its own accord. "This side of what?"

"What?"

"You said this side and the other side. What sides are we talking about?"

"Ya see," carried on Rupert, "it's a security measure so that people can't steal the soap, no one wants to steal liquid soap. It really takes the fun out of it all."

"There is no side, it's the name of the realities," explained Lily.

"So there are two realities?"

"Yes. Thiside and Othaside."

"So this reality is Thiside?"

"Other way around, this is Othaside."

"Of course nothing can beat those little seaside resorts up in Blackpool, they have custom made soaps in their very own little boxes."

"Will you shut up!" said Lily. "We don't care about your bloody soaps."

"I was just trying to make polite conversation," said Rupert.

"Well, make it with someone else. Look, Robert, it's all very simple, I'm part of an Agency that makes sure no one from Othaside goes to Thiside and that the residents of Thiside don't cause any trouble in Othaside."

Robert stared at her blankly in much the same way that cats stare at pretty much everything. "What does any of this have to do with me?"

"I'll leave that for Jack to explain; he's going to meet us at the Exchange."

"Okay, so what's the Exchange all about?"

"We're here," said Rupert in a sulky voice.

"I'll explain once we're inside."

"The Royal Exchange?" said Robert as they stepped out onto the soggy sidewalk. "What are we going to do, shop for shoes?"

"No, we're here for blood."

Lily led Robert down the right-hand side of the large building.

"What do you mean, blood?"

"The two realities have always been separate but thousands of years ago there were doors, like a hole in reality, and they were everywhere so residents of both sides could cross over whenever they liked. This caused more problems than you could ever imagine. Some people simply fell through the doors by accident, others abused the fact that they could skip between two worlds. It caused a great deal of chaos. Ever heard of the Dark Ages?"

"Of course."

"That whole time period came about because of the doors. In the end, the Four Witches and the Wizards of Oz banded together to create a Regulator for the doors. One being who could control the passage of anyone between Thiside and Othaside. Now all the doors in Othaside are hidden unless you're carrying a passport. The Wizards did that to protect your world. The central office for the Regulator was built into the basement of the exchange in 1844. Now if you want a passport to cross between the two worlds, this is where you come."

"Did you just say the wizards of Oz?" asked Robert.

"Shush, we're here," said Lily.

Lily and Robert reached the doorway at the back of the Exchange and Lily knocked three times. The door swung open and the pair entered.

"It smells like rabbit droppings in here," said Robert.

"They're actually very clean creatures once you get to know them."

They walked down the stairs into the antechamber. Lily took up the quill pen, jabbed herself in the back of her hand and scrawled her name in the leather-bound book. She held the quill out to Robert.

"Your turn."

"My turn to what? I'm not jabbing myself with a pointy feather."

"You need to sign your name so we can enter the Exchange."

"I'm pretty sure I have a pen here somewhere."

"Doesn't work, the ledger needs your blood to let you through the wall."

Robert started backing up against the wall as Lily advanced with the feather. "Look, I appreciate everything you've told me, it's all very interesting and practically believable, probably more so after a few drinks, but you know I just don't think I'm cut out for all this. I like living on this side. I mean Othaside. Whatever the hell side this is. I'm happy with it."

"Aren't you curious?"

"You keep asking me that but you refuse to tell me anything!"

"It'll be so much easier to explain all of this once we're in Thiside but we can't waste any more time. The Dwarf may have come and gone already."

"Forget it, I'm not jabbing myself with that thing."

"Fine." Lily turned to walk back to the table with the ledger but quickly spun around and lashed out with the quill, cutting Robert across his cheek, instantly drawing blood.

"What the hell?"

She quickly wrote Robert's name in the ledger and placed the quill back in its place.

Robert held a hand over his cheek.

"It's just a scratch, Robert. Don't be a baby."

"What now? Why does everything feel different down here? I feel misplaced and yet right at home."

"The Exchange is the only place on the entire planet that exists in your world and mine. Think of it as a border crossing."

"So it's here in Othaside but also in Thiside? And who the hell named these places?"

"Maybe you should calm down, count to ten?"

"Do you have any idea how confusing this all is?"

"Look, you're getting a little frantic."

"Frantic!" Robert's voice notched up an octave. "Who's getting frantic? I lost my girlfriend last night, lost my job this morning, was almost attacked by a Dwarf in my bathtub, was knocked out by a Fairy, dragged across town by you who won't tell me anything other than there's two worlds with ridiculous names, you attack me with a feather—"

Lily slapped Robert. There was a momentary pause, during which Lily's cool exterior was thawed ever so slightly by the smile that crept onto her face, and Robert's blood pressure dropped back to its usual level.

"Thank you," he said, "I think I needed that." The light from the hanging bulbs reflected off her eyes, causing the amber colours within them to dance.

"It's a lot to take in but let's go inside and talk to the White Rabbit."

"The White Rabbit? From Alice in Wonderland?"

"Don't mention that to him, it's an unfavourable subject. Come on."

Lily pushed through the wall and vanished, leaving Robert alone in the antechamber.

Come on, Robert, pull yourself together. Your life has never made much sense, too many unexplained things and now this whole situation makes even less sense. Maybe somewhere along the line, all this nonsensical stuff will suddenly end up making sense. Or at the very least, there's no harm in trying, it's not like life can get any worse.

And with that rather stupid and presumptuous thought Robert closed his eyes and pushed against the wall that Lily had vanished through.

The wall was cold and felt like a gooey sort of liquid that for a moment enveloped his entire body, slid across his skin, into his ears, through his fingers and then all of a sudden there was a rush of warm air as he came out on the other side. The first thing he noticed was that the room wasn't much bigger than the one he had left, although it looked more like a professional interior designer had a hand in its creation. The second thing he noticed was that the colour had completely drained from Lily's face. The final, and possibly most prominent, thing he noticed was the presence of several dead rabbits littering the floor immediately in front of them.

CHAPTER FIVE

THE WHITE RABBIT

The Warrior Gnomes of the Grimm Mountains watched the Dwarf as he emerged from the Exchange in Thiside. He was limping, favouring his right leg, and clutched a bloody rag to the left side of his forehead.

"He's injured," said General Gnarly.

Gnomes were exceptionally strange creatures. Their creation had occurred thousands of years ago when an extremely inexperienced witch had cast a spell to create a new breed of Dwarf that would serve only her. She had measured out the right ingredients, had dug up the bones of an ancient Dwarf, mixed everything in a cauldron, lit the right kind of fire, using the right kind of wood, and then completely skipped the last page entitled *When and Where* because she got bored. The explosion it caused was seen for miles, mostly due to the pretty colours it created.

The witch was completely obliterated in the explosion, but when the smoke cleared there sat two tiny figures with little beards and pointy hats. Standing just over a foot tall, the Gnomes began to breed at an exceptional rate. The intricacies of Gnome mating, especially since there are no females or even sexual organs of any kind, are far too complicated for any mere human to comprehend.

The Gnomes were born as one-foot-tall men with beards and pointy hats. They had a life expectancy of exactly seventy-three years. Like any species, except dolphins, the Gnomes did not get along and fights broke out. The fights resulted in tribes being formed and the Gnomes split. Many tribes headed for the mountains, others moved into the forests of the Northern Regions, and one unfortunate tribe found a curse inherent in their creator's spell. It seemed that an unfortunate side effect of their creation caused the Gnomes to be drawn to the doors like a moth to a flame. As a result, the Gnomes were constantly falling through the doors to Othaside. Gnomes feared Othaside as it was quickly discovered that they couldn't survive in that world. Whenever a Gnome crossed over, it instantly turned either ceramic or plastic, and the residents of Othaside used the petrified Gnomes to decorate their gardens.

The Warrior Gnomes settled themselves at the foot of the Grimm Mountains and were known to be the toughest and most dangerous Gnomes of all the tribes. They had commissioned themselves to watch over the Exchange, as it was the only static door between Thiside and Othaside. The tribe figured it warranted guardians and they were just the Gnomes for the job. Numbering almost two hundred, the Warrior Gnomes watched over the wooden door that was set at the very bottom of the mountain.

Today, the mountain felt unsettled and General Gnarly himself had taken to watching the doorway from one of the many ledges set into the rock. A small contingent of his best warriors had just joined him on the ledge when the doorway below had swung open and the Dwarf had staggered out.

"What shall we do, General?" asked Gnorman.

"Let's kill him," suggested Gnick.

"Easy, soldiers," said General Gnarly, an aged Gnome who was drawing close to his seventy-three years and had already survived the Great Gnome War of 1952. "Gneil and Gnelly, head down to the Exchange and make sure everything's okay. Return to us quickly."

"Sir, yes sir," chimed Gneil and Gnelly and took off down the mountain toward the entrance.

"It's strange," said Gnorman, "I've never felt this unsettled in a long time."

General Gnarly scowled through his little white beard. His experience had taught him not to jump to conclusions. "Keep an eye on the Dwarf but let's wait and see what the scouts have to report before we act."

Robert covered his nose to dampen the smell of blood. The small room had a tiled marble floor, cream-coloured walls similar to ones often found in an old folks' home, a long oak counter, and bright fluorescent lights. Set into the wall to the right was a large wooden door, much like the entrance to the Exchange in Othaside. Behind the counter was an intricately carved circular door that stood next to a large metal refrigerator.

Robert counted at least sixteen fluffy white dead rabbits littered around the floor, on the counter and one that had been impaled by a knife to the adjacent wall.

"What happened here?" asked Robert.

"Stay here." Lily jumped the counter, swung open the circular door, and dived through the hole, closing the door behind her. Robert stood alone in the Exchange, now a tomb for dead rabbits, and took a moment to examine his life to date. Something deep down was stirring inside of him and he wasn't sure he liked it. It felt as if, up until the moment he'd walked into the Exchange, his life wasn't completely real, that the feeling of not belonging he'd experienced even before he'd found out he was adopted was totally validated. Despite being in an unfamiliar world, despite being dragged around by some strange woman whose pet Fairy had knocked him unconscious, despite being surrounded by the small fluffy corpses of dead rabbits, despite all these things, Robert felt for the first time that the world had a place for him.

The moment was fleeting as he realized someone had killed these rabbits and that someone could still be around. The knife he recognized as the same one the Dwarf had been holding in his bathtub that morning. He pulled the knife out of the wall, letting the rabbit slide to the floor.

The wall Robert and Lily had entered through shimmered slightly, and a tall man with long blond hair, chiselled features, and bright blue eyes stepped through. Robert looked from the tall man, to the bloody knife in his hands, to the dead rabbits scattered about the room, then back to the tall man again, whose face had now adopted a look of rage and anger.

Robert realized how this must seem and instantly dropped the knife, which he then thought probably made him look even guiltier.

There was a creak somewhere off to his left and before Robert could begin explaining his innocence, two Gnomes flung themselves at his head, causing him to stagger backward, slip on a dead rabbit, and smash his head into the counter. Unconsciousness, who was quickly becoming a fast friend of Robert's, came to visit once more.

The cataclysm he had caused had been purely accidental. It was the complete opposite of the dull mediocrity that had caused him to slumber in the first place that had pulled him back to consciousness or maybe even back into existence. Out of everything in any of the worlds he had visited in the past, present, or future, he understood himself and his own existence least of all.

For thousands of years he had slipped out of reality and dwelt where no one would ever dare look for him. He was distinctly aware that he was not fully in control of himself yet and though he had tried, couldn't yet take corporeal form. Wherever he drifted, sparks of his abilities ran amok. He knew it would be this way until he could contain himself.

His essence floated now in Othaside over the wooden shards of a broken coffee table in Robert Darkly's apartment. Whatever had drawn him back had happened here in this apartment. Some event, although the only current casualty appeared to be a coffee table, had caused just as big an impact on his home reality and on this one as the cataclysm he himself had caused. His essence giggled in the only way that a non-corporeal creature can. Madness, he thought with a smile, is fundamental.

Robert's landlady, Gertrude, was on the phone with her friend Beatrice, a semi-retired schoolteacher who lived her life with rigorous structure. Gertrude and Beatrice had discovered long ago that they were far too self-involved to be friends and as a consequence they hadn't actually seen each other in over five years. Instead, they resigned themselves to a weekly phone call where Gertrude would complain about the hardships of her own life and Beatrice would respond by complaining about her latest ailment. As far as definitions went, it could barely be considered a conversation.

"It's my arthritis, ya see, flares up every time it rains," complained Beatrice.

"I always had high hopes of being a prima ballerina in the London Ballet, you see," responded Gertrude, "but then that bus hit me back in seventy-nine, ruined any chance so when my Jim bought this place it's where I ended up. Never wanted to be a landlady, bloody ungrateful tenants the lot of them."

"Feels like someone's turned my bones to ice, can barely get out of bed and you know how I like to get up early."

"I slave all day to make sure the building doesn't fall down and chase them to make sure they pay rent on time but they don't care, you know, they just don't care!"

"And then there's this rash I got. I think it's because I switched my laundry detergent, never should have don't that, it's all itchy and red."

"Of course I still like to watch the ballet on the telly when it's on."

"The doctor gave me some ointment but I don't think it's working. And it smells funny."

"I'm very partial to the tutus. Always liked a good tutu. Of course I'd probably look like a hippopotamus in a tutu if I tried one on now."

"And then my dog got into the ointment, poor thing hasn't been able to stop pooping."

"You know what else irritates me is this weather, this one tenant came in today and dripped water all over my clean floors. Of course I'm going to have to call the cleaner to come back and redo them and you can imagine how much that's going to cost."

"Of course that's nothing out of the ordinary, he has a very sensitive digestive system, does Rexworth."

"Although he's a very nice man is the cleaner, a bit young for me but I often catch him looking at me when I've got my rollers out. It's flattering, of course, but completely inappropriate."

There was a knock at Gertrude's door. Unbeknownst to her, the fabric of reality was being disturbed by the non-corporeal creature currently floating up on the third floor in Robert Darkly's apartment. Such knowledge, had she possessed it, may have affected her decision to open the door.

"Oh, Beatrice, I'm so sorry but there's someone at the door. I'll have to call you back," said Gertrude and hung up without waiting for a response. Most of their conversations ended this way.

Reality as she knew it outside of Gertrude's small apartment ceased to exist and was replaced with something completely different. Gertrude swung open her door with the confidence of a woman who had every intention of berating what she expected to be one of her tenants complaining about something leaking, not working, or smelling funny. It came as a surprise to her when she found that the hallway outside of her room had turned into a jungle, complete with a waterfall, colourful flowers, and an assortment of animals, the most outstanding of which was a hippopotamus wearing a pink tutu.

Gertrude shrieked, causing one of her rollers to dislodge, and slammed the door. She ran to her kitchen cupboard, grabbed her portable phone and a bottle of Scotch, then flung open her living room curtain to find that London had turned itself upside down, literally. The entire city was hanging upside down from where the sky normally was and people were falling down toward where the sky was now sitting. A hippopotamus wearing a pink tutu fell past her window. She closed the curtain again.

Gertrude prided herself on her ability to remain cool during a crisis. She took a long swig from the bottle of Scotch and dialled 9-9-9.

"Emergency service, how may I direct your call?" came the serious voice on the other end of the phone.

"Get me the police, and the fire service, and the mayor! You need to alert the army. London's upside down and there's a jungle in my hallway."

"Ma'am, have you been drinking?"

"No," said Gertrude and took another swig from the bottle. "Listen to me, you idiot, do you think I could make this up? I'm not drunk. There's a hippo wearing a tutu outside my door. Come down and see for yourself. Oh, you probably can't because you're upside down. Now I think of it, you're very calm for someone who's upside down."

"Look, lady, just sleep it off and I'm sure everything will be fine," said the operator and hung up.

Gertrude downed the rest of the Scotch and turned it upside down to brandish the bottle as a weapon as there came another knock at the door. She crept over to the door, tightened her grip on the bottle, swung open the door and let out a war cry that would have made an Apache Indian proud.

Mrs Tibbot from the first floor was quite unprepared when Gertrude lunged at her, swinging an empty Scotch bottle.

Gertrude realized at the last minute that she was about to assault a seventy-year-old woman who was possibly the furthest thing from a hippopotamus wearing a tutu. Everyone knew that a seventy-year-old woman isn't really the furthest thing from a hippopotamus wearing a tutu. The furthest thing was actually a wombat wearing a negligee, a sad but true fact of life.

She released the empty Scotch bottle, which shattered against the hallway wall, raining glass upon Mrs Tibbot, who screamed and shuffled off down the hall as fast as her seventy years would allow.

"Mrs Tibbot," shouted Gertrude, "it's quite all right, I just thought you were a hippo!"

Gertrude stalked back into her apartment and closed the door.

"Bloody stupid tenants," she said to herself. She grabbed a broom and dustpan to clean up the glass in the hallway, swung open the door, and almost tripped over an alligator. The hippopotamus, which was still sporting the tutu, stared at Gertrude with love in its eyes.

Gertrude shrieked and ran back into her apartment, slammed the door, and locked all seven of the deadbolts she'd had installed. She grabbed a second bottle of Scotch from her liquor cabinet, settled down into the corner of her living room and resolved to keep drinking until all this madness ended.

At that moment, the creature in Robert's apartment vanished and reality as Gertrude knew it, without alligators, hippos, and tutus, returned to normal.

Robert regained consciousness and immediately began to panic. For some reason, he couldn't see, he was completely blind, he couldn't be blind, what had happened? Had those small men plucked out his eyes? He didn't want to live blind, he liked looking at things, he liked having the use of his eyes and... Realization dawned on him and, feeling like a complete idiot, Robert opened his eyes.

Several things were staring down at Robert as he lay on the floor. The first one he noticed was Lily, because she was beautiful; the second was the angry-looking blond gentleman who looked only a little less angry than before. The two small men who looked to Robert a lot like garden Gnomes were whispering between themselves while casting sidelong glances down to where he was lying. They seemed to be arguing about something. The last person staring at him was not a person at all but a giant white rabbit wearing a red housecoat. The rabbit looked sad and clutched its left shoulder with a fuzzy paw. It looked injured.

"What?" was all Robert could come up with.

Lily and the blond man helped him up so he was standing face to face with the giant rabbit.

"Robert," began Lily, "this is the White Rabbit. He's the Regulator. He lives here at the Exchange. All of these other rabbits worked for him."

"What?" said Robert again.

"A bit slow, isn't he?" said the White Rabbit with a flawless British accent that sounded a lot like Noel Coward. It was the kind of accent that indicated to everyone else in the room that the owner of the accent was far better than anyone within ten square miles. "I would have thought that with his lineage he would be a bit quicker on his feet. Why don't you all come into the back room and we can talk about this."

"You two," said the blond to the Gnomes, "go and report back to your general."

"Go to hell, ya Giant-killing moron," snarled the Gnome on the left. The Gnomes hopped down off the counter they had been occupying and vanished out the door.

Lily took Robert's hand and guided him through the circular door behind the counter. The White Rabbit looked at his dead rabbits and shook his head sadly before climbing through the doorway.

The back room was basically how the average person's living room would look if it was moved into a cave that had been carved out by rabbits. There was a coffee table, a couple of end tables, a rather nice couch, a beat-up looking recliner, a blazing fireplace, and a big screen TV. A small kitchenette had been built into one corner. The overall feeling was warm and cosy.

"Be a darling, Jack, and make us some tea. I dare say we could all use a cup right about now," said the Rabbit.

The blond man, Jack, busied himself in the kitchenette.

Robert took a seat on the couch next to Lily while the White Rabbit settled into the recliner. He pulled his paw away from his shoulder to reveal a deep knife wound that was still trickling blood.

"Are you going to be okay?" asked Lily.

"I should be fine," said the Rabbit, "in a matter of hours this will be nothing more than a scratch and a painful recollection. One of the advantages of being imbued with magical significance, you know."

Jack brought over a tray of cups and handed everyone their tea, then sat down in front of the fire. Robert noted that Jack must have played rugby in his younger days; he looked strong, well built but a little worn around the edges. His blond hair was tied back; his eyes looked stern but tired. Robert would have placed him in his mid-forties.

"Robert, this is Jack," said Lily. "He's an Agent, like me."

"I'm sorry about before," said Jack, "you can imagine how it looked, you standing there with the knife and the dead rabbits everywhere."

"Uh, yeah, I can see how that would be a bad first impression." Robert could tell that Jack was hiding something. There had been some sort of recollection in his eyes in that moment when he had entered the Exchange and seen Robert holding the knife. Robert's thoughts were interrupted by the White Rabbit.

"Clearly the events that have transpired here today and the tragedy that has occurred within these walls have not happened without reason. I assume that you, Lily, and you, Jack, have come to explain just what is going on. What I don't understand was why the Dwarf attacked me and killed my staff and why there is an Othasider sitting here in my living room. An event that I can assure you has not happened in a very long time. So, let's start at the beginning shall we?"

CHAPTER SIX

BEST LAID PLANS

A million thoughts buzzed around in Robert's head and not one of them made sense. "Look, I know that something serious is going on and I'm all for going with the flow but I would like to know what's going on here. I have so many questions and it seems that things just continue to get more and more confusing. I'd honestly be happy understanding maybe a quarter of what's happened today."

Lily, Jack, and the White Rabbit stared at Robert as if they'd momentarily forgotten he'd been in the room. Ten minutes of chatting had taken Robert from slightly confused to very confused. He had so readily accepted the fact that there was a completely new world hiding behind the reality that everyone else knew but now he was feeling more and more like a tourist being dragged around by people he didn't know. And to what end? In a way, he was honoured to be here in the living room of a giant White Rabbit, but why had he been dragged along in the first place? The Dwarf that had randomly appeared in his bathtub had obviously known who he was.

"My dear boy," began the Rabbit, "I would have thought that you had been brought here armed with at least some information."

"No, not in the slightest, I just followed her here," said Robert tilting his head toward Lily, who had a slightly bemused smile on her face. "I mean, you're... well, you're fairy tale characters, aren't you?"

The temperature in the room dropped a couple of degrees. Two humans and a three-hundred-pound rabbit stared at Robert. Jack's hands tightened around his teacup until his knuckles turned white. No one breathed.

"Do I look like a fairy tale character to you?" growled Jack.

"Jack..." began Lily.

"Look, I'm sorry," said Robert, "But—"

The Rabbit coughed the kind of cough meant to gain the attention of everyone in the room. "Obviously, I assumed incorrectly that you at least had some idea what was going on around you rather than just following our pretty Lily here wherever she led you. It's a widely shared opinion that the term fairy tales when applied to Thisiders is somewhat derogatory. But your perception is not entirely mistaken."

Casting a cautious glance at Jack, who had relaxed only ever so slightly, Robert said, "So you are the White Rabbit from Alice in Wonderland?"

"You make it sound as if the book produced the characters. What I can tell you is that you're looking at it backwards, as only an Othasider could. Yes, we inspired many of the stories that you know as fairy tales but the vital piece of the puzzle that you're missing is the *how*. Of course, it's all to do with the doors. Many Othasiders used to fall through the doors into Thiside but thanks to improved and stronger magic, we have all but abolished the problem. Long ago, it was a common occurrence. Most Othasiders fell through doors by accident and were quickly delivered back by members of the Agency. In fact, as I recall, the Agency spent much of its time chasing down Othasiders, performing forget-me-not spells and dropping them back off in Othaside."

"Then how did your likenesses," said Robert carefully casting a quick glance toward Jack, "end up on the pages of some of our greatest literature in... Othaside?"

The Rabbit sipped his tea. "Probably the story I can best relate to is the Alice in Wonderland that you mentioned. In 1852, a young man named Charles Dodgson fell through a door in North Wales and ended up not two miles from where you're sitting. He is probably the most well-travelled

Othasider ever to come here, as he made it all the way to the Northern Territories before the Agency caught up to him. The forget-me-not spell was performed, and he was dropped back into Othaside. The spell works extremely effectively when an individual is conscious. However, it was discovered that when the individual is asleep, the spell has no effect and their experiences in Thiside often creep to the surface. It was further discovered that if the individual suffered any kind of sickness that affected the mind, then the influence of the spell would waver. As was the case with Charles Dodgson, who you probably know better by his pen name: Lewis Carroll. Charles suffered from a combination of epilepsy and micropsia, which caused cracks in the spell and caused recollections to float to the surface of his conscious. Believing them to be the result of a vivid dream, he wrote the story of Alice and her adventures in Wonderland. Some of the fairy tales in your reality date back hundreds and hundreds of years. And as you're probably now realizing, the fairy tales, although they may have similarities, are not entirely accurate."

"This is amazing. Those stories, those fairy tales are a basis for life lessons in Othaside. They're taught to children, parents read them at bedtime, movies are made about them."

"It's all real," assured Lily. "The folks who wrote all those stories, or at least the original writers of the original fairy tales and stories, had probably been here."

"So you are the White Rabbit. Who is the Dwarf? He can't be one of the seven Dwarves?" ventured Robert.

"Don't be preposterous; those Dwarves are miners, not killers. They're good working folk and I have the utmost respect for them," said the Rabbit. "The Dwarf who appeared in your bathtub is Rumpelstiltskin. And the fact that he appeared in your bathtub is very interesting indeed."

There was a crash as the door swung open and a bright blue ball of light hurtled into the room. The ball hovered and the light dimmed to reveal Veszico.

"I see your Agency Fairies are still ignorant of all manners," complained the Rabbit.

Lily held out a hand, and Veszico landed softly into her palm. The Fairy threw a dirty look at Robert before looking at Lily and speaking. To Robert, the sound of her voice was nothing more than the ringing of a tiny bell but he could tell from her body language that the Fairy was distressed. She pointed back toward the Exchange several times.

"Do you understand her?" asked Robert.

Veszico looked at Robert with her dark eyes and shouted in her tiny ringing voice.

"Yes, we all can," said Lily. "She says don't interrupt her."

"Oh, I'm sorry, uh… miss."

Lily turned her attention back to the Fairy, standing with her arms folded across her chest. Her wings twitched impatiently. "I understand your kinship with the rabbits and I know you're upset…"

Veszico shook a fist and pointed back to the door.

"Yes, it was Rumpelstiltskin who slaughtered the rabbits but that doesn't mean you should…"

Veszico leapt into the air and began to glow red, then white, then burst into flames. Many people kept their emotions hidden, others wore their emotions openly. Fairies preferred a much more dramatic display; when angry, they simply burst into flames.

"Veszico!" shouted Jack but it was too late. The Fairy took off out the door. "Damn it, Lily, you could have grabbed her first!" Jack jumped to his feet. "Take the Othasider and go visit the Historian."

"Jack, you know I can't."

"You can and will; we'll need to know what the Dwarf is planning. He hasn't been out of the Tower long but it seems he already has an agenda. Find out what it was he was trying to do before we put him away. I'm going to go after Veszico and hope I can find her before she finds Rumpelstiltskin. Thank you for your hospitality, White Rabbit; next time we meet I hope it's under better circumstances."

With that, Jack left the room.

Robert turned back to the Rabbit.

"You said before that the Dwarf, Rumpelstiltskin, showing up in my bathtub was very interesting. Why is that interesting?"

"I wish we had time to stay and chat," said Lily, "but we need to get moving. It'd be an advantage to get as far North as we can before sunset."

"I'm sorry to see you leave so quickly but I suppose I have my own work to do here. A word of advice for you, Lily, my dear. Don't underestimate the Dwarf. If Jack is right, and he already has an agenda, he's probably several steps ahead of you in this dance and you've yet to even learn the tune. And moreso, your unlikely partner here probably can't even hear the music yet. What I can tell you is that the Dwarf came for my blood and he took it straight from the source." The Rabbit placed a paw over his bloodstained fur where the wound had been. "This means he intends to travel to Othaside again soon. It was nice to meet you, Robert Darkly. While I fear your life will never be the same again, maybe that's just the way it's supposed to be. My thoughts go with you both."

Lily and Robert stood as the Rabbit hefted himself from his recliner.

"Actually, there is something else we need from you. Robert doesn't have a passport, and if he's to come with me on this chase he'll need one."

Robert shook the tiny vial of blood attached to a silver chain around his neck.

"This is a passport?"

"Yes, the blood of the White Rabbit will allow you to pass through any door and it will take you to a location in Othaside," said Lily, "Travelling through a door without the passport will just send you to another location in Thiside. The contents of that vial are highly coveted. All Agents have the same blood that you have around your neck and there are some people who would kill to have it."

The White Rabbit had shuffled back to his living room to pack some food for Lily after furnishing Robert with his first ever piece of jewellery. The tiny vial was made of glass but the silver necklace was intricately woven. Its actual origin was the Northern foothills of the Grimm Mountains where the seven Dwarves had mined for the last three hundred years.

"But why? Couldn't anyone just come here and purchase some blood? You said it was a commodity. Commodities can be bought and sold."

"It's true and sometimes people are granted temporary passports, a watered-down version of the Rabbit's blood, which diminishes in power within a certain time. In order to obtain a passport like that there has to be a good reason for the individual wanting it, and they must have something to trade. Not just anyone can get one."

"But then the one I have and that you Agents have isn't temporary?"

"No, it's pure blood. That's why people would kill to have it. One of the Agency's primary missions is to monitor the use of passports and punish those who abuse the privilege."

"Is that the Agency's only mission?"

Lily stared into Robert's dark eyes. "No."

Something about the answer disturbed Robert and he felt there was more in that answer than a simple one-syllable word but the fact was that Lily's eyes caused his brain to get butterflies and all curiosity was instantly dispelled.

The Rabbit ducked through the back door of the Exchange and handed a leather satchel to Lily.

"Thank you so much; we'll send word when we find the Dwarf."

"I'd certainly appreciate it. Robert Darkly, something else occurred to me while I was preparing your food. May I have a word with you in private?"

Robert looked to Lily, as if for permission, but found that she was staring sternly at the Rabbit who completely ignored her. A look like that would have turned any normal man to stone. As the Rabbit was a rabbit and not anywhere close to being a normal man, he was obviously perfectly safe from any such looks.

"I'll wait outside," said Lily resolutely. "Make it quick, we're wasting time."

Lily cast a warning glance at Robert and left through the large wooden door. Through the doorway, Robert could see what looked like a myriad of colours blending together as if someone had painted a watercolour picture and then left it out in the rain. Lily walked through the image in the doorway and the colours flowed over her until she vanished completely and the door creaked closed behind her.

"As much as we are cordial when in each other's presence, there is a certain animosity that exists between the Exchange and the Agency." The Rabbit shook his head sadly.

"Why is that?"

"It comes down to purpose. Without the Agency, life would go on. Without me, the Agency would have no purpose. I'm a threat and a necessity all at once. But let us talk about you for a moment. I imagine that you believe you are here on this magical journey for a reason, maybe to give your own life some purpose, but please don't deceive yourself about the severity of the world that you now occupy. If you want my honest opinion, you'd be better off turning around and leaving the Exchange and all this behind you."

"Look, Mr... Rabbit, I got fired from my job today and last night my girlfriend broke my heart. I don't really have any friends or anyone I would call a friend, I'm not particularly handsome or smart and the only really significant element of my life is that weird, unexplainable things happen to me on a regular basis. I really don't have much to lose, to be perfectly honest."

The Rabbit scratched one of his long white ears. "Well, then, if you're committed to remaining here, there are three things that I must impart to you. Firstly, you always have something to lose. Your blood is as valuable as mine, as valuable as anyone's. It's a commodity. Always remember that. Secondly, I packed a special little something in the passport that I gave you."

Robert had absentmindedly been playing with the tiny vial around his neck, and he now looked at it.

"If you travel through a door without a passport it'll just send you somewhere, randomly, within the same world which you currently occupy. If you travel with a passport you have the option to travel within the world or between them."

"Allowing me to go back to Othaside, I know. But I don't want to go back—"

The Rabbit held up a large, fuzzy paw to interrupt Robert and rolled his large, glassy eyes in his large, white, furry head. "Like I was saying, there's something extra. The passport you hold gives you, and only you, the ability to enter a door that will take you anywhere you want to go. You can use this gift only once, so don't waste it. In fact, maybe save it for when you end up in inescapable peril which, on your current course of action, you'll undoubtedly run into fairly soon."

"And the third thing?"

"The third is the most important. Under no circumstances should you seek out your father."

Robert and the Rabbit stared at each other. After never hearing about his father for several decades and assuming that he was probably dead, this was the second instance within a three-hour period that someone had mentioned his existence.

"What do you know about my father?" asked Robert. He couldn't help it.

Robert never saw the punch coming and when thinking about it later, he wondered if the term *rabbit punch* had been coined in Thiside. The Rabbit struck him hard across the face. The look of shock that Robert knew had plastered itself across his stinging face was completely ignored by the Rabbit who continued as if nothing had happened.

"I know enough that you should not seek him out and that's all I'm going to say. Good luck, Robert Darkly. Travel well." The Rabbit turned and began cleaning up his dead employees.

The White Rabbit in *Through the Looking Glass* was an adorable little rabbit of a nervous disposition who had an obsession with keeping time. The real White Rabbit was a five-foot-tall melodramatic creature who dealt in blood, spoke like a British noble and, as it appeared to Robert, had a slightly violent streak.

Robert left the Exchange through the same door as Lily. The watercolour wall on the other side of the door felt like motor oil as he pushed a hand through it. He pulled his hand back and considered, for the last time, whether what he was about to do was the right thing. He thought briefly about his life in Othaside. The job he had hated, the girlfriend who didn't love him, friends who barely knew he existed, an angry landlady... It was a laundry list that didn't bring him any sort of happiness.

But here, an opportunity had been presented to him. It could have been the thrill of uncertainty or maybe the beautiful amber-eyed woman waiting for him on the other side, or maybe it was the simple fact that all the weirdness that he had experienced in his life didn't seem all that weird anymore. Robert Darkly took a deep breath and stepped through the doorway.

Back in the Exchange, the White Rabbit shed a tear for the seventeen rabbits lying dead around him. He glanced at the door as it creaked itself closed and he hung his head low. He'd seen the inevitability in Robert's eyes and he knew what it would mean. He couldn't predict the future, not by a long shot, but he had a good idea where events were heading.

CHAPTER SEVEN

THE MATING RITUAL OF THE JUBJUB BIRD

Robert stepped out through a doorway set into the foot of a tall mountain. The sun sat almost too comfortably high in a bright blue sky; green hills rolled away into the distance before ducking down somewhere beyond the horizon. A road made up of square bricks stretched away from the entrance to the Exchange.

Two birds, each the size of a small horse, with bright yellow feathers, dark blue plumes, and blood-red beaks flew low over the hills as if playfully chasing each other. They ducked and twirled, spun and plummeted, crash-landed into a grassy hill, rolled down to the bottom near a babbling brook, and began making passionate love as only two giant yellow birds possibly could.

"They're Jubjub birds," said Lily.

Robert hadn't noticed Lily, who was standing a few feet away with two small men who looked similar to the two small men who had attacked him in the Exchange.

"I didn't know that's how birds, ya know, did that."

"That's not how birds do that, you idiot. That's how a Jubjub bird does that," explained the small man with a scar across one eye, his pointy red hat sitting slightly askew upon his tiny head.

"They look like they're in pain," commented Robert.

"Sqquuarrkkk," screeched one of the birds.

"They're fine, moron," said the other Gnome.

"And who are you, shorty?" asked Robert.

Lily grabbed Robert's elbow and led him away from the two angry-looking little men. "Listen very carefully, Robert."

"Yes."

"Ssqquurriinnkkaaka chaka chaka chaka nee," squawked the birds in unison.

"Seriously," said Robert, "are you sure those birds are okay?"

"Yes, they're fine; in fact they're almost done. Those two men—"

"Look exactly like the two that attacked me inside the Exchange. I wasn't ready, I can tell you that. I'd like to see them try it again when I'm more aware," said Robert as he peeked around Lily at the two little men who stared back intently.

The younger-looking one pulled a tiny dagger from somewhere within his jacket and started cleaning his fingernails, never taking his eyes off Robert.

"They're not the same Gnomes, they're two different ones."

"Gnomes, even! Like the one's my mother keeps in her garden I suppose?"

"Wooot wooouut chika," ended the two birds abruptly.

"Does that mean they're done?" asked Robert.

"Yes. The Gnomes are exactly like the ones your mother keeps in her garden. Don't take them for granted and stop trying to look around me at them. They don't take rudeness lightly and they don't like being stared down. They're also not partial to threats, insults, bad manners, short jokes, or being referred to as lacking in size in any way, shape or form."

"Anything else?"

"Yes. The two standing behind me are General Gnarly and his Lieutenant, Gnick. They are the leaders of the Warrior Gnomes of the Grimm Mountains, which we are currently standing in front of. The Warrior Gnomes are among the most deadly of their kind."

"I never thought I'd hear the words *deadly* and *Gnome* used together in the same sentence."

"They're a complex race and not to be taken lightly," advised Lily.

"Yes, you mentioned that. I don't like them," said Robert, shaking his head.

"You don't have to like them," assured Lily.

"Good."

"But you're going to have to get used to them," said Lily, "they're coming with us."

"What? Why?"

"Because they offered and because the road may not be all that safe. They can provide protection."

"I could provide protection," said Robert without even a hint of confidence.

"Let's not be silly, Robert."

"Right," agreed Robert.

Lily turned back to the two Gnomes.

"We'd be honoured to have you accompany us," said the Agent.

General Gnarly had been waiting at the door with Gnick ever since Gneil and Gnelly had returned with their report of the slaughter that happened within the Exchange, right under their noses. It was an outrage! One of his best trackers had monitored the Dwarf's movements until losing him at the border of the North Territory. The tracker had hijacked a Jubjub bird and brought his report back to the General as quickly as possible.

Gnarly had decided quickly that in order to regain their position as the guardians of the Exchange they would temporarily need to align with the Agency in hunting down the murderer. Since then, an angry Fairy and the other Agent, who no Gnome could stand, had exited the Exchange and followed the Dwarf's path themselves, which meant the Agents knew something. As much as he hated the man, Jack would have been the best candidate to join forces with, but he'd been too busy chasing his Fairy to notice them, which left Gnarly with only one other option.

The beautiful female Agent and the idiot from Othaside stood before them.

Gnarly and Gnick bowed ever so slightly. "It'll be our honour to protect you both on your journey," said General Gnarly. "We pledge our services to you, Agent Lily, and to you, idiot, from Othaside."

The tall lanky one began to speak but the girl silenced him with a jab to the ribs. Gnarly had always admired the Agent called Lily. She carried the dignity of a warrior with her and her reputation was unquestionable.

Gnarly looked up to the mountains where a couple hundred Gnomes stared back at him. He gave some quick hand signals and the Gnome known as Gnorman, who was perched on a ledge sixty feet up the side of the mountain, nodded his head solemnly. The General had left Gnorman in charge as, beside himself and Gnick, he was by far the most deadly and most able to lead the tribe.

"Let's move out, shall we?"

Robert already didn't like the Gnomes and they'd been walking for only five minutes. Lily had set a steady pace and Robert walked beside her. Every now and then, he'd glance back to see the two Gnomes marching along twenty feet behind, deep in conversation. Every so often, they'd both glance up at Robert and laugh. Robert didn't understand why he had to be so polite to the two little bastards, or even why Lily thought they needed them so much.

The road wound past the babbling brook where the two giant birds were lying across each other, panting heavily. Yellow and blue feathers were scattered around. It seemed like they were sleeping with a determination and resilience that most people display when they've climbed Mount Everest.

"What's the deal with the giant birds? Are they dangerous?"

"It's hard to say. Jubjub birds are highly passionate creatures. They approach everything with such a high intensity, no matter what it is. I suppose if they ever got angry they would be quite vicious."

"And the... er... sex?"

"It's a trait of their species to be sex obsessed. They're rarely a problem, as they always travel in pairs. It's rare to find a Jubjub bird that travels alone, and frankly, you don't want to meet one."

"Why not?"

"Because if they can't find another Jubjub bird to mate with they'll try and mate with pretty much anything."

"I used to have a friend at school who was very much like that," said Robert.

Lily laughed a shrill laugh. "I think most of the male gender, no matter what their species, are very much like that."

"Well, I wouldn't say all of us are that way."

"Oh yes, all of you."

"Well, then."

"In fact, if the male species all got together, I mean all of you in one place, I bet the IQ level would probably jump over fifty."

"I don't think there's any need for—"

"Although that much testosterone in one place would probably cause some sort of ecological explosion."

"So, who's this Historian we're going to see?" said Robert.

Lily threw him a dirty look. "He's a record keeper. In the same way that the Rabbit was appointed to be the Regulator, the Wolf was appointed Historian."

"He's a wolf?"

"Mostly wolf. He served many years in the Tower before he was deemed too old and decrepit to be a threat any longer, and due to several hundred years of good behaviour and an interest in the histories, he was appointed to be a record keeper; the Historian."

"What's the Tower?"

"It's the prison, you moron!" said General Gnarly.

Robert looked back to see the Gnomes had caught up and were only a few steps behind. He ignored the two little men.

"And how is the Historian going to help us?"

"Rumpelstiltskin escaped from the Tower last night. Since then, the only notable things he's done are visit you and break into the Exchange. We need to find out what he was doing before he was sentenced to the Tower."

Robert had been meandering around the intricacies of conversation in the fond hope of asking Lily where she fit into this world, and he felt the pathway of revelation opening up ahead of him.

"Lily," began Robert.

"Yes."

"Can I ask you a personal question?"

"No."

It appeared to Robert that a tall tree had fallen onto the pathway of revelation, blocking his approach, and he found that he was completely lacking a chainsaw and would have to find a way to meander around it. Unfortunately, meandering wasn't really Robert's strong point. In fact, now he thought about it, he really didn't have any strong points.

The bleeding had almost stopped but Rumpelstiltskin still felt lightheaded. He had expected that it would be difficult to get what he wanted from the White Rabbit, which was why attacking him directly seemed to be the better option rather than trying to convince the annoying beast verbally that he should simply give up his blood voluntarily. What he didn't consider were the obvious dangers of attacking a three-hundred-pound giant rabbit. Despite the Regulator being a pompous, over-articulate ass, he could also pack a hell of a punch.

When he had attacked, the Rabbit had moved with the distinct speed of, well, a rabbit. What Rumpelstiltskin had thought to be a stealthy attack had turned into a fight to keep the Rabbit's claws from getting close enough to rearrange his insides. It'd been more luck than anything that had allowed the Dwarf to leave with only a minor head wound and a limp.

The blood-soaked cloth he'd used to clean his knife was safely tucked away in his pocket. His only regret was leaving the knife behind; it was well balanced, freshly sharpened, and if Rumpelstiltskin appreciated anything, it was a well-balanced, sharp knife. His desire to continue his plan had been thwarted for the last half an hour as he searched in vain for a weapon. The Agency wouldn't be too far behind and even the White Rabbit might seek retribution. It wouldn't be long before he was in the City of Oz and he'd feel a whole lot safer if he had a good knife with which to defend himself or, alternatively, murder without remorse. The Dwarf giggled at the thought.

He'd followed the Eastern Yellow Brick Road, which was overgrown and broken to the point of being all but invisible. He'd passed through Miller's Forest without encountering any inhabitants or travellers. Most forest dwellers were nocturnal, and the sun was only now beginning its dramatic dive toward the horizon.

The sun completed this complex manoeuvre every day and had done so since the beginning of time. In Othaside, the sun rose and set in a continuous arc that rarely changed. In Thiside, the sun had a creative sense of purpose that sometimes gave it the inclination not only to rise and set but to rise and set with a style and panache that would make a French Olympic figure skater blush. On this particular day, the sun planned to complete a complex triple axel jump with a twist before sinking below the horizon.

Rumpelstiltskin now stood on the edge of Miller's Forest which opened out onto a steep rocky hill that led down to a small settlement a hundred yards below. The settlement contained four large houses with thatched roofs built around a ten-foot wooden statue. The statue was a female figure with long, flowing hair made out of braided straw. The statue's hair flowed down to the ground and spread out in all directions.

A shrill scream echoed in the back of the Dwarf's mind; a memory of his time in the Tower, and one inmate in particular crept to the forefront. The witch, Rapunzel, had been locked in the Tower for several thousand years. Even as a prisoner, he'd heard rumours of an uprising of followers who believed Rapunzel was some sort of wrongfully imprisoned goddess. They worshipped her, believed her hair to be magical, longed for her release, and had petitioned to the courts of Oz several hundred times for them to do just that. After the appeal was turned down for the six hundred and thirty-second, time the followers disbanded to create settlements to help grow their numbers until such time as they had enough manpower to storm the Tower and release their deity. The only drawback was that most normal people believed that the followers were insane and the concept of following a witch that was responsible for killing hundreds was a little on the strange side. As a result, their numbers grew slowly.

Smoke rose slowly from all four stone chimneys in the settlement, suggesting that occupants were more than likely inside. Rumpelstiltskin wanted to avoid confrontation but had no desire to continue his journey without some sort of weapon. His answer lay beneath him, at the bottom of the rocky hill. As the sun completed its triple axel, its rays glinted off the metal of a hatchet stuck in a stump used as a platform for splitting wood.

Perfect! The Dwarf began to look for safe passage down the hill. The last thing he wanted to do was get any more beat up or bloodied before the day was done.

No sooner had he finished the thought than a fiery something flew like a bullet out of Miller's Forest and slammed into the back of the Dwarf. The little man was not simply pushed over the edge, but was rather flung without the slightest bit of grace. The jagged rocks of the steep hill were horribly inconvenienced in the course of their stony lives as a surprised and enraged Dwarf bounced across them.

Rumpelstiltskin landed in an uncomfortable heap at the bottom of the hill, his clothes shredded, blood seeping from various gashes, and although he wasn't a doctor, he was pretty certain that several of his ribs were broken. He rolled himself onto his back and began scanning the skies for whatever it was that had struck him from behind. The darkening sky revealed nothing out of the ordinary. At the moment, this was perfectly fine as he was quite content to just lie still and bleed quietly. He felt coldness seep into his bones and the fear of losing consciousness edged into his mind.

A dark shadow appeared above him. *The Jabberwocky has come to collect.*

"Who are you?" said a childlike voice from the shadow standing over him.

Rumpelstiltskin blinked, and then squinted his eyes. A young girl, around six years old, stood over him. One of the settler's daughters, he assumed. She had long, blonde hair as was traditional among the witch's followers. A round face with rosy cheeks and the innocence that everyone loves to see in young children stared down at him. A spark of hope ignited somewhere behind the Dwarf's eyes and he whimpered a little for effect.

"Hello, little girl," he struggled.

"Are you okay, mistuh?"

"I was"—cough, cough—"resting at the top of the hill enjoying the sunset when I lost my footing and here I am," moaned the Dwarf.

"Want me to get dada?"

"No, no, I want you to help me."

A small fireball blazed across the sky. The source of his current predicament suddenly occurred to him. A Fairy! An angry one!

"What can I do?" squeaked the girl.

"Well, you see, little girl, I don't think I can move, and you see, it's my puppy I'm worried about."

The little girl's face brightened. "You have a puppy?" she asked, excited and totally oblivious of the growing pool of blood beneath the small man lying in front of her.

"Yes." Rumpelstiltskin could taste blood and his vision was going blurry. The fireball flitted across the sky again, closer this time. The damned insect was making sure she'd done the job properly. Time was of the essence. "His name is Foofoo and he's my best friend."

The little girl screwed up her face in disgust. "A boy puppy? I don't like boy puppies."

"Did I say he? I meant she. A little girl puppy."

The girl's face brightened again.

"I bet she'd love you. But I fear I'm dying down here and I won't be able to take care of little Foofoo anymore. I won't be able to feed her. She's probably so scared."

The little girl's face looked panicked and she clasped her hands together nervously. "I could take care of her for you?"

"Well, yes, that would be an option. But... uh... I would still need to go get her for you and I'm in no condition to do so."

"You could tell me where you live?"

"It's very hard to find!" snapped the Dwarf.

The girl looked a little taken aback.

"I mean, I'd be happy to take you there if I could just get better. Don't you wish I was healed so that I could take you to see little Foofoo?"

The little girl nodded enthusiastically. Rumpelstiltskin would have rolled his eyes if he thought the effort wouldn't make him pass out.

"I need you to say it."

"Say what, mistuh?"

"That you wish I was better," suggested the Dwarf.

The little girl tilted her head. "Why?"

Rumpelstiltskin tried to move and screamed in pain.

"Ohh, poor Foofoo," he cried.

The little girl gasped.

"I wish you were better and not bleeding everywhere or making that little gurgling sound."

A smile crept across the evil little man's mouth. "Granted!"

His bones cracked back into place, the blood that had soaked into the earth retreated into his body, filling his veins and pumping through his evil little heart. The skin knitted itself together and his bruises vanished. Even the wounds inflicted upon him by the Rabbit were gone.

The Dwarf jumped to his feet and grabbed the hatchet from the stump.

"Aha!" he shouted triumphantly. For all the limitations of his magical powers, sometimes he had moments of brilliance.

He turned on the little girl who was slowly backing away, her bottom lip quivering. Should he simply take her head off or knock her out? A little girl was no threat, really, but she could alert others to his presence. He shifted the hatchet in his hands so he could strike her with the blunt end and swung for her tiny, terrified-looking head.

Out of nowhere, the Fairy, still doused in flames, flew in front of the girl, taking the full force of the blow. Veszico's tiny body hurtled toward the giant wooden statue in the middle of the settlement and was lost from sight somewhere in the straw hair of the fake deity. The dry straw promptly ignited and began to burn, slowly at first, before building into a raging fire that consumed the statue within moments and started to spread to the structures.

Rumpelstiltskin turned and fled around the back of the settlement, picking up the Eastern Road, and kept running until his Dwarf lungs gave out two miles later and he stopped to rest for the night.

The fear that compelled such speed was the possibility of discovery by the witch's followers which, as it turned out, wasn't a possibility at all as they were far too busy trying to stop their settlement from burning down. Later that night, the followers failed to believe the little girl's story about a Dwarf who had almost died and had a puppy called Foofoo and then got better and then hit a burning Fairy into the statue causing the complete destruction of their settlement. *Too farfetched* and *stop being ridiculous* were muttered and the girl was chastised for making up stories. It was then decided that the fire and consequent destruction of their homes was a sign from Rapunzel that the time to free her from her prison was growing close and all her followers should be prepared. They were wrong, of course, but when it came to religion, truth and fiction often made a cute couple.

What was strangely coincidental was that the settlement disaster wasn't the only fire that happened in Thiside on that particular night. Several miles away and a few more hours into the night, a second blaze erupted, and once again, no logical cause could be determined.

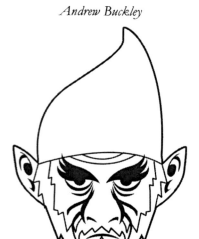

CHAPTER EIGHT

THE GOATHEADS

The minutes turned into hours and the hours turned into more hours as darkness descended on Thiside with as much passion as the absence of light could possibly muster. Robert hadn't exercised this much since secondary school physical education classes, where he was forced to run cross-country over the desolately damp and cold fields in Southern Yorkshire. He managed to run for only the first five minutes before giving up, walking the rest of the way, and always came in dead last.

In truth, he barely noticed the time passing as he took the opportunity to learn as much as he possibly could about Thiside. His fond hope was that he could figure out why he was along on this ride in the first place. Lily was extremely patient with his obvious ignorance and answered most of his questions about the world they currently occupied to the best of her ability. Robert had learned about some of the inhabitants of Thiside. He now knew that humans only made up half the population. Other inhabitants included Humanimals: half human, half animal. There were also Dwarves, Fairies, Gnomes, Munchkins, Giants, Goblins, Ogres, Mermaids, and a variety of creatures that he'd never heard of, even in stories in Othaside.

It had taken a while, several explanations, and some fairly strong insults to his intelligence by the Gnomes until he finally understood how the doors worked. If someone with the Rabbit's blood as a passport passed through a door, he would go to an equivalent location in Othaside.

Equivalent probably wasn't the best way to describe it, as locations between realities could sometimes shift as if both realities were blankets that had been stitched together at random points by a deranged sewing woman driven mad by the intricacies of needlepoint and occasionally felt the need to undo her work and re-sew elsewhere.

If the traveller didn't have a passport, they would be transported quite randomly to another location in Thiside. Doors moved constantly, as if they had a mind of their own. They weren't driven by anything; they had no purpose except to link locations and worlds and over the past several decades, according to Lily, the amount of doors had diminished considerably. She hinted that there was a moment in their history when a great source of magic had vanished from their world and ever since then, the amount of magic in Thiside began slowly to decline.

After the first hour into their journey, Robert had resolutely decided to ignore the Gnomes. It seemed the best course of action, as any verbal sparring ended in them winning; it appeared that the Gnome race had developed a keen sense of how to insult people. It was a skill they had sharpened throughout the last several centuries until it was as dangerous and as deadly as the weapons they kept concealed upon their person. It was also obvious that the Gnomes had no respect for Othaside or any of its inhabitants, although Robert had no idea why. When he'd asked the Gnomes why they hated Othaside so much, they made a statement that compared Robert to the passing of gas from an elderly female Rath.

He later discovered that a Rath was a pig-like creature that was coloured bright green. Not many people ate them, partially because of the unappealing taste, but mostly because Raths had the ability of speech. They weren't classed as a Humanimal because they weren't half of anything. Their simple life functions consisted of eating, sleeping, excreting, and talking single-mindedly to anyone and everyone about current events and local politics. Raths were known to be so boring that they could make people's appetite vanish completely. Some thought this was a defence mechanism to stop anyone from killing and eating them. The Raths didn't support such accusations and claimed that they simply enjoyed a good conversation.

The path Robert and Lily had been following finally wound out of the hilly region surrounding the Exchange and led them through a dense forest known only as the Dark Forest, so named because the trees were so dense that they practically blocked out the sun and the closeness of the trees made it impossible to deviate from the path. Lily had said that the Historian lived on the border between the Northern Territory and the Central Region, where they were currently located. Thiside was split into several different provinces, each one controlled by a different ruler, or in some cases, several rulers. Lily explained that they would reach the Historian sometime in the morning and that they'd need to stop for the night, as the Forests of Thiside were dangerous at night.

"Where will we stay?" asked Robert.

"There's a halfway house in the Dark Forest. I've stayed there before. It'll be a good experience for you; it's owned by a Humanimal couple."

"Really?" asked Robert, far too excited than he probably should have been but he couldn't help it. Everything was new to him today. It was like being born, if being born meant getting dumped, fired, hit by a Fairy, attacked by Gnomes and witnessing a sordid sexual act by a couple of giant birds.

"Thank you," said Robert to Lily sincerely.

"For what?"

"Just for everything really. Bringing me along."

Lily smiled a coy smile that Robert had barely seen since first meeting her. As quickly as the smile appeared, it was gone. "Well, it makes sense. Obviously you're involved in all this somehow."

"I wish I knew how." Robert looked around and realized that they were alone. "What happened to the Gnomes?"

"They're around somewhere, probably scouting ahead."

Robert had wanted to bring up a subject with Lily but it didn't seem that she was overly interested in talking about herself at any point. "Lily, where do you fit into this?"

"I work for the Agency."

"I know, you've told me that. Not what the Agency does, but I know you work for them. I was thinking more along the lines of how do you fit into this world? Everyone here seems to have an origin in Thiside."

"I don't want to talk about it. If you're here long enough, maybe you'll figure it out."

Gnick and General Gnarly dropped through the overhanging trees and landed lightly in front of Lily and Robert. Gnarly always addressed Lily, rarely even acknowledging Robert's presence.

"The halfway house currently holds no travellers. Maureen and Melvin Goathead will be happy to accommodate us for the night. They know nothing of the escaped Dwarf."

"Thank you, General," said Lily. The Gnome nodded and, with Gnick, turned and carried on along the path. Robert had found it amusing when Lily had told him the Gnomes were warriors. He could scarcely believe that any person so small could be dangerous. Not long after they'd left the Exchange, General Gnarly had announced that he was hungry and in one fluid motion Gnick had produced a dagger from his sleeve and thrown it with pinpoint accuracy at a small bird in a tree at least fifty feet away. Much to the bird's dismay, its head was severed clean off its shoulders and the carcass was quickly cooked over an open flame and eaten by two hungry Gnomes.

"How far to the halfway house?" asked Robert. Lily simply pointed up ahead. He could see that the pathway widened to accommodate a large stone building with a thatched roof. The windows indicated that the building featured two floors. Smoke billowed from the stone chimney and a warm glow emanated from the windows, making him feel comfortable and cosy just by looking at it.

The incorporeal creature drifted somewhere between the realities as orange and purple colours of no significance swirled around in the nothingness, riding on winds that didn't exist in a space where no living thing could survive. It had taken time and some searching, but he'd finally found his prey. He had tried again to take corporeal form, but the only result had been an extremely surprised young poet from South America who had been snatched out of his morning shower, propelled across the ocean at the speed of dark and dropped, stark naked, in front of the Sydney Opera House in Australia. A performance of the stage show *Cats* had just come to an end and the audience was exiting the Opera House into the warm night air.

The poet, who had always been good at making the best out of any situation, got to his feet, cleared his throat and recited a haiku he'd written a couple of months ago. He received an encouraging round of applause. He went on to recite a limerick that made everyone laugh and ended with a heart-wrenching allegory that caused the audience to shed a few tears. As the final stanzas rang out into the night, the crowd cheered and screamed for an encore. The South American poet went on to be known as the *Naked Poet* and lived out his days travelling around Australia and drawing crowds wherever he went.

The mystical creature had come to terms with the fact that he had two choices. He could remain incorporeal and ineffectual and do absolutely nothing but float around and observe as best as he could the events unfolding in the universe. Or, he could throw caution to the wind, create a corporeal vessel, and slowly filter himself into it. It would be slow and although the vessel would, in essence, be him, he understood that for a time he would be completely unaware of himself but at least he'd be in the thick of the action. Eventually he'd be himself; it was just a matter of time. And when one is a mystical, slightly omnipotent creature that transcends space and reality, time is meaningless.

With no more than a thought, he began to reintroduce himself back into the world.

"Look, I didn't mean anything by it," said Robert with an insurmountable amount of conviction.

"Shut up, Robert," snapped Lily.

The Gnomes snickered.

Two angry-looking Humanimals glared at Robert, their arms folded assertively across their chests, as Lily tried to rectify the situation. Robert was sitting at a table near the door, feeling like an idiot. The Gnomes perched at the bar, wearing large grins.

Maureen and Melvin Goathead stood seven feet tall. They had the legs of a goat, a human upper body, human arms, and a long goat's neck topped with a goat's head. Maureen had a ring in both of her ears, ample breasts, and a stern look that could turn men to slush. Melvin had a simple look about him that would lead anyone with eyes to believe that Maureen was definitely the boss in this household. Maureen wore a dress tied at the middle with a braided rope while Melvin sported a pair of stonewashed jeans, a white shirt with a high collar, and a green blazer. A pair of spectacles perched haphazardly on the end of his long goat nose.

Robert, Lily, and the Gnomes had entered the halfway house, which to Robert looked very much like he would have imagined a medieval tavern to look. It occurred to him that, so far, everywhere he'd seen had held the same Olde Worlde sort of look. It should have seemed strange to Robert but for some reason it felt completely natural.

Lily had informed Robert that the names of the owners of the halfway house were Melvin and Maureen Goathead, but failed to mention that their animal half was, coincidentally, a goat. The revelation had taken him by surprise. As they entered the halfway house and were greeted by the couple, Robert had been shocked by their height and the fact that they spoke just like a human. Coupled with the many surprises of the day, the first rather stupid words out of Robert's mouth were "You're goats!"

There was nothing more insulting to a Humanimal than being referred to as an animal. The pair demanded that Robert leave.

Lily had come to his rescue and explained that he was an Othasider who knew nothing about this world until a few short hours ago and that the stress of the day was getting to him. The Gnomes added that he was a moron and couldn't help it.

Finally, the Goatheads agreed that they'd overlook the rude comment and that they were all welcome to stay the night, took their food orders, and vanished into a back door that he assumed led to a kitchen.

"Nice first impression, Robert," said Lily with a smile.

"Good one, moron," said Gnick.

The Gnomes jumped down from the bar and the four of them moved to a larger table by the fireplace at the far end of the room.

Robert hadn't realized how hungry he was until Maureen dropped a plate of something brown and roasted accompanied by fresh vegetables and boiled potatoes smothered in some sort of rich gravy in front him, along with a large glass of beer. Realistically, he hadn't eaten since before he was fired from his job that same morning. It seemed like a lifetime ago.

After dining, Lily retired to her room to get cleaned up, leaving Robert alone with two slightly intoxicated Gnomes and Melvin, who had joined them for a nightcap. Maureen could be heard clattering around in the kitchen. Thanks to his underwhelming first impression, the conversation had been as comfortable as barbed wire underwear. As the night fully took effect and the alcohol slipped slowly into the bloodstream, Melvin started to warm toward Robert. After a while, the Gnomes started telling jokes about wizards that amused Melvin to no end. Robert did his best to laugh where he thought was appropriate as he didn't really get some of the jokes and assumed he needed to know something more about wizarding-kind to appreciate fully the humour. Melvin on the other hand had a hearty laugh that often ended with him bleating, which caused him to laugh more.

After some time, the conversation turned to Robert. Melvin asked if there was anything he'd like to know, as he was a newcomer to this world.

"Well, I only have around a million questions," replied Robert.

"As you should," agreed Melvin.

"Moron," stated Gnick. Even the Gnomes had ceased to annoy Robert; he was getting used to their general lack of manners and consistent insults.

"How about money?" asked Robert. "What kind of currency do you use in Thiside?"

Melvin reached into his jacket and pulled out a small, leather, drawstring pouch. He loosened the strings and shook several gold coins of varying sizes out onto the table.

"Is this real gold?"

"There are several different forms of currency here," said Melvin, "information, for example."

"Blood," added General Gnarly.

"And gold," finished Melvin. "The blood is regulated by the White Rabbit. Information belongs to the knowledgeable and the gold is mined and coined in one location on the far side of the Grimm Mountains."

"By the Seven Dwarves Mining Corporation," added Gnick.

"The Seven Dwarves? As in *the* Seven Dwarves?" Two pairs of tiny Gnome eyes and one pair of spectacled goat eyes stared at him blankly. "You know, small cottage in the forest, hi-ho-hi-ho, Snow White? The Dwarves took her in after the evil queen threatened to kill her?"

"That's not exactly the way it happened," said General Gnarly. "As Lily told you, the stories you know aren't exactly reality."

"Well, there are obviously seven Dwarves," said Robert.

"And there was a Ms. White," said Melvin with obvious contempt in his voice.

"Thieving bitch," agreed Gnick.

"What?" said Robert, taken aback.

"The woman was a dirty thief," snarled General Gnarly.

"She was stepdaughter to the evil queen who tried to have her killed because she was too pretty," explained Robert.

"Moron," stated Gnick.

"You see," began Melvin, "Snow White was a famous cat burglar in Thiside. She robbed everyone. She was the only person to ever break into the Wizards' Council Chambers in Oz and steal one of the seven sacred books of magic."

"There was... is an Evil Queen. Snow White broke into her castle and tried to steal her cauldron," said General Gnarly.

"When running from the Queen's guards, she found refuge in the Dwarves' summer cottage," added Gnick as he started in on his second plate of food. The little man had a considerable appetite. By Robert's reckoning he must already have consumed his own weight in food and for the life of him couldn't figure out where Gnick was putting it all.

"And the Dwarves took her in, right? Took care of her?" asked Robert, who was trying to hold onto the last vestiges of the stories from his childhood. "Until Prince Charming could come back to her."

"There is no Prince Charming."

"There *is* no Prince Charming?"

"There's a very nice Frog Prince who lives in the swamps in the South of Munchkinland," said Melvin.

"Actually, he's a King now," said General Gnarly.

"Really? Good for him."

"I met him a few years ago, nicest Frog I've ever met."

"Excuse me!" cried Robert. "Can we stay on topic for a minute? What happened to Snow White if there was no Prince Charming?"

"I'll get us another round of drinks," said Melvin and headed for the bar.

"Are you okay, moron? You're looking a bit pale."

"It's a lot for him to take in," said Lily's silky voice from behind him. "Imagine, General, if you'd grown up believing that Thiside was nothing but make-believe? Just stories in a book and then one day you find out it was all real. But not exactly the way you were told."

Robert turned around to find Lily standing at the bottom of the stairway. Her hair hung freely around her shoulders and she wore a black nightdress that clung to all the right places, outlining a fiendishly lovely body. The hem had been pinned up to accommodate Lily's shorter stature and Robert assumed Maureen must have loaned it to her for the evening.

"Well, yes… uh, well," stammered Robert. Lily's dress felt like a slap across the back of his eyeballs. "It is all a bit overwhelming. So what happened to Snow White?"

Melvin returned to the table with four tankards of beer and a glass of wine for Lily, who pulled up a stool.

"Are you sure you want to know?" asked the Humanimal.

"To be honest, no. But I suppose I have to get used to things like this."

Melvin settled back into his seat, adjusted his glasses so they were still slightly crooked, only at a different slant, and began. "You have to remember that this was a long time ago, long before I was born, before the Agency ever existed, before the Tower. There was no form of policing or security in Thiside. It was very much every man, woman, Humanimal, whatever, for themselves and the population had no trouble taking matters into their own hands. The Dwarves returned to their summer cottage the day after Snow White attempted to steal from the Evil Queen and found the young girl trying to break into their safe. As a rule, most Dwarves are kind and reasonable folk. They're the kind of people that if you were down on your luck, they'd offer to help you out. But if it ever entered your mind to attempt to steal their gold, they'd rather decapitate you than look at you."

"They didn't?" said Robert, mouth agape.

"They take the theft of gold very seriously. She was executed and her body was fed to the animals of the forest."

"I think I'm going to be sick."

Lily sighed and took a sip of wine before placing a comforting hand on Robert's shoulder. "I know it must all be a bit of a shock, but you've got to try and forget what you already know. You're going to find a lot of discrepancies in the stories of Othaside."

"Didn't they put her head on a stick and place it outside the cottage to warn other thieves of what would happen if they messed with their gold?" asked Gnick through a mouthful of food.

"Oh god," said Robert who was beginning to feel queasy.

"Those were darker times," said General Gnarly nodding.

"You should drink up, Robert," said Lily, "and we should all get to bed; I want to get an early start in the morning."

Lily got up and offered her hand to Robert, who thought she was being overly nice considering her hot and cold mood throughout the day.

"Uh, thanks for the food, Melvin," said Robert.

"Don't mention it."

"And for the hospitality."

"It's what we do," grinned Melvin.

"And I'm sorry for the goa—ehh, the comment earlier."

"Moron," said Gnick.

"Already forgotten," said Melvin.

Lily pulled on Robert's hand and led him up the stairs. The stairs doubled back on themselves and opened up into a narrow hallway lit by candles hung on the wall. Ten wooden doors lined the hallway.

Lily stopped at the third door and let Robert in.

He slid past her into a small room lit with a single oil lamp. The room was sparsely furnished with a desk and chair and low bed with a large feather mattress piled with warm-looking blankets and fluffy pillows. The furniture was all roughly carved, causing the lamp light to throw angular shadows across the wall. The room felt so warm and cosy that Robert felt he could sink into the bed and lie there happily for the rest of his life.

He turned to see Lily leaning against the doorframe, her arms crossed, her dark hair slightly tousled, the lamp light gleaming playfully in her amber eyes. If a simple look could offer a suggestion, Robert would have guessed that Lily was tempting him in some way.

"Have a good sleep, Robert Darkly. I hope you find a place in this world."

Or maybe it was just the beer talking. Lily smiled and closed the door behind her. She was beautiful; no question about it, but there was something mysterious about her that he couldn't put his finger on. Of course, females had always presented themselves as a complete mystery to Robert, and most of mankind, he expected. He'd long ago concluded that men and women were never meant to understand each other. If the world would accept that one simple truth, then everyone would be a lot better off.

Robert sat on the bed and sank into the soft mattress. The Goatheads had left a pile of clothes on the chair in his room that consisted of a pair of oversized pyjamas, a pair of pants made from some sort of rough material, a leather belt, a long-sleeved shirt, and a thick woollen sweater. *Nice people, these Goatheads.*

The surrealism of the day washed over him as he stripped down and pulled on the pyjamas. He was careful not to remove the necklace the White Rabbit had given him. It was hard to believe that just this morning, he had been fired from his job and had spent the early morning trudging through the rain-soaked streets of London. And now, here he was in a completely different reality, chasing an evil Dwarf, sleeping in a house run by two Humanimals, travelling with two Gnomes and a beautiful young woman. His thoughts faded as he settled down on the bed; seconds after his head hit the pillow, the lamp winked itself out and Robert was asleep.

His sleep was deep and his dreams confusing. He stared out from behind the bars of a prison, then he was in the White Rabbit's living room, and then a bustling city with high green towers and bells chiming all around him. He was back in the halfway house and Lily was in his bed, naked, blood dripping from her mouth, and she smiled to reveal a set of fangs; she growled at him and lunged for his throat. Everything was black and then it was white. A maddening laugh screamed through the emptiness. A cat meowed and the world exploded into a million points of light, fire rose up all around him, someone screamed. Robert sat bolt upright in the bed.

The halfway house was burning down around him.

Chapter Nine

Fire, Cat, & Rats

Jack had been jogging for almost three hours when he reached the end of Miller's Forest. He'd seen the smoke from miles away and immediately assumed the worst. The settlement was nothing more than a smouldering mess. Jack climbed down the same hill that the Dwarf had bounced down and where he'd almost died not too long ago. The followers who had inhabited the settlement had already moved on to find shelter for the night. A light rain fell, causing steam to rise from the smouldering rubble surrounding the charred statue. *Followers of the Witch.* He hadn't seen the body of the Dwarf, so Veszico must have failed in her vengeance. Jack felt relief and sadness all at once. He quickly checked himself, pushed his emotions deep down as he had a hundred times before, and started searching for the remains.

After an hour of searching and digging, he found the small body of Veszico buried beneath what remained of the statue. Jack lifted her to his ear and heard nothing. He let out a sigh, dropped to his knees, and began to dig a hole in the dirt beside the burned statue. After he had dug a foot deep, he dropped Veszico's body in and covered it over. He muttered a small prayer to the Jabberwocky, stood, and brushed himself off.

A single thought rang through his mind. *Find the Dwarf.*

Robert was panicking. And not just panicking, he was close to hysterical. Back in the normal world, in Othaside, sometimes bad things would happen. His alarm wouldn't go off and he'd be late for work so he'd panic. He would forget his adoptive mother's birthday and he'd panic. Even during one of the many weird events of his life, like when he was seventeen and he'd fallen asleep in his own bed and had woken up on his neighbour's kitchen table with no memory of anything. His neighbours were members of a local militia group known for their short tempers and large guns. He'd panicked.

Yet even during any of those times, he'd never felt hysterical. But being in Thiside and feeling the ease with which he was sliding into this new world, hysterical didn't just feel like the right thing to do; this world felt comfortable. Like a pair of warm socks on a cold day. There was a prime example; the building was burning down around him and all he could think of was warm socks!

He grabbed the stack of clothes from the chair, which wasn't completely on fire just yet, and assessed the situation with a hint of insanity playing on the edge of his mind. The walls were on fire, the ceiling was looking precarious, the heat and smoke blinded almost all his senses, the floor creaked beneath him, but somewhere in the chaos he heard Lily's voice screaming, "Get away from the door."

Robert, in his hysteria, stood in his pyjamas holding a pile of clothes and waited patiently for his brain to comprehend the words.

Melvin obviously wasn't operating on the same wavelength as he kicked open the door with a strong hoof, smacking Robert in the head. Melvin ducked his head through the door.

"Don't just stand there, Robert," said Melvin, "the whole building's on fire!"

Robert let out a tiny laugh that seemed a little inappropriate, considering the situation. "Yes, I had noticed."

Melvin pulled him to his feet and dragged him out through the door. Lily was pulling on a pair of pants underneath her nightdress as Melvin grabbed her hand and pulled her down the tight hallway. The far end of the hallway was already consumed by fire and the smoke was so thick that it was almost impossible to see. Robert and Lily were dragged down the stairs into the barroom where Melvin stopped and shielded his eyes. The room was an inferno. The flames twisted and contorted in ways that Robert had never seen, swirling here, zigzagging there, climbing the walls, and shooting along the ceiling, eating at the rough woodwork that made up the halfway house.

Melvin began to make his way toward the door, letting go of Robert and Lily to fend for themselves. Robert assumed that his job as their host had abruptly come to an end. Lily grabbed his hand and kicked over a nearby table, flattening some of the flame and taking them a few feet closer to the exit. Melvin had vanished from view.

"This is ridiculous," shouted Robert. "We're not getting out of here." The fire flared up around them in agreement.

"Don't be hysterical," shouted back Lily.

"And why not? This seems like the perfect time to be hysterical!"

The beam above them cracked. Robert hit the ground and assumed the foetal position. He was mildly surprised when he wasn't crushed like an egg, as was his expectation. He looked up to see Lily, the short woman he'd spent most of the day with, holding the beam over her head as if she was competing in the Olympics. The beam must have weighed the same as a small car.

"Uh," was all Robert could come up with.

"*Move*, Robert! I can't hold this forever," said Lily as her stance weakened slightly. She bent ever so slightly and threw the beam into the air. Robert scrambled back the way they had come and Lily dove forward, toward the exit, as the massive piece of wood crashed down, raining cinder and a good chunk of the upstairs into the barroom.

Fire surrounded Robert as he edged his way around a pile of rubble and crawled into the large stone fireplace that wasn't on fire. The irony of the situation made Robert laugh inappropriately again and he began to wonder what was wrong with him.

"Meow," said the kitten.

Robert had crawled as far back into the fireplace as he could and was surprised when he looked down to find a tiny kitten brushing up against his leg. The kitten was coloured an unusual orange and black, with fluffy fur and deep yellowish-green eyes. The kitten blinked at Robert.

"Huh," said Robert. The kitten chased a couple of loose embers and seemed completely at home with the building burning down around it. It crouched, twitched its little tail, and dived after a rampant ember as it drifted out of the fireplace into the inferno.

"No!" shouted Robert, but his concern was unfounded. As the cat scampered toward the fire, the flames moved away from it, as if they were afraid of the tiny creature. Robert reached forward and grabbed the kitten by the scruff of the neck. He held the cat out in front of him, stood up, and left the safety of the fireplace. The flames backed away from him as if running for cover and a pathway quickly revealed itself. It took a while to get around some of the debris, but soon enough he was through the billowing smoke and stumbled out the front door into the cold night air. He made his way to where the Goatheads stood holding each other while Maureen sobbed quietly as their home burned down.

"Robert?" said Lily.

Robert coughed in reply.

"How did you make it out of there? The fire was everywhere; we sent the Gnomes back in after you."

As the adrenaline flowed away, Robert realized his lungs were heavy and his throat felt as if he'd swallowed a handful of gravel.

"Cat," was the only reply he could come up with as he coughed again and held up the kitten as if to prove the point.

Lily turned back to the halfway house and let out a loud whistle. In reply, the two Gnomes crashed out of a second floor window and landed smoothly on the ground. The tip of Gnick's pointed hat was on fire, making him look like a giant novelty candle. General Gnarly blew it out.

"Nice to see you got out okay, moron," said Gnick.

"Thanks for going back in for me."

"Thank Lily; our vote was to let you cook for a while."

"Oh, well, thanks anyway."

"Robert?" asked Lily.

"Hmm?" said Robert.

"Where did you find the cat?"

Melvin let go of his wife, who crumpled into a heap and was hugging her knees.

"Cat?" said Melvin.

"He was inside. I assumed he was yours."

"No, we don't own a cat."

"No one owns a cat," said Lily, a stern look chiselled into her soot-blackened face.

"Well, I... did I do something wrong?"

"I've never seen a cat before, except in pictures, of course," said Melvin as he examined the kitten that kept trying to swat at Melvin's floppy goat ears.

"What?" said Robert.

"Robert, there are no cats in Thiside. Anywhere. There hasn't been any for a long time."

"I just found him inside."

"You did this!" shouted Maureen as she struggled to her feet. "You lot brought some sort of evil magic in here. And now look what happened."

"Maureen—" said Lily.

"No, I don't believe you, Lily! You should all leave right now. We have to rebuild our home."

"We didn't start the fire," said Robert.

"Get out!" screamed Maureen.

"Come on, Robert," said Lily and grabbed him by a pyjama sleeve. The Gnomes gave a slight bow to Melvin who was once again consoling his distraught wife and followed Lily and Robert as they walked away from the halfway house.

Robert, Lily, and the Gnomes had been walking in silence through the dark for almost thirty minutes. The Dark Forest's name was well deserved, as any remote source of light was quickly chased away. It seemed to Robert that the forest didn't want any light intruding upon its murkiness.

Robert still held the kitten firmly curled up and fast asleep under one arm and the clothes he'd grabbed from his room in the other. He hadn't even stopped to lace up his boots yet, and every so often his oversized pyjama pants would slip slightly, causing him to re-adjust awkwardly.

The Gnomes had vanished up ahead not too long ago and Lily didn't look like she was in the mood to talk. She walked, stern-faced, and was probably cold, wearing only her pants and nightdress.

As they rounded a sharp bend, they came upon the Gnomes who had built a fire in a more open area of the pathway and were cooking two small rat-like creatures on a spit.

"I thought we should stop and get a few more hours' sleep before the sun comes up," said General Gnarly. "It's never a good idea to travel through forests at night."

Lily simply nodded and sat down by the fire.

Robert dropped his clothes and placed the sleeping kitten near the fire. He couldn't help but notice the fire no longer seemed afraid of the little cat. Robert picked up his change of clothes and looked around for somewhere semi-private to change.

"Just change, I promise I won't look," said Lily, without looking.

"What about them?" asked Robert looking at the Gnomes.

"Although we have no desire to see you naked, moron, you do smell funny and could use a change of clothes," said Gnick.

Robert changed clothes as quickly as possible and sat on the opposite side of the fire to Lily, who looked like she was trying to extinguish the flames with her eyes. The clothes fitted him loosely and felt scratchy in places, but he imagined they were good for travelling and could stand up to a variety of elements.

"Will the Goatheads rebuild the halfway house?" asked Robert.

"Aye," said General Gnarly. "The Goathead family have managed that halfway house for the better part of a century; they'll want to continue the tradition."

"Strange fire," said Gnick as he launched into one of the rat creatures.

"Never seen anything like it," agreed General Gnarly.

"How did it start?" asked Robert.

"I was downstairs when it started," said General Gnarly, "looking for a nightcap. It just started from nowhere. One minute the room was quiet and dark, and the next it was ablaze. It doesn't make any sense."

Robert ran a hand over the sleeping kitten, who began to purr loudly.

"I wonder where this little guy came from?"

"Cats are a bad omen," said Gnick.

"Why?"

"There are no cats in Thiside, Robert," said Lily.

"But why?"

"Because the Emerald Guard was ordered to kill them all."

Robert looked from Lily to the cat to the two Gnomes who were both tearing the dead cooked flesh from the rat creatures' bones.

"I don't understand."

"You've heard of the Cheshire Cat?"

"From *Alice in Wonderland?*"

Gnick snorted and almost dropped his creature.

"Yes," said Lily. "I don't know where the Cheshire part came from, must be a British thing. But the Cat was real. Probably still is real."

"That's ridiculous," said General Gnarly, "he died."

"He vanished," argued Lily.

"Died."

"Either way, he's no longer in Thiside and hasn't been in a long time."

"What was so special about him?" asked Robert.

"He was powerful," said Lily.

"Magically," agreed Gnick.

"Yes, magically powerful. He was believed to be a great source of magic in Thiside. The Wizards of Oz consulted him from time to time. He was there in the beginning before the Emerald City fell to ruin, before the Gnome wars, before the Giants, maybe before Thiside itself. And then all of a sudden, he vanished."

"Died."

"Shut up, Gnick," said Lily, and smiled for the first time since the fire. "He vanished because the Wizards of Oz decided they should control the Cat's power and in doing so, they tried their best to bind and imprison him."

"But it wasn't enough," said General Gnarly. "They failed, and the Cat vanished, taking a lot of the magic of this world with him. But just to be on the safe side, the Wizards ordered the Guard to hunt and kill all cats."

"That's horrible," said Robert.

"It is what it is," said Lily. "But what's strange is that after there being no cats in Thiside for the last four centuries, we have a kitten sitting next to us right now."

All four of them looked at the sleeping kitten, who looked adorable in a way that only sleeping kittens can.

"You're not suggesting that this little thing is the Cat you're talking about?"

"No not at all. It's just weird."

"You know what else is weird," said Robert sounding more defensive than he meant to. "How about you lifting that huge beam over your head?"

There was a moment of silence as everyone stared at Lily, whose amber eyes reflected the flames that danced before them. The purring of the cat was all that could be heard for several long moments.

"I don't know what you're talking about," said Lily matter-of-factly. "We should all get some sleep." And with that she lay down, facing away from the fire.

"Nice one, moron," said Gnick.

"Get some sleep," commanded General Gnarly.

Robert lay down on the hard earth with his head next to the kitten and drifted off into a dreamless sleep.

The ink black trees of the Dark Forest rustled restlessly while the four travellers slumbered in a deep and uncomfortable sleep. Not all in the forest were sleeping, though. The forests of Thiside were well known for the amount of sleep that its inhabitants did not get during the night hours. One such creature, the Warzgurt, was one of those especially adept non-sleepers.

The Warzgurt was widely regarded as an unsociable creature, the sort that never got invited to a birthday party or afternoon tea. This was partially because the Warzgurt was the size of a compact vehicle, with two bright, orange, lemon-sized eyes, had six legs, was covered in shaggy hair, sported talons like kitchen knives, and had a large, melon-shaped head with a wide crescent-shaped mouth that housed hundreds of very sharp teeth. The other reason a Warzgurt would never be invited to a birthday party or for afternoon tea was because it loved the feeling of warm flesh, mostly in between its teeth.

It was a Warzgurt that now emerged from the forest onto the open path not far from where the group slept. A Warzgurt could be compared to a hundred-year-old ninja in that they could move with a stealth and conviction that almost made them seem invisible and yet they didn't really have to move quietly at all, as they had the ability to kill a person before one had a chance to say, "Wait, don't kill me." Although tests on the subject matter didn't exist, it was highly suspected that a victim probably wouldn't even get to the word "wait," let alone anything else.

The Warzgurt's gaze penetrated the darkness and realized that this was his lucky day. Not only had he stumbled across four victims quite accidentally, he didn't even need to stalk or hunt them; they were laid out like a buffet just asking to be eaten.

The large beast moved without a sound and took a closer look, sniffing each one as he examined the soon-to-be dinner. Two single-bite Gnomes, always tasty, and rare in the forests, a smelly human that he'd save for dessert, and another human with long hair, and… The Warzgurt froze solid in mid-sniff over Lily. Its hind legs began to tremble and although it was covered in hair, the skin beneath turned pale. It scrambled back as quietly as possible before losing control of its bladder, creating a nice-sized puddle of green fluid.

The Warzgurt, one of the most feared creatures of the Dark Forest, turned and fled into the trees like a little girl running from a spider.

Lily began to snore softly.

Rats in Thiside were very much like rats in Othaside. They were small, furry, grubby-looking scavengers with long tails and pointy teeth. The only difference was that the rats of Thiside could speak. Some could even sing. Before the Emerald City was destroyed, the Emerald Opera House often played host to the Travelling Rat Chorus, a group of rats who enjoyed wearing frilly collars and singing opera music.

The only issue with the rats of Thiside having the ability to speak was that they lacked the ability to keep their thoughts to themselves and instead verbalized every single last one of them. Everything they thought came out of their mouths.

Around the same time that the Warzgurt was fleeing into the Dark Forest, an especially grubby, overweight rat named Albert was scurrying around the remains of a burnt-down settlement. He hummed to himself as he sifted through the remains of a wooden statue looking for something to eat or possibly something shiny that he could take home to decorate his hole in the wall.

"Looking for garbage looking for garbage," muttered Albert. "Hmm hmm *hmm* hmm," hummed Albert, "ohhh that looks nice, what's that? Could be a piece of fruit nope definitely a piece of wood ooh maybe that's a piece of fruit nope that's a rock definitely a rock looked like fruit boy it smells funny here wonder where the other rats are they always leave me by myself I get so nervous so nervous when I'm by myself. What was that?"

Albert wasn't particularly smart even by rat standards and when the ground beneath him began to move around he assumed it was just his feet doing something funny.

"That's strange," he said, "that's very strange my feet have never done that before nope never before."

When a small hand exploded up out through the earth and grabbed a handful of Albert's fur he assumed that he was experiencing a very intrusive itch.

"Hmm, that feels itchy."

When a second hand grabbed another handful of fur, he began to worry.

"Wait a second that's not right."

When the hands repositioned and clamped onto Albert's groin it began to dawn on him that it might not be an itch at all. It took a while for the electrical impulses to reach his brain telling him that he was in a great deal of pain but once they did, he took off like a rat whose testicles had been grabbed firmly by a Fairy.

"It's got me it's got me! Something's got me I don't know what it is but it's got me by a very awkward area and it doesn't feel comfortable at all, at all! This is bad oh this is very bad."

Veszico held on tight and was dragged from the earth by the retreating rat. The Fairy released her grip and watched Albert run as if his testicles depended upon it.

"Help! Someone help! There's a creature around here trying to hang on to my groin what kind of animal does that ow it's hurting to run but I'm not stopping because that thing might still be behind me and I do not want it to grab me again no I don't definitely not. Oh the pain's getting worse so much worse and everything going a little blurry oh dear I think I'm passing out yes definitely passing out."

Veszico watched as Albert the rat passed out in mid-run and slid to a stop.

Fairies were created by a random burst of magic that had transformed a group of shiny rocks into the first Fairies. The Fairies quickly discovered how to breed and the three groups of Fairies quickly became obvious. Because they were descended from rocks, Fairies were incredibly tough and could transform back into rocks at will. As their emotional state resulted in a chemical reaction through their sweat glands that caused either glowing or spontaneous combustion, they were impervious to high or low temperatures. It wasn't the fire that had hurt Veszico, but the impact from the axe handle that had struck her. She had tried to turn into a rock but was too late and had been rendered unconscious. Why she had been buried was completely beyond her comprehension. She carefully stood up and brushed herself off. Thinking back to the Exchange, the last thing she'd heard was something to do with the Historian.

She tested her wings, jumped into the air, and began to glow bright blue. She swished and she swerved, she flipped and she spun, and then she took off into the darkness.

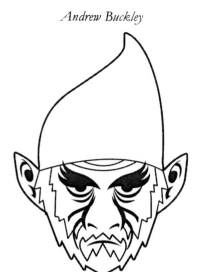

CHAPTER TEN

BANDITS OF THE OLD FOREST

Robert awoke as the sun began to rise. Much like its setting, the sun had a much more adventurous way of rising. Rather than peeking over the horizon and slowly creeping out, the sun in Thiside preferred to jump out, so the transition went from dark to slightly dim as the sun approached the crest of the horizon to sudden daylight!

Robert was used to sleeping in his apartment in a dark room with curtains on the window and a comfy bed. Sleeping under the stars on the hard ground was not something that he was used to. He'd tried camping once when he was younger and, as usual, his general weirdness had intervened. He'd woken up in the morning to find an elderly badger in his tent. Finding a badger in his tent was weird enough but what was strange was that the badger appeared to be humming to him. And not humming just anything; he was humming *Rock-a-bye-baby*. Robert had stared at the badger. The badger had stared back, winked at him, and vanished. Since that moment, the thought of camping had disturbed Robert in ways he couldn't describe and he chose not to sleep in the wild ever again.

The Gnomes had cooked everyone a breakfast made up primarily of large eggs and some sort of leafy herb that the White Rabbit had packed for them. As obnoxious as the two little men were, they were among the most amazing cooks that Robert had ever experienced. Their ability to make a meal out of anything was remarkable.

Lily had taken Robert's pyjama shirt to wear and looked very much like an outdoorsy person with her thick, rough pants and baggy shirt. Her hair was messy and her face still held traces of soot. Her eyes seemed less bright this morning, and much to Robert's joy, she had lost the sternness he had experienced in her last night. Lily's mood swings were extremely random and always seemed worse at night. Robert was having trouble figuring her out and it didn't help that he'd yet to figure out any female he'd ever met.

The Gnomes extinguished the fire and the foursome prepared to make their way along the dim path out of the dark forest. Robert felt like he was forgetting something, something important.

"Where's the kitten?" he remembered.

The Gnomes finished kicking dirt on the fire and looked at Robert as if he'd lost his mind.

"What are you talking about?" asked Gnick.

"The kitten from the halfway house; he was asleep here last night and gone when I woke up this morning."

"Maybe you dreamt it," suggested General Gnarly.

"You guys are just screwing with me, right? Bloody hell, you didn't cook it, did you?"

"Look, moron," said Gnick, "I promise you, we don't know what you're talking about."

Lily was looking at him in complete confusion.

"Lily," pleaded Robert, "you must remember the cat. You told me about how there are no cats in Thiside."

"That's true, there are no cats in Thiside," agreed Lily.

"I know! You told me why, about the Cheshire cat and how he vanished and the Emerald Guard were ordered to kill all the cats."

"Where did you learn all that?"

"You told me!"

"I don't remember that at all," said Lily with complete sincerity.

Robert rubbed his temples. Something in his mind twitched uncomfortably. He felt for a moment that he was back home and he'd just woken up in his elementary school teacher's flower garden with no memory of how he got there. "Look, what do you remember about the halfway house?"

"There was a fire," said Lily, "we all got out alive and then spent the rest of the night here."

"But you don't remember the cat?"

"What cat?"

"He was small and fuzzy, black and orange, and the fire didn't like him. He's the only reason I made it out of the halfway house in the first place."

"Robert," said Lily as if she was talking to a little boy in kindergarten who had just wet himself, "you've been through a lot during the past twenty-four hours. Maybe you dreamt it and it just felt real?"

The twitch in Robert's mind turned into an itch, then it pulsated, and then it burned, and then... nothing. It was as if something clicked. A little voice in Robert's mind that sounded a lot like Robert said, "Maybe she's right, maybe we dreamt it."

"Who the hell was that?" said Robert.

"Who was what?" said Lily, looking concerned now.

Robert looked around and saw nothing out of the ordinary. "Maybe you're right, maybe it was a dream," he agreed.

"Are you sure you're okay?" asked Lily.

"Yes, we're fine," said the voice in Robert's head.

"Yes, I agree we're fine," said Robert. *This is it. I'm losing my mind.*

"Oh no, I'm sure we're okay," said the voice.

"All right, if you say so," conceded Robert.

Lily and the Gnomes stared at him.

"What?"

"I think we should get moving," said Lily in the fond hope that changing the subject would make the weirdness go away. "If we absolutely have to speak to the Historian, I'd rather do it well before nightfall."

Lily and the Gnomes set off along the path, Gnick and General Gnarly deep in conversation. Maybe it was Robert's paranoia but he felt like they were talking about him.

"They're probably talking about us," agreed the voice.

"Really, you think so?" Robert asked the voice.

"Most likely."

"Well, what do you think they're talking about?"

"Probably about how you're standing here talking to no one in particular."

"Well, you're me, right? So really I'm just talking to myself."

"That's just as weird, you know?"

"Look, just shut up, I'm having enough trouble with everything today without me making it worse."

"Yeah, that's strange about the cat."

"I'm not talking to you anymore," said Robert resolutely.

"Suit yerself," said the voice.

It should have worried Robert that he was not only hearing voices but also holding full conversations with them.

"Voice," said the voice.

"What?" said Robert.

"Voice, not voices. Singular, not plural. You're just hearing the one voice."

"Oh right. Thanks."

But for some reason, and just as equally disturbing, it didn't feel weird at all. It didn't worry him. It simply felt like it was the right way for things to go. The disappearance of the cat actually worried him more.

Robert took a moment to examine his surroundings. It's true that there were no signs of a cat being anywhere in the area, although aside from maybe a hairball or poop, Robert couldn't think of anything else that would show the presence of a cat.

Did I really dream it all?

"Who knows?" said the voice in his head.

And now his own mind was arguing with him. It had never done that before. Robert felt different today and he couldn't decide whether it was a good different or a bad different or a completely indifferent different. But whatever it was, as Robert turned and followed the others to find that Lily was waiting for him, he decided that today was probably going to be *one of those days*. Whatever that meant.

After several failed attempts, Robert's mind gave up on trying to make conversation with itself and committed to humming which, to Robert, was much more favourable.

They'd exited the Dark Forest around mid-morning into what was a very dreary day. The grey clouds hung low in the sky and occasionally spat on people. The forest opened out into a large valley with lush green fields, copses of trees, and the occasional stone structure. Lily had explained that there was a great deal of farmland in the North. Robert could see mountains that disappeared into the low clouds off to the West. Far off in the East, barely visible, he could see a storm brewing. Three high mountains surrounded the valley. Before them, the brick road split into three.

"There are no signposts anywhere," commented Robert.

"Why does that matter?" asked Lily.

"How do you know where you're going all the time?"

"I've been around for a while. Each path leads to different kingdoms in between each of the mountains. The one to the West runs out to the Northern Peak of the Grimm Mountains and the Seven Dwarves Mining Company. The Eastern road leads to the Kingdom of Hearts. The Northern road, which we'll be taking, leads through the Rose Kingdom to the Beast's Kingdom."

"So many Kingdoms," said Robert.

"They spend a lot of time at war with one another. There's currently a peace treaty in place to prevent the fighting, but it's just a matter of time before one of them oversteps the boundaries."

"Does that happen often?"

"About once every two weeks. In fact, all three Kingdoms have special departments whose sole job it is to watch the other kingdoms and find out what they're planning."

"Can't they just negotiate something?"

"The Wizards Council of Oz tried and failed miserably. Even the Agency stepped in and tried."

"And what happened?"

"The result was a war that raged for almost a year."

"I see."

The group continued down the Northern path toward a far-off gap in between two of the three mountains. Ahead of them, the path entered a large copse of trees. Robert thought he saw something moving through the trees but the humming in his head was making it difficult to concentrate on more than one thing at once.

"The problem," said Lily, "is that they're very difficult rulers in the first place. Queen Aurora is extremely nice on the surface, but a cunning and extremely smart strategist. The Queen of Hearts is slightly crazy, and the Beast, well, he's a Beast."

"A literal Beast?"

"Yes, fur, sharp teeth, very angry."

"Like Beauty and the Beast?"

"Poor girl," said Gnick.

"Let me guess," said Robert, "she's dead?"

"As a doornail," agreed General Gnarly. "The Princess Belle was given as a gift by the Queen Aurora's great-great-great-grandfather to the Beast in order to keep him at bay and away from their kingdom. The Beast was insulted and tore her to pieces."

"Why on Earth did he do that?"

"Because she was ugly."

"Not just ugly," said Gnick, "I heard that her looks were comparable to a troll."

"Still seems like a bit of an overreaction," said Robert.

The copse of trees loomed up ahead of them, throwing dark silhouettes against the grim sky. The path ran for about a mile through the trees before emerging at the other end. Dry leaves blew across the cracked and faded yellow brick road and swirled through the trees.

"Why's it feel so intensely creepy in here?" asked Robert. There really wasn't any reason for it. The trees were alive and rustling to the melodic tunes of the breeze, the green hills and pastures could be seen in breaks through the trees. It was nothing like the Dark Forest, but it still felt chilling.

"Some say that the trees are angry," said Gnick. "This entire valley was once forest but it was felled to make the farmlands for the three kingdoms. The copses that remain are in a constant state of aggravation at losing their tree brethren."

Lily laughed. "What a load of crap."

"Yeah but it adds to the effect," said Gnick grinning.

Robert noticed something through the trees to the left and for a moment, thought he saw the lost kitten playing in the leaves. "Did you guys see th—?"

"Shh!" said General Gnarly and everyone came to an abrupt stop. "We're being watched."

"General, if this is more crap about angry trees—" said Lily.

"Shh!" he said. And then in direct paradox, he yelled "Come out, we know you're there!"

"Look," said Robert, "how do you know…"

Six men emerged from the trees not far in front of them. Four of them looked like they were made for hiding behind trees. They wore ragged looking, tree coloured clothing and their limbs were long and spindly. They wore large brimmed pointed hats and gave off a sense that everyone should probably just do what they say. In order to back up that particular sense, the fifth and sixth members of their group were extremely large and Robert wondered how they had missed them as hiding behind a tree would seem like a physical impossibility for them. They were tall and broad, wearing similar clothing as their companions, although somewhat tighter, with fists the size of a good ham shank and faces that looked like they were chiselled from granite.

One of the thin ones stepped forward, removed his hat to reveal a completely bald head, and bowed low. "Greetings, fellow travellers, it is a good day to walk the yellow road, a good day indeed."

"It is that," said General Gnarly.

"No argument here," agreed Gnick.

"I wonder, might you move aside, as we still have a ways to go and as you mentioned, it is a good day to travel," said Lily diplomatically.

"You should say something," said the voice in Robert's head.

"Hello," said Robert.

"Bold and moving all at the same time," said the voice with only a hint of sarcasm.

"Of course we'll have you on your way in no time. Allow me to introduce ourselves. My name is Arollis. My three brothers here are Mikolin, Gaulo, and Jillik. Our two larger cousins are Gruntnard and Abbigail."

Robert noted that Abbigail had started to drool.

"And in whose company do we find ourselves today?"

There was a pause while General Gnarly weighed up the six men.

"I'm General Gnarly of the Warrior Gnomes of the Grimm Mountains and this is my Lieutenant, Gnick. Lily here is an Agent assigned out of Oz and the moron on the end there is Robert."

Robert barely even noticed the insult. He was watching Gruntnard and Abbigail as they appeared to be flexing their fists.

Unbeknownst to Robert and his companions, Abbigail had originally been named Bockrick but had voluntarily changed his name to prove a point. That point being that if one were big enough, mean enough, and had the ethical capacity to turn a grown man literally inside out, then it really didn't matter what one was called.

"An Agent, well, well. And you, General, we've definitely heard of."

"Aye," agreed the General, "and I know of you as well. You're the Bandits of the Old Forest."

Arollis clapped his hands in delight. "I'm so happy that our reputation has spread so far."

"It's true," agreed Lily, "we've heard reports of you as far as Oz."

"Splendid," said Arollis, "then we can dispense with any further pleasantries, I suppose. Normally I have to speak at length about what we do and why we're here and so on. It actually gets boring after a while but being that you already know us, then you know what the next step is?"

"You'll be expecting us to hand over all our belongings," said General Gnarly with a bit of a grin that suggested he had no intention of handing anything to anyone.

"Gentleman," began Lily, once again diplomatically, "I'm sure you understand the gravity of robbing an Agent, and as you have heard of General Gnarly, then I assume you also know that he is actually quite dangerous. I'm willing to overlook this interruption in our journey if you'll just step aside and we'll pretend that none of this ever happened."

The skinny bandits laughed in a way that Robert found condescending. His impression of Agents was that they were feared but disliked, sort of like a fairy tale Gestapo. But any authority that instilled even a small amount of fear usually garnered at least some respect.

"Well, I see that this conversation has gone quite as far as it can," said Arollis.

"Oh dear," said the voice.

"What?" said Robert.

"What do you mean, 'what'?" asked Arollis.

"There's going to be a fight," said the voice.

"Surely not," said Robert.

"Surely not what?" said Arollis, who was clearly getting thrown off his game. He was used to a standard order of things. His family would fall upon travellers, Arollis would act as the spokesman, always the gentleman, and then they'd rob the travellers of everything. If they resisted in the slightest the bandits would beat the travellers within an inch of their lives. Sometimes less than an inch.

"You should apologize," suggested the voice.

"Will you please shut up!" said Robert.

"All right I think I've had quite enough," said Arollis, losing his temper.

"Sorry," said Robert, "got lost in my own mind, carry on."

Lily and the Gnomes were staring at him. General Gnarly had a glint of realization somewhere behind those old eyes.

Lily tried diplomacy one more time. "Arollis, you have a lovely family and I'd hate to see anyone get hurt here today. We've never met before and I keep the knowledge of my existence to a minimum and even then only among those I trust. I can however assure you that if you continue along this particular path of trying to rob us that it will end badly for you and your kin."

The bandits laughed again. Even Abbigail let out a giggle. It sounded a lot like someone chewing on rocks, but still, a giggle, nevertheless.

"Gruntnard, please take care of the one they refer to as the *moron*; Abbigail, please take care of our friendly Agent, and brothers, we will take care of our two small problems."

Abbigail moved with surprising speed to grab Lily but was met with a very diplomatic kick to the testicles that caused him to literally rise off the ground a few inches. Lily grabbed a handful of the large man's shirt and heaved him backwards over her head into a tree, causing a cracking sound that could have been the tree trunk or possibly the permanent realignment of Abbigail's spine.

The four brothers dived for the Gnomes, who were now brandishing shiny, sharp weapons, and Lily moved to help them.

Robert was left facing Gruntnard who, after seeing his own brother thrown aside by a small female, was proceeding with caution. Gruntnard wasn't known for his thinking skills. There was a very good chance he couldn't spell *skills*. He was more known for his ability to snap bones and cause internal bleeding. Normally, he would have lunged at Robert, who would quickly be rendered unconscious and then relieved of all his worldly possessions.

"Uh," said Gruntnard.

"Don't be rude," said the voice in Robert's head, "say something."

"Please don't hurt me," said Robert meekly.

"No, be more confident," demanded the voice.

"I mean, don't even think about hurting me, or, ehh...."

"Or else," suggested the voice.

"Or else!" finished Robert.

"Or else wot?" said Gruntnard

"Or else what?" Robert asked the voice.

"That's wot I sed," grumbled Gruntnard, scratching his head. This was more conversation than he was used to with his victims. He raised a fist like a sledgehammer and waved it menacingly as if trying to figure out the best place to hit that would cause the most damage.

"Maybe we should change the subject; ask him about his family?" suggested the voice.

"How's your mother these days?" asked Robert with as much sympathy as he could muster.

"Well, we don't talk anymore, do we," said Gruntnard lowering his fist a little.

"Well, that's no good, everyone needs a mother," said Robert.

"Uh yeah. Do you 'ave a muther?" asked Gruntnard.

"No, I'm an orphan. Never knew my mother. Why don't you talk to your mother anymore?"

"She don't like tha' bizniss I'm in, she thinks it's too ruff."

"You know, she might have a point," said Robert.

"Oh nice, I see where you're going with this," said the voice.

"Well, it's all I'm good at really. Hurting people's what I do."

"Surely there's something else you'd like to do, maybe something that your mother might not mind so much? What else are you good at?"

Gruntnard dropped his fist to his side. "Well, I like to bake every now un then."

"Baking... really?" said the voice.

"Shut up," said Robert.

"No really, I love to bake every now un then. Nothin too complicated, just bread or some scones or maybe a nice apple pie."

"Well, maybe you should do that? Think how much better your mother would feel. I'm sure she loves you a lot and probably doesn't like all the bone-breaking you're probably used to."

"Well, yes," said Gruntnard, tearing up slightly, "she'd be much happier if I'd stop making people bleed all the time."

"And she probably works hard," suggested Robert. "Must break her heart to see you not doing what you enjoy doing. And I'm sure you don't want to break her heart."

Gruntnard started sobbing slightly. "Well no…"

"Of course, you'd have to stop what you're doing right now but just think how happy she'll be. I'll bet she'll have a twinkle in her eye when you tell her you're going to become a baker."

Gruntnard's large shoulders were shaking as the tears began to flow freely. "I wanna see my mummy!"

"You should hug him," said the voice.

"Are you sure?" asked Robert.

"Look at him; he's bawling. The least you can do is give him a hug."

Lily ducked beneath Arollis' arm as he swung a dagger in a wide arc. She grabbed his wrist and swung her head up, breaking his arm. She punched him in the stomach, then threw him onto the pile with his brothers as he doubled over. General Gnarly was re-concealing his weapons while Gnick dusted himself off.

"Robert!" said Lily. She often got lost in the moment when fighting and Robert had slipped her mind completely. She and the Gnomes turned around to where they'd left Robert before the fight started. What they saw was surprising.

Robert was hugging and consoling a blubbering Gruntnard, who was crying uncontrollably.

"There, there. You should probably get your family and head home. I look forward to tasting one of your pastries one day."

"I'd like that," said Gruntnard.

"Now go on, run along," said Robert.

"Thanks ver much," sniffed Gruntnard and shuffled off past Lily and the Gnomes and began gathering up his unconscious family members.

"Robert, what the hell happened?" asked Lily in disbelief.

"And you thought I couldn't handle myself," said Robert confidently.

"Why was he crying?"

"Obviously he was scared of me," said Robert.

"She's never going to buy that," said the voice.

"There's no way that's true," said Lily.

"Told ya," said the voice.

"I appealed to his better nature. He's going to be a baker now and give up beating the hell out of everyone."

One of those moments took place where no one really knew what to say. When someone should say something profound but can't figure out who should say it or what they should say. The four of them just stared at each other.

"You're weird, moron," said Gnick finally.

"Good job not getting killed," said General Gnarly. "Lily, we need to talk, now!"

The pair of them moved away, leaving Gnick and Robert wondering what had just happened.

As Lily followed General Gnarly farther into the forest to escape earshot, she was surprised by the emergence of a feeling. She felt a sudden wave of admiration for Robert Darkly. She wasn't used to feelings and she wondered what it could mean.

CHAPTER ELEVEN

NIGGLE

The concept of having a City of Oz that resided in the province of Oz was completely lost on many residents of Thiside. When the Emerald City had been left in ruins almost three hundred years ago, the best architects in all of Thiside were commissioned by the Wizards of Oz to build a new city. The architects charged an extortionate amount of money but no one batted an eyelid as they were, after all, the best. Despite many residents of the ruined Emerald City being homeless and living in overcrowded camps, the architects took almost a year to design and release their first plans for the new city, but this was completely understandable because they were the best.

Once the plans were released, most people had to look twice out of sheer disbelief. Upon review, the Wizards of Oz became severely confused. Instead of carefully laid out plans for an entire city, there were several large sheets of paper with some of the nicest finger-painting seen anywhere in Thiside or Othaside. The architects explained that they were the best at what they do and that drawing up plans was beneath them and that if the wizards wanted something more coherent than their highly detailed finger painting they should have said so. The architects were promptly fired.

The second group of architects to be hired had to be brought out of retirement as they were once the best but had since retired to a nice cottage on the Fairy Islands. They were Humanimals with the heads of pigs and the bodies of humans and there were three of them. They had built a great many houses in their time but had retired when an economic downturn, in the form of a particularly mean dragon, stole a large store of gold from the Seven Dwarves Mining Company, caused the bottom of the housing market to drop out entirely.

As construction of the city was already a year behind schedule, the Wizards of Oz agreed to use magic to help move the construction of the City of Oz along quickly. The three architects drew up plans, masonry was shipped in, the Wizards garnered the necessary magic, and construction of the city was completed in just under two weeks. The River Oz separated the city itself into two halves. It was a sad fact that, although steeped in magic, the Wizards of Oz had the creative capacity of a brick. When it came to naming the city, its landmarks, and other important elements, all the names ended up having *Oz* in the title somewhere. On the north side of the river lived the downtown and industrial areas and the south comprised the residential end of the city. The roads were all cobblestoned and narrow to maintain the look and feel of the old Emerald City. The buildings were tightly packed and stacked high and the High Castle of Oz that housed the City Guard and the Council of Wizards was built out of emerald stone quarried from the ruins of the Emerald City.

It was the tall green towers, sparkling despite the overcast sky, which Rumpelstiltskin observed from his hiding spot in a nearby alleyway. He needed to talk to someone in those towers, one wizard in particular; an old acquaintance. The Dwarf guessed that the wizard probably wasn't going to be happy to see him but Rumpelstiltskin needed a favor; a favor that only a wizard could do.

He pulled on the ragged cloak he'd found in the alleyway and kicked the old man he'd found wearing it as he groaned on the alley floor. The Dwarf slipped from the alley, quickly crossed the street, and scrambled up and over the emerald wall, then dropped heavily into the Castle gardens.

The gardens were created by a colour-blind wizard horticulturist by the name of Eric. He didn't want to be a wizard; he just wanted to grow pretty flowers. It'd been Eric's parents who had forced him into wizardry, although really no one was forced into wizardry, it just naturally found them. No one really understood how, but it had something to do with magic accidentally penetrating the womb not long after conception. The wizarding community experimented with forcing magic into the wombs of several pregnant women, but the result was a group of children who came in a variety of interesting and unique shades of purple. Magic accidentally had to intrude upon the foetus for it to produce a wizard, concluding with a certain amount of finality that even magic likes to have a little fun now and then.

Eric was found to have the wizard's gift at a young age when he blew up his aunty Flo's pet borogove. His love of gardening always intruded upon his magical training but he was overjoyed to find that he could blend his necessity for magic with his love of horticulture by creating and growing fabulously strange plants and shrubs. The other wizards avoided the Castle Gardens at all costs, as they often failed to perceive the beauty that Eric saw in his beloved creations.

It was these horrifically multi-coloured creations that now stared at the Dwarf with looks ranging from bewilderment that someone was actually in their garden to anger that someone had the audacity to intrude upon their garden. A horrible side effect of creating plants using magic was that they were often not only self-aware, but also aware of everything that was going on around them. Many of them also had the capacity to move and in some cases to talk, although not always in an understandable language. Magic being an ancient force, it was sometimes associated with the language of the Jabberwockies which was simply called *Jabberwocky*. Some believed it to be a grand language full of wisdom and the hidden meaning of the creation of all things. Others believed it to be a load of crap.

"What you doin' ere ya lil blanderskite?" said a particularly offensive orange and purple fern.

Rumpelstiltskin had heard of the garden and understood the best thing to do was ignore the plants altogether.

"Wargen you baraganth mankdweller?" intruded a group of tulips who were a sharp shade of grey.

"You," began a giant pink-leaved grassy sort of bush, "are intruding on private property. I suggest you leave."

Rumpelstiltskin waved a dismissive hand toward the grassy bush and walked on.

The grass whipped out a long tendril and wrapped itself around the Dwarf's wrist.

"It's very rude not to answer when you're being spoken to," said the bush.

"Kigan landagger dagga doo," said the tulips.

"Feed him to the bandersnooter!" shouted the fern.

"Get off me, you damned plants!" said Rumpelstiltskin.

"Ahh, so you *can* talk," said the bush.

"Bandersnooter!" shouted the fern again.

"Easy, my orange friend. Let's hear what he's doing here. Maybe he's simply come to converse with us."

"No one ever talks with us, yer manky little shrub!" shouted the fern.

"Do you see what I have to deal with?" said the bush to the Dwarf. "Any company is good company when you're rooted to the spot but they're all such Neanderthals that a fresh conversation is always welcome. So how about it? Care to stay a while?" The bush nonchalantly wrapped a few more tendrils around Rumpelstiltskin's mid-section.

The hatchet he'd stolen from the settlement hung at his side under his cloak.

"Well, I suppose if you'd care to loosen your grip, I could stay for a little while," smiled the Dwarf.

"Splendid! Fetch our guest a seat."

A large ornamental boulder sprouted spider-like legs and half walked, half scrambled its way over to where the Dwarf stood. The bush released him and he sat down on the rock as the legs disappeared beneath it.

He made himself comfortable, adjusted his weight, and slipped his hand under the cloak, gripped the handle of the hatchet, and waited.

"So…" said the bush. It was as far as he got. The Dwarf hurled himself toward the bush, swinging the hatchet directly at its roots.

"Eekk!" screamed the bush.

"Ee's got a blade ee has! Kill him! Kill him!" screamed the fern, helplessly swaying from side to side.

"Cardoosh!" shouted the tulips.

The garden seemed to lean in toward the action as the Dwarf hacked mercilessly at the bush, which was lashing out with every strand of grass at its disposal. A long length of climbing ivy with a crazed look in its chlorophyll joined the fight, wrapping itself firmly around Rumpelstiltskin's head, blinding him. Anything that could move, or at the very least lean, closed in on the struggling Dwarf and began to attack him by any means possible until he was completely lost from view. All that could be seen was a violently shaking group of psychotically coloured plants and shrubs accompanied by the rustling of foliage.

A few moments later, the garden was quiet once more.

Robert left Gnick by the scene of the fight and went to look for Lily and the General. Gnick was happily sharpening his knives with a small piece of stone. The other two had been gone for only a few minutes but something about the way the conversation abruptly ended and that the pair felt the need to move away out of earshot wasn't sitting comfortably with Robert. He didn't like to intrude but he had to assume they weren't talking about Gnick, which left only one subject of conversation.

The brush became denser away from the path, and Robert crouched low and moved as quietly as possible until he could make out Lily and General Gnarly's voices not far away. He stopped and listened intently. The voices had a distinct sense of urgency about them.

"There's something you're not telling me," accused Gnarly.

"As a member of the Agency—"

"Ahh, don't feed me the Agency line. I'm too old to care. You told me he came from Othaside but there's something very strange about him and I think you know more than you're telling. First the fire at the halfway house and then the cat he may or may not have seen and just now—"

"All right, all right!"

"He was talking to himself, wasn't he?"

"Well, not exactly."

It sounded like General Gnarly was pacing. "I know you think I don't know much of the goings-on of the world outside of my mountains."

"That's not true, General."

"But we receive reports from everywhere."

"Well, I'm sure—"

"Reports about you, for example," stated the Gnome with the obvious maximum effect, as there followed an uncomfortable pause. "If what I've heard is correct, and what I saw today leads me to believe that I am, then you may as well come clean and tell all of us the truth before it's too late."

"It's not easy to talk about," growled Lily.

"Aye, but I'll wager that the Historian has a loose tongue."

"As far as Robert is concerned," said Lily changing the subject, "he was born here in Thiside but his mother was an Othasider."

General Gnarly sighed. "The man I assume is his father was well-known, wasn't he?"

Robert guessed that Lily must have nodded as Gnarly continued, "I encountered him around forty years ago. We were hunting food through the Southern edge of the Dark Forest and all of a sudden, he was there. Standing as if he was expecting us. He's a strange character and I can only assume by his long life that he's not human?"

"It's hard to explain, and even I don't fully understand it. He's a sort of human but something to do with the way his mind works causes a discontinuity in his life cycle."

"You're right, that doesn't make much sense."

"It does to him, and that's all that matters, I suppose."

"So Robert is his son. And very much his father's boy, from what I saw today."

"We've watched him for some time. He's survived in Othaside for all this time even through all the strange events that come naturally to him."

"Why watch him? He's not the first kid to be born here and grow up in Othaside."

"You know where his father currently resides. There was always the concern that he would go the same way, but his personality turned out to be quite boring. All the weirdness surrounded him and affected people and the environment around him but never actually touched him."

"Until he came here," said General Gnarly.

"Wow, this is interesting stuff, isn't it!" shouted the voice in Robert's head.

Robert made a sound of surprise, something of a *bwehar* kind of sound, jumped to his feet, tripped over a tree root, and fell backward.

"Robert!" said Lily and stared sternly.

Robert struggled to his feet. "What the hell is going on?"

"Don't get hysterical, Darkly," said General Gnarly.

"Hysterical? Why would I be hysterical? Because you know something about me that I don't know? That there's something weird about you too? And you, well, you're a Gnome, aren't you? 'Nuff said about that. And don't mention your short stature, although it's plainly obvious." Robert was breathing heavily.

"Robert," said Lily, "you're hyperventilating. Try and calm down."

Robert sat himself down and tried to control his breathing.

General Gnarly shook his head and headed back to where they had left Gnick. "We should be going soon; don't take too long."

Lily crouched down next to Robert and put a hand on his shoulder.

"Why can't you tell me about my father?" asked Robert.

"I've been ordered not to. And to be honest, it's not important as far as our current mission is concerned."

"And what about your secret?"

"Even less important. Come on, we need to get to the Archives and speak to the Historian, otherwise Rumpelstiltskin's trail will be too cold to follow."

And with that, she stood and walked away, leaving Robert sitting on the forest floor more confused than he felt he had any right to be.

A little-known fact about Dwarves is that they're short. And not just short in the terms of stature but they are also short-tempered, short on patience, and constantly short of deodorant, thus coining the well-known phrase, "It smells like a Dwarf in here." Dwarves didn't believe in body odour and chose to ignore any such way of remedying that which they didn't believe in and had no reason to acknowledge. Another little-known fact about Dwarves is that they have a tremendous lung capacity, which makes them amazing miners. They require very little oxygen to function as almost everything about them is anatomically smaller than that of a human.

They could survive in deep tunnels where the oxygen is thin for hours upon end where a human would simply pass out and die, wishing that he had been born a Dwarf and probably contemplating why he had even considered entering such a deep tunnel in the first place.

It was this increased lung capacity that had allowed Rumpelstiltskin to lay as if dead, unmoving beneath the ground, surrounded by angry plants, for the better part of an hour. The plants had begun to drift off to sleep and slowly moved apart, back to their original rooted spots. Rumpelstiltskin took the opportunity to thrust forth his hatchet and break the ground above him before scrambling out. He'd taken some good swipes at the over-articulated bush before he was overcome and dragged into the earth. His face was bleeding in several places where he'd been slashed with vines and he was almost certain that a particularly strong lavender bush had succeeded in dislocating his right shoulder.

He was also covered in leaves, dirt and matted blood, and looked a lot like a man from Liverpool after he's had a good solid night out on the town. Or, in Thiside, a man from the Three Fairy Islands who'd just visited the Dockside district of the City of Oz. Rumpelstiltskin walked to the edge of the garden and leaned against the wall. It was at times like this he wished he had control over his own magic. But all the wishing in the world would do him no good, at least not while he was the one doing the wishing.

The evil Dwarf headed along the edge of the garden, being careful to stay away from the slumbering plants. He pushed open a door set into the emerald wall at the back of the garden and found himself in a long courtyard crisscrossed with lines of laundry; wizard's hats and robes and colourful pairs of underwear hung everywhere. Wizards believed in colourful underwear the same way that water believed it was wet. It was just natural.

Rumpelstiltskin looked toward the Eastern tower where he believed he would find the wizard he was looking for. Niggle was a member of the Wizards' Council who suffered from a nervous disposition that made him stutter uncontrollably. He'd also had the misfortune of having his life saved by Rumpelstiltskin not long before the Dwarf was incarcerated in the Tower.

It was by the Dwarf's own hand that the then-apprentice wizard Niggle found himself in peril. Rumpelstiltskin had been looking for an apprentice wizard whom he could manipulate and control, and Niggle had turned out to be the perfect victim. Rumpelstiltskin set up an elaborate trap by which he could save the wizard and have him in his debt. At his request, the wizard had then performed a spell for Rumpelstiltskin that allowed him to continue with his plan. Not long after the spell casting, the Dwarf was apprehended and escorted to the Tower by the Agency. That was the last time Niggle had seen him. Until today.

The wizard Niggle was not a particularly good wizard, although that was not to say he didn't have the skill. It was more that he had a very comprehensive fear of everything, including his own powers. As a result, he spent a lot of time locked in his chambers trying to avoid the practice of magic. He held the opinion that the fact wizards spent all their time *practicing* magic was a clear indication that they shouldn't be using it at all. As soon as

Niggle passed his final exams and was admitted into the Wizards' Council, he resolved to attend council meetings only when absolutely necessary and remained locked in his apartment chamber passing the hours by reading books and trying different types of tea. He was called upon to work magic only once, a few years ago, to magically reinforce a cell of particular importance in the basement of the Tower prison. Since then, most people seemed satisfied just to leave him be and keep their distance.

Something that the Wizards' Council did know that Niggle didn't was that he was actually one of the most powerful wizards in all of Thiside or Othaside. Thankfully, he was too scared of his own power ever to test it out. It was for this reason that the Wizards' Council let him remain on the council despite his lack of involvement. They never knew when such power might come in handy, especially if it was on their side.

Niggle was happily boiling water for the latest batch of tea he'd received from some far-off place and was scanning one of his many bookshelves for something to read. Along with his nervous stutter came an equally nervous twitch that caused his right eye, neck, and left shoulder to spasm in unison every thirty seconds or so. He'd grown to live with it, but the rest of the world found it very unsettling. Accompanied by the stutter, his unique appearance made most people find it difficult to hold a conversation with him.

There was a distinct knock at the wizard's chamber door that made Niggle jump. It was Wednesday; no one ever visited him on a Wednesday. Incidentally, Thiside only had five days of the week: Monday, Tuesday, Wednesday, Sunday, and Snarfday. To make matters worse, the days occurred in different and random order every week, as laid out by the Thiside yearly calendar. This made keeping track of appointments very difficult but made the embarrassment of forgetting someone's birthday or anniversary much more understandable. Every Snarfday, an apprentice wizard would stop by to drop off the council news, but other than that, Niggle never had to interact with anyone. A surprise visit from an unknown someone made him nervous, which wasn't really a stretch of the imagination when everything made him nervous anyway. On a scale of one to ten, where one is a little bit nervous and ten is an extravagant sort of nervous, with a paling of the skin and hot sweats, this was around a seven.

The someone at the door knocked again, this time with clear impatience. Niggle realized he'd been staring at the door hoping they'd go away but their persistence was apparent as there came a third knock. Niggle made his way over to the door and cracked it open and peered through with his left eye, the one that didn't twitch. Niggle stood almost six feet tall, and was happy to see that no one was there. His mistake was quickly realized when a voice from below the five-foot mark said, "Hello, Niggle, nice to see you after all this time."

Through a face covered in dried blood, leaves, and, dirt Rumpelstiltskin grinned up at him from beneath a wizard's hat that was obviously too big for him and, knowing the Dwarf, more than likely stolen.

"Aren't you going to invite me in?" asked the Dwarf.

Rumpelstiltskin didn't wait for an invite and pushed his way through the door into the chamber. He noted that almost everything was covered in dust and the whole place smelled like must, tea, and self-indulgence, much like the smell of Ukrainian cooking.

Niggle stood with the door open, mouth agape.

"You can close the door, Niggle. And your mouth."

"J-j-j-j-yes," said Niggle and closed the door. And then slowly closed his mouth. "Y-y-you were in p-p-p-pr-pr—in the Tower."

The Dwarf pulled the kettle away from the fire, as it was starting to boil over. "I know you're probably surprised to see me but as you can plainly see, I'm no longer in the Tower so we can stop stating the obvious."

"How d-d-d-did you g-get out?"

Rumpelstiltskin waved a dismissive hand. "Not important. The important part is that I'm here now and could really use your help."

Niggle twitched uncontrollably. It looked a lot like someone had dropped an ice cube down his shirt. "W-w-what happened to your f-face?"

"I had a run-in with the Castle gardens. Evil bloody plants. Actually," said the Dwarf with an evil glint in his eye, "let's start there. How about you wish me healthy again? I think this shoulder is dislocated."

"C-c-c-an't d-do that, you know that, w-w-w—"

"Oh right, wizards can't make wishes, yada, yada, yada. How about you magic me up some first aid then?"

"W-w-w—"

"Oh, come now, my friend, let's not forget who saved you those many years ago. By the way, you haven't aged well."

"Th-th-th—"

"No need to thank me again. It was just lucky I was outside your parents' cottage when that seven-headed poisonous snake was thrown—uh—jumped at your head. The least I could do."

"B-but I p-paid that d-d-debt."

"That is true, yes. But what I'm asking this time, aside from a quick fix-me-up, is for you to perform the exact same thing you did for me before I was sent to the Tower."

Rumpelstiltskin leaned back in the chair and winced a little at the discomfort of his shoulder.

The wizard Niggle was sweating profusely and his twitch was now occurring every twenty seconds.

"B-b-b…"

Rumpelstiltskin used his good arm to loosen the hatchet from his belt loop and idly examined the sharpness of the blade.

Niggle observed that the loudest and most threatening words in the room were those that were not being spoken.

"O-o-o-of course," said the terrified wizard.

"I'm glad you see it my way."

Niggle twitched and hastily wiped the sweat from his forehead and rolled up the sleeves of his robe. Rumpelstiltskin watched as the wizard silently called into the room the magical essence of nothingness and moulded it into somethingness. He moved his hands in a circular gesture and the room around him began to glow blue. Niggle moved closer to the Dwarf and with his eyes still closed, he pointed a steady finger at Rumpelstiltskin and pushed it to his forehead.

Rumpelstiltskin's body became rigid as the magic did its work, coursing through his body, his veins, his muscles, and his bones. He felt his shoulder snap back into place, the broken skin where the plants had lashed at him knitted back together, and even his muscles that were tired from all the recent running felt refreshed and made anew.

The blue glow diminished and the wizard Niggle resumed twitching and sweating. He sank into a chair and rubbed his temples.

"Th-th-there ya go. G-g-g-g-good as new."

So easy. "And now the girl. I need you to tell me where she is."

"I haven't d-d-done a finding sp-sp-spell in a long time."

"No time like the present," said the Dwarf and grinned maliciously.

114

CHAPTER TWELVE

THE HISTORIAN

General Gnarly and Gnick led the way as the foursome followed the North Yellow Brick Road through the valley. After their encounter with the bandits, Gnarly and Gnick had scouted ahead to make sure the way was clear. Aside from a couple of farmers and an oddly shaped cow-like creature, their contact with anyone but each other had been limited.

Robert and Lily walked together in silence. Lily's mind seemed to be elsewhere and Robert noticed that she seemed to be growing anxious as the day marched forward.

Robert was trying to ignore the way that General Gnarly glanced back at him every now and then. He now felt that the Gnome saw him as a threat, which was hilarious on various levels. To those who knew him, Robert was considered to be one of the least threatening things on Earth. Some people would have gone as far as to say that cotton wool or a really well made ham sandwich presented more of a threat than Robert. Robert was one of those individuals that people didn't mind meeting in a dark alley because he would provide comfort in the sense that if there was anything bad lurking in the alley, it would attack Robert first because he looked like an easy target.

Robert was taking the silence as a time to reflect and plan.

"You really don't have a plan," said the voice in Robert's head.

Robert ignored it.

Although, it was true. He'd considered using the vial of blood that the White Rabbit had given him. He'd said it would take Robert anywhere he wanted if he went through a door.

The problem was that he'd never seen or been through a door and the prospect scared him. The other reason was that he felt he needed to be here. Needed to stick to Lily because… well… he couldn't actually come up with a reason.

"It's because she's beautiful, and despite all outward appearances she seems to care about your well-being," said the voice.

Robert didn't reply. He didn't want to give off the impression he was going crazy to the others. Even though that was obviously what was happening, he didn't feel the need to advertise it any more than he had to. Either way, he felt this was where he was supposed to be for the time being. The one thing that was still bothering him—

"One thing?" said the voice.

—was the cat. The voice in his head was strange, definitely. The fire that had started at the halfway house was very suspicious. The cat, however, he was certain had been real. He hadn't imagined it; he'd held it in his hands.

"Maybe you didn't?" said the voice.

"Shut up!" said Robert.

Lily jumped. "Damn it, Robert!"

"Sorry," said Robert sheepishly. "I don't have any control over it."

"I know it's not really your fault."

Robert was a little surprised. This was the first time that Lily had admitted any hint that she knew what was going on with him.

"So," began Robert, hoping to get back on speaking terms once again, "tell me about the Historian?"

"Well, for starters, he lives there," said Lily as they crested the high ground of the pathway to reveal the foot of one of the surrounding mountains. Set into the foot of the mountain was a medium-sized castle built of a dark grey stone, with three tall towers and guarded by a high wall. Robert noticed that there were flocks of birds flying close to the castle walls and around the towers.

"I thought it'd be bigger," mused Robert.

"The castle is just the front of the Archives. The mountain behind it is largely hollow. It was mined by an ancient group of Dwarves. There are countless rooms and passageways; many haven't even been explored. It was originally supposed to be some sort of Dwarf kingdom but the Giants wiped them out."

"How did the Giants get in there?"

"The Dwarves were so impressed with themselves for hollowing out an entire mountain and turning it into their kingdom that when the Giants rampaged across the land, the Dwarves felt the need to defend their mountain."

"Wouldn't they have been safer *in* the mountain?"

"They weren't the smartest of the ancient races. They marched out to meet the Giants and were consequently crushed. The Giants wanted nothing to with the Dwarves or anyone else. They just wanted to get from the Southlands, where they had originally lived, to the North where they wanted to re-settle. The Dwarves just got in their way."

"And now the mountain's a library?"

"Precisely. It was taken over by the first Wizards' Council and became home to our history. It was managed largely by wizards for many years until just over a hundred years ago, when the Historian was appointed to watch over and catalogue the Archives."

"Over a hundred years? How old is he?"

"He's getting close to his nine-hundredth birthday."

"So he's not human?"

"No."

"Dwarf?"

"No."

"Wizard?"

"No."

"Look, it'd probably help if you gave me a hint."

Lily stopped and turned to face Robert and he realized then that he had been wrong about her seeming anxious. She wasn't anxious or nervous, it was fear he saw in her. She was scared of the Historian.

"Lily, what is he?"

Lily bit her lip and looked to the ground. "He's a werewolf, Robert."

Robert didn't know why the thought of werewolves existing was any stranger than anything else he'd seen today but the concept struck him as amusing.

"Well yeah, of course he is. Now it just seems silly that I even guessed a wizard. I suppose he has an assistant that's a vampire?"

"Don't be ridiculous, there's no such thing as vampires," said Lily and continued walking.

Robert followed behind her. "So when it's a full moon he turns into a wolf and terrorizes the local farmland?"

"No, he doesn't do that anymore."

"Ohh, so he's a nice werewolf," said Robert with a laugh.

Lily turned around and stood in Robert's path. Her eyes were moist with tears.

Robert's smile instinctively dropped from his face.

"He's not a *nice* werewolf. There are no nice werewolves. He terrorized Thiside for many years and killed a lot of innocent people. He stole a passport and fled to Othaside in the early eighteenth century and hid in France quietly for thirty years. But he couldn't keep his blood lust in check and he finally snapped. Othasiders named him the *Beast of Gévaudan* because that's the province he was terrorizing at the time. Your history books actually have some of the details. He attacked two hundred and ten people and killed one hundred and thirteen of them. A special task force had to be assembled to cross over to Othaside to hunt and capture him. He was dragged back here and served a hundred and thirty years in the Tower before being released and appointed, at his request, to be the Historian. He's a murderer, a killer of men, women, and children. He's not nice, Robert."

"I'm sorry, Lily, I didn't know."

Lily wiped a sleeve across her eyes. "Well, now you know. Let's make this visit short."

She turned and walked away, passing the Gnomes who had stopped to see what the shouting was all about.

"You've got a real way with the ladies, moron," said Gnick.

"Who's that?" asked General Gnarly who had been watching Lily.

Robert looked down the road to see that Lily was talking to a bright blue glowing ball.

"That's her Fairy. She went after the Dwarf."

Lily beckoned the three of them over. "Veszico had an altercation with Rumpelstiltskin but essentially she lost. The Dwarf was heading toward the City of Oz which means he definitely has an agenda."

"How do you know?" said Robert.

"Because he's heading toward one of the most populated areas in Thiside. If you're an escaped convict on the run, then staying away from people is normally the best thing to do."

"So there must be something there he wants."

"Or needs," added the General.

"Hopefully, the Historian can tell us what he was doing when he was caught, which might give us some idea of where he's going," said Lily.

Veszico's little voice rang like the tiniest of tiny bells.

Lily looked confused.

"No, I haven't seen Jack since he went after you."

The Fairy's voice rang again but this time with urgency.

"I'm sure he's fine, and regardless, I have a different task for you. I need you to fly to the Kingdom of Hearts. Agent Tweedle is on assignment as council to the Queen. I need you to send him to the Tower as quickly as possible. There's a prisoner there who needs interrogating; the Guard Troll will know which one. He might be able to shed some light on how and why Rumpelstiltskin escaped but tell him to use caution."

The Fairy nodded, shone brighter, and flew off toward the East.

"Come on, we've lost enough time already today," said Lily and started a quick pace toward the Archives with the Gnomes running on ahead.

Robert stayed where he was until they were out of earshot. "Uh, voice in my head?"

"Who, me?" said the voice.

"Yes. Do you think she was telling the whole truth about the werewolf thing?"

"You think she wasn't?"

"Well, it just doesn't feel right."

"Are you asking my opinion or just looking for someone impartial to talk to?"

"Your opinion."

"Well, if I'm you, then we actually share the same opinion. Which is…"

"…she's not telling the whole story."

The castle loomed up ahead of them as they got closer. The sun was beginning its downward spiral, quite literally, and the shadows of the Western mountains began to point dark fingers across the valley.

Robert noticed what he had thought were birds weren't birds at all.

"What are those things?"

"They're pixies," said General Gnarly and spat on the ground. "Sodding awful creatures!"

"I thought they were supposed to be nice creatures?" said Robert.

"Someone really ought to slap you up the side of the head every time you make an assumption in this world that begins with *I thought*," said Lily.

"I'll do it," said Gnick.

"Oh, I'm sorry," said Robert sarcastically, "but I'm sort of new here and the only thing I have to go on is the Fairy Tales from Othaside. And in those stories Pixies are cute, happy, magical creatures."

"Well, here they're not cute, they're never happy, and they're certainly not magical," said General Gnarly.

"Sort of like Gnomes, then, are they?" said Robert, grinning.

"Good one, moron," said Gnick.

"Hmph," said the General.

"Oh, c'mon, General, that was a classic, coming from the moron."

"I suppose."

"Think of Pixies as guard dogs," said Lily. "They generally only ever listen to one master and they're very protective. They're not overly smart but they do have the ability to perform simple tasks.

"And why don't Gnomes like them?"

"Because they're too short," said General Gnarly gruffly and knocked on what looked to be the only door set into the castle wall.

Robert mouthed the word *seriously* to Lily, who just shrugged.

There was the buzzing sound of wings flapping extremely fast, and a small black creature, about half the size of a Gnome, flew down from above and hovered in front of them. It had large, black, marble-like eyes set into an oval-shaped head above two slits that Robert assumed were its nostrils. It smiled a wide mouth full of tiny sharp teeth and a green tongue. Its arms and legs were short but the hands and feet were larger, disproportionate. The creature was completely naked but didn't seem to care in the slightest. Its manhood, in this particular case, dangled for all to see. On its back a pair of almost transparent wings flapped like a hummingbird's and smelled faintly like oranges. To Robert they looked like mini-demons; this was reinforced by two small red horns protruding from its head. It looked at Lily and Robert in turn and then finally decided to address Lily.

"Whats you want?" said the Pixie.

"We're here to see the Historian."

"Ee's bizzy, go way."

"Let us in, you ugly little piece of bandersnatch excrement!" said General Gnarly.

The Pixie looked down as if surprised. Robert noticed that more Pixies were now lining the walls above them, intently watching the scene.

"Ohzie, Gnomes izit? Never sawz ya down there," said the Pixie and snickered.

Gnick produced a small dagger from his sleeve but General Gnarly waved him down. "Unless you'd like those wings clipped, you'd better go tell the Historian we're here."

"Gnomes iz nasty. Don't like. Go way."

"We're here at the request of the Agency. I'm an Agent. And your Historian knows me well," said Lily.

"Eazy t' say youz agent. Arder to prove."

Lily rolled up her right sleeve to show a tattoo that Robert had never noticed before. An intricate blue dragon with a red eye coiled around her forearm.

"Ahhright," said the Pixie, "Namez plez."

"This is General Gnarly and Lieutenant Gnick of the Warrior Gnomes of the Grimm Mountains."

The Pixie rolled its eyes.

"This is Robert Darkly and I'm Lillian Redcloak."

This was the first time that Robert had heard Lily's full name. He repeated the name in his head and something in the back of his mind clicked. Something familiar? A memory? But he couldn't place it.

The Pixie giggled. "Oh I seez. Whats biznezz you ave with thistorian?"

"We need access to some records."

"Waitz here. Gnomes don't cause no problemz, or elsez!"

And with that, the Pixie buzzed off over the castle wall.

The wizard Niggle was beyond what a normal person would constitute a nervous wreck. He'd already tried three times to pour himself tea but he was shaking so badly that the liquid never reached the flower-imprinted cup. *Why hadn't the Dwarf just let the seven-headed poisonous snake tear me to pieces all those years ago?*

His fourth pot of tea was now beginning to boil and he used his favorite oven gloves to remove it from the fire. He'd performed the spell that the Dwarf had asked and found what he wanted and told him exactly where he could get it. Rumpelstiltskin hadn't wasted any time leaving, although he did pause long enough to let Niggle know that if he breathed a word of his visit to anyone that he'd return and perform some nasty things involving a freshly sharpened knife and Niggle's favorite body parts.

The spell Rumpelstiltskin needed performed was a simple one that Niggle had learned early on in his training. It wasn't the spell that worried him, but the purpose behind it. Niggle did not know what the Dwarf had been up to the first time that he had performed the spell all those years ago, and he still had no idea. Part of him thought that he was much safer not knowing what was going on, but part of him, that little tiny obscure piece of him that wasn't a nervous wreck, was full of confidence, and had amazing control over his immense power, wondered what it was all about.

He shakily carried the kettle to a large oak table that was mostly covered in books, scrolls, and half-burnt candles. He set his teacup on the table and lifted the kettle carefully. All his concentration was focused on getting the tea into the teacup. The hot liquid shifted in the kettle as he tipped it and the first droplets appeared at the end of the spout…

The front door was suddenly kicked open with a loud *thump*. Niggle's entire body twitched in one massive spasm of fear and he dropped the metal kettle, spilling hot water all over the floor. He lost momentary control of his bodily functions and piddled himself just a tiny bit.

Jack stood in the doorway, red-faced and out of breath.

"Where's the Dwarf?"

"I-I-I-I-d-d-d-d-bah-bah-bah," said Niggle nonsensically.

Jack strode over to the wizard, pushed him into a seat, picked up his flower-imprinted cup and threw it against the wall where it shattered into many flowery pieces. He leaned over the horrified wizard and with a calmly terrifying voice said, "Tell me where Rumpelstiltskin is or I'm going to throw you out of your own window."

The wizard's delicate bladder gave up completely and wet his robe.

Robert, Lily, and the Gnomes had been waiting for almost thirty minutes. The Gnomes were carefully eyeing the Pixies, who continued to line the castle walls and chatter and giggle amongst themselves while pointing at the visitors. Lily hadn't stopped moving since the Pixie had left. She stalked back and forth in front of the door, alternating between glancing at the door and up at the setting sun. Incidentally, the sun was feeling adventurous and was attempting a triple salchow, which most considered impossible without ice skates, but the sun could not be deterred.

Robert slouched against the castle wall, preparing himself for the monster that Lily had described the Historian to be. A werewolf, of all things! He vaguely remembered the tale of the Beast of Gévaudan from Ms Windle's History class. It was one of the few things any adolescent British schoolboy would remember, as it involved a mysterious creature that was never caught plus the violent murder of many French people. He began to wonder how many other crossovers there had been that simply melted into Othaside's history books.

"Lily?"

"Yes, Robert," said Lily, still stalking back and forth.

"Are the authorities in Othaside aware of the existence of Thiside?"

Gnick raised an eyebrow and leaned over to Gnarly. "That was almost a smart question."

Gnarly nodded in agreement.

Lily stopped stalking. "They used to be," she said thoughtfully. "I imagine that somewhere in Othaside, some sort of government agency is aware of us. When the Agency was first established, it decided that we should reveal ourselves to the authorities of Othaside. With so many of our geographical locations coinciding with areas of England or Europe, we first spoke with the Director of the British Secret Service. As you can imagine, he was sceptical. The liaison finally had to bring the Director across to Thiside to make him believe."

"And what happened?"

"He took one look at the White Rabbit and lost control of his mental faculties. After that, it was decided that it was best just to pretend none of it ever happened. I'm sure he reported it somewhere and it's filed away in an obscure filing cabinet in a forgotten basement."

"Are there many crossovers from Thiside to Othaside?"

"Not really; we police both sides. It's easier and more common for an Othasider to trip into Thiside. With the requirement for a passport to go from here to there it's rare that someone gets across whom we don't know about."

Robert wondered who was at the head of the Agency but before he had a chance to ask, the Pixie returned.

"Soz ta keep ya waiting."

"No, you're not," said Gnick.

"No is not," agreed the Pixie. "Istorian wills see ya now."

The Pixie waved an oversized hand toward the large wooden door, which slowly creaked open to reveal an overgrown and cracked courtyard, steeped in shadows and hovering Pixies.

Lily walked through the door, followed by Robert. As the Gnomes approached the archway, the Pixie buzzed in front of them and waved a stubby finger.

"Ah, ah, ahhh, no Gnomesez. Youz stay ere."

General Gnarly waved his hand and produced a dagger from nowhere, causing the Pixies within the courtyard to hiss.

"It's okay, General," said Lily, "we won't be long. And if we're not out before sunset, feel free to kill the Pixies and storm the castle."

General Gnarly smiled a half-smile and bowed slightly before hiding his dagger back in his sleeve. The door creaked closed and Lily continued walking. The Pixies, and there must have been at least two hundred, hovered out of the way to allow them through. Robert wondered how they could tell each other apart, as they all looked the same.

The courtyard looked like it used to circle the entire castle but as parts of the castle and wall had fallen to ruin. It was now blocked on either side and overgrown with grass and climbing ivy.

Two large, wooden, double doors rose up before them nestled into the dark stone of the castle wall. As they came closer, several Pixies flew against the door and with great difficulty pushed it open. It was dark within, but Lily walked with purpose as if she could see just fine. Robert stumbled with less purpose and not an ounce of grace, as he couldn't see anything. There were slits cut into the rock wall high above them but the sun was no longer at the right angle to allow the light to enter.

As his eyes adjusted to the darkness, he made out a large stone room with no doors and a long, stone staircase that went down. The only reason he could make out that the staircase went down was because a light was slowly making its way up the steps. The silhouette holding the light was short but stocky, walked with a slight limp, and grunted every third step.

The figure held a candlestick, and as he reached the top of the stairs, Robert could see that he was a lot bigger than originally thought. His limp and stooped frame made him look small but Robert could clearly see that the Historian was not a small person, although it seemed as if his nine hundred years were taking their toll.

The man stopped short of Lily and Robert, raised his candlestick, and squinted at them.

"Hello, Lillian," he said in a gruff voice that sounded harsh and cold. His face was hard and chiselled, with shaggy grey stubble that was separated down one side of his face by a long scar that ran from his temple to beneath his chin. One eye was white with cataracts, while the other eye was bright amber.

"Hello, Bzou," said Lily.

Robert noted that she seemed tense all over. If she had hackles, they'd be up.

"I never thought I'd see you again. It's been a very long time. You've grown some," said the Historian.

"I didn't want to come."

The Historian barked a laugh. "I'll bet you didn't. Who's your friend?"

"This is Robert. He's an Othasider and he's helping with an investigation."

Robert opened his mouth to say *hi* but other than a quick once-over, the Historian continued speaking to Lily.

"And why did you come here? I know it must have been difficult, so it must be important."

"We need access to any records you have pertaining to the Dwarf, Rumpelstiltskin."

The Historian looked hard at Lily.

"Come with me." The old man turned and started to head back down the stairs.

Lily reached out for Robert's hand and led him down the stairs. Robert was taken aback by the contact and thought maybe she was just assuming it was too dark for him, but her grip was so tight that he knew she was actually looking to him for support. This worried Robert for several different reasons as, for one, he wasn't very good at supporting people, even himself, and two, his feelings for Lily seemed to be on a yo-yo depending on her mood. She was weird and quirky, mysterious and beautiful, ridiculously strong...

"Beautiful," added the voice in Robert's head.

Got that already.

"Oh, sorry, wasn't fully listening," said the voice.

Over the last twenty-four hours, he'd definitely developed a feeling for her, maybe multiple feelings. But he'd felt extremely let down when she hadn't believed him about the cat and then again when she and Gnarly had been speaking behind his back in the forest.

His thought process jarred when they reached the bottom of the staircase, which he now realized had been very long. They must be quite a ways beneath the surface, which made sense if, as Lily said, the archives stretched back into the mountain.

The staircase opened out into a long hallway that led to a doorway at the far end. A bright light shone from the door and from the flickering, Robert assumed that the room was lit by firelight. The farther they walked, the harder Lily gripped his hand. He began wondering how long before he lost feeling in his fingers.

Despite the limp and his age, the Historian had no problem taking long strides ahead of them. Robert could now see that his grey hair was shabby and hung just beneath his shoulders. He wore a red robe, dark pants, and black boots.

When they reached the doorway, the cold feeling of the castle changed considerably. The room was large and warm and looked like it belonged in a stately home. A hearth burned brightly in the centre of the far wall. The furniture looked like it was covered with velvet, and all the tables and chairs were carved from wood and featured clawed feet. Bookshelves surrounded the rooms from floor to ceiling. Papers and scrolls spread across numerous tables. Another large door was set into the wall to the far right and Robert could see that the hallway beyond was lit by wall-mounted candles that stretched far into the distance, out of sight.

The Historian motioned to the chairs by the fire.

"Please, have a seat." He sat down in a large chair covered with red velvet. As he did so, he pulled a tiny silver bell from the pocket of his robe and rang it once.

Stiltskin

Lily didn't move to sit down or let go of Robert's hand, so he stood awkwardly, not really sure what to do.

A Pixie flew into the room and hovered by the Historian.

"Fetch me the file on Rumpelstiltskin. It'll be in the Eastern wing on one of the upper levels."

"Yez zir," said the Pixie and flew off down the candlelit hallway.

"They're not the smartest or most articulate creatures but they make good servants. Really, why don't you both sit down, it's perfectly safe."

Lily pulled Robert with her to a loveseat and they both sat down, facing the old man.

The Historian eyed them both and sniffed the air.

"It'll take him a few minutes to find the right section. You probably both need the rest; you smell like you've been doing a lot of walking. You smell like dead rabbits, goats, and fire, and…"

He sniffed the air again and looked directly at Robert. His eyes grew wide. He moved from his chair so fast that Robert barely had chance to notice the movement until the old man was inches from his face and sniffing him.

Lily had completely tensed and paled a little but she made no move to help.

"Uh, look, I know I don't smell that good, it's been a while since I've had a bath, but would you mind not doing that?" asked Robert.

The Historian stopped and looked him in the eyes. "There's something special about you, isn't there, boy?"

"Well, I suppose so."

"You have a very strange smell."

"I'm sorry about that. I haven't had any access to deodorant for the last twenty-four hours."

"I'm surprised you can't smell it, Lillian."

"I've spent a lot of time with him. I'm sure whatever it is, I've become immune," said Lily.

The Historian barked a short laugh again and retook his seat.

"So what's this all about?" said the Historian.

"Rumpelstiltskin escaped the Tower yesterday morning. We're searching for him."

The Historian smiled.

"You mean you're hunting him," he said matter-of-factly.

"No, we're searching for him, and when we catch him we'll arrest him."

"You still try so hard to hide your true nature, Lillian; it must be exhausting."

"And you wear your true nature so openly, *that* must be irritating to everyone around you."

There followed the kind of pregnant pause which wasn't just pregnant but had quickly ventured through the third trimester and was imminently about to give birth to triplets.

"So," said Robert, "you're a werewolf?" It was all he could think of to say.

The Historian fixed his old eye, the good one, on Robert in much the same way that a lion fixes its gaze on a three-legged, blind, deaf gazelle with a bell around its neck.

"Well," continued Robert, "it's just that I've never met a werewolf before today, you see. And, uhh..." The Historian's stare was getting to him. "Are you going to blink anytime soon?"

"Probably best not to provoke the creature responsible for a great many deaths," said the voice in Robert's head.

"Right," said Robert.

The Historian looked from Robert to Lily and his face broke in a whimsical smile.

"He doesn't know, does he, Lily?" growled the Historian.

"Know what?" asked Robert.

Lily turned to Robert and there were actually tears in those amber eyes. Although he didn't know why she was so upset, Robert felt a rush of anger that something had dared upset her like this.

"Amber eyes," said the voice in Robert's head.

"Amber eyes," said Robert out loud.

Lily closed her eyes, and then opened them again.

"I don't underst—"

"They both have amber eyes," said the voice.

"Oh," said Robert. "Oh shit, you're a werewolf too."

As if it was the simplest statement in the world. He turned to the Historian. "Bloody hell, you're not her dad, are you?"

The Historian laughed and the sound of it bounced around the chamber. The firelight flickered, casting his shadow against the far wall and for a moment, Robert thought he saw his true shape silhouetted there.

Lily took both of Robert's hands in hers.

"This isn't easy for me to talk about." Lily's eyes were moist as she looked past Robert into the fire.

He felt a pang of sadness override the anger. Then he realized he was holding hands with a werewolf. Then he realized that he was currently sitting in a room with two werewolves.

"You're over-thinking this," said the voice in Robert's head.

Lily seemed to collect herself, and shifted her gaze to Robert.

"I was born to a family of Lords over three hundred years ago. My father's name was Randolph Redcloak. He owned a great amount of farmland along the Southern edge of the Enchanted Forest. When I was twenty years old, I spent the summer at my grandmother's estate not far north of here. I spent the summer hunting and fishing, learning how to run the family business, and enjoying the time with my grandmother. At the end of summer, I set out with two friends to hunt for Jingraz, a sort of deer, but the day drew to an end far too quickly. It was a horrible day of hunting, we didn't catch anything, and it wasn't until we were a couple of miles from home that we realized why we hadn't caught anything. We came across a field filled with half-eaten Jingraz. And at the centre of the field sat a giant, wolf-like creature."

Lily glanced at the Historian, whose face was unreadable. "The creature attacked us, violently, and killed my two companions before we even had a chance to run. I was carrying my father's hunting blade and it was pure luck that saved my life that night."

The Historian snorted.

"The creature stood over me while I sobbed and struggled. Blood dripped from its jaws and its amber eyes shone in the moonlight. It sank its teeth into my shoulder and it felt like it would tear me in two, so I lashed out with the blade, a silver blade, giving him the scar he now wears so proudly. I ran like I'd never run before but the change was already upon me. It hurt like nothing I'd ever felt before and I stood and screamed. But all I heard was a howl."

"Lily, I don't know what to say."

"I change with the moon, and at will, if I so choose. I can heal from any injury but silver, and you've seen how strong this curse has made me."

"It's not a damn curse, you ungrateful whelp," growled the Historian. "What I gave you was a gift."

"You would've murdered me!"

"That's why you joined the hunting party to cross over to Othaside to catch the Beast of Gévaudan," said Robert.

"Because he infected me, we were... are... commonly bound. Even when we're miles apart, we can still sense each other. I can smell him infinitely clearer than anything else. I was the best person to hunt him down."

"I don't think your sense of smell is that good, my dear Lillian," said the Historian. "If it was, you'd be able to smell the distinct feline scent on your companion."

Lily looked at Robert, who felt embarrassed although he couldn't figure out why.

"You can smell the cat on me?"

"It's as plain as day."

"But there was no cat," said Lily. "It was all in Robert's head."

"I highly doubt that," said the Historian.

"I knew it was real!" said Robert.

"No you didn't," said the voice.

"Well, I did start to question myself after none of you believed me," agreed Robert.

The Pixie was suddenly hovering in between them, holding a massively thick book with the name *Rumpelstiltskin* inscribed in gold on the black leather cover.

"Ah, good," said the Historian and pointed to one of the large reading tables. The Pixie flew over to the table and dropped the book with a thud. The Historian was already making his way over to the table, as if the conversation regarding his murderous intentions and consequential infection of Lily was over. But Robert couldn't bring himself to say anything. Lily was still looking at Robert, maybe trying to gauge his reaction.

"I'm sorry, Robert; as my travelling companion, you should have known. I endangered you. Are you... okay?"

"Well, yeah, I suppose. It's just another weird thing to get used to really. How come you couldn't smell the cat on me?"

"Oh sure, completely ignore her inner turmoil and focus on your own preservation of sanity. She's not going to like that you're not being sensitive," said the voice in Robert's head.

"I think it's because I've been with you the whole time, I'm somewhat desensitized to your scent. Thank you for understanding."

"Or maybe not," said the voice.

"Uh yeah, no problem. Not like we can change it, I suppose."

The Historian coughed loudly. "If you two are finished being ridiculous maybe you'd like to tell me what it is you're looking for?"

There it was again! As Lily moved over to the table along with Robert, she felt the same wave of admiration for her new travelling companion. It was warm and fuzzy and entirely unfamiliar to her. He didn't seem to mind that she had a vicious killing machine hidden inside of her. Over the years, Lily had confided in very few people. Those who knew her secret had never acted the same around her again. Robert didn't seem to mind. She couldn't help but find that an admirable trait.

Outside the castle, General Gnarly and Gnick sat with their backs against the castle wall. They were making themselves look busy and keeping the Pixies at bay by sharpening various pointy kinds of weaponry.

The Pixies hovered above the castle wall, staring down at the Gnomes and chattering amongst themselves. Pixies hated Gnomes and Gnomes hated Pixies. This point was proven when a brave Pixie had chosen to spit on General Gnarly. The spit had barely touched his red pointy hat when he'd flung a blade, cleaving the Pixie's wings from its back and causing it to plummet to Earth. Pixies, being the cannibalistic carnivores that they were, swooped down to tear the injured creature to shreds. After that, the Pixies kept out of what they hoped was throwing distance.

The tip of the sun could still be seen peeking over the tip of the Western mountains. Without any provocation whatsoever, the sun dropped beneath the mountain and darkness flooded the land. The sun kept to common rules of rising and setting in that it rose in the East and set in the West. But outside of that, it did whatever it damn well pleased. The moon shared this attitude of indifference and didn't feel it needed to adhere to any such simplistic rules such as the so-called *lunar cycle*. The moon came out whenever it pleased. As if shot out of a cannon, the moon rose from behind the mountains and attached itself firmly in the sky over the mountains, throwing moonlight across the fields and against the castle walls of the Archives.

The Pixies all froze in unison and General Gnarly was on his feet.

"No!"

"Eh?" said Gnick.

"The moon's full. There was no indication of a full moon tonight."

The moon, although ignoring astrological law, usually appeared on the first night of its chosen lunar cycle as a crescent moon. The moon, being nonsensical and feeling in a smug sort of mood, had chosen to appear in the sky only once this lunar cycle and that appearance would be in its full glowing glory. Tomorrow, it might change its mind.

"Did we bring any rope?" asked Gnarly.

"Of course," said Gnick, "why?"

"Because we're going to need it."

Gnick began to pull thin strands of rope from somewhere in his trousers. General Gnarly turned to look up at the castle to see that the Pixies now lined the castle walls. They were no longer watching the Gnomes. They were now watching expectantly, their gaze focused upon the courtyard inside the castle wall.

The entity who now knew himself to be the Cat, who was once again incorporeal, was shocked at how weak he'd become. Floating through what could only be the nether regions of space and time, due to his surroundings being warm and squishy, he now maintained only a small strand of connection to the world. He'd appeared as a kitten and had funnelled his entire being into the creature to the point where he almost felt whole again, but it seemed that he could not anchor himself to the world he once occupied. There just wasn't enough magic left there anymore to sustain his arrival. So for the moment, he dedicated himself to doing what he had done for centuries and simply floated lost in his own thoughts and occasionally plucked on the single strand that held him to the world of Thiside. Mainly because he liked the twangy sound it made.

The Historian quickly flipped through the pages, stopping every now and then to read.

"Hmm," said the Historian, and then, "harrumph."

The firelight danced shadows across the wall. The Pixie had long since vanished from the room after fetching the Historian an ancient map of Thiside. Lily and Robert stood on the opposite side of the table from the old man.

Robert was taking the time to reflect on everything that had happened today, from the cat disappearing, the fight in the forest, the voice in his head, the revelation that he'd not only met a werewolf but had been travelling with one for the last day and a half. The same question still kept nagging at him: *Why me?* He was afraid he knew the answer. He must have been born here and crossed over at some point. And from the hushed conversations he'd heard today, his father was here. Maybe his mother, too. But why had they given him up?

"All right, I think I have it all together now," said the Historian, looking up from the book.

"So what was Rumpelstiltskin doing before he was caught?" asked Lily.

The Historian paused, shook his head a little as if something was buzzing inside his head. He looked toward the ceiling for a moment. A broad grin cracked his old face and he looked back to Robert and Lily.

"Sorry," said the Historian, "dizzy spell." He flipped back through a few of the pages. "It's strange that you, Lily, as an Agent don't already know this as he was caught and transported to the Tower the same day. Although Jack is possibly the worst Agent I've ever encountered for his record keeping, he did file the report and eventually it ended up here."

"Jack was the Agent who caught him?"

"No, but he was his interrogator at the Tower. Like I said, strange that you didn't know that."

"This was fifty years ago; I was on sabbatical."

"Ah yes, your voyage across the seas. I recall hearing about it. Strange, though, that he'd send you here to find out what he himself already knew, as it was he that filled out the report."

"But what about the Dwarf?" asked Robert, who was growing more and more anxious to get out of the Archives. Something didn't feel right, and he had a severe dislike of the Historian. He'd been waiting for the voice in his head to say something but it had been quiet since the werewolf revelation.

"The Dwarf known as Rumpelstiltskin is not like a normal Dwarf. He's a wish granter."

"Like a genie?"

"Robert…" said Lily.

"I know, I know, there's no such thing as genies."

The Historian shook his head. "Similar concept as a genie, but there are no limitations to wish granters. They can grant or deny any wish that's made in their presence, so it always pays to watch what you say."

"We already know this," said Lily.

"I didn't know," said Robert.

"Regardless," said the Historian, "his power is relevant. Jack's interrogation notes are sparse, at best, but they do indicate that Rumpelstiltskin was trading wishes for different objects of varying value before he was caught. What's interesting is that wasn't the reason he was arrested. He was arrested for attempted murder in Othaside."

"How did he obtain the passport to get through to Othaside?"

"The notes say he threatened a farmer who wished him to see a particular person, the one he tried to murder, in Othaside."

"Who was the victim?"

"Her name was Elise Marie Palmer."

"What was so special about Ms Palmer?" asked Lily.

"Her birth name was Elise Bastinda."

"Oh," said Lily.

"Makes sense, doesn't it?"

"Can you two just pretend I'm actually here in the room and know nothing about what's going on?" asked Robert.

Lily sighed. "The Bastindas were a family of witches. Evil witches. The main members of the Bastinda family were wiped out during the Munchkin Wars almost three hundred years ago, but it was rumoured that a few escaped and were granted asylum by the Wizards' Council, although they continued to be hated for their past transgressions."

The Historian lifted a separate piece of paper and squinted at the scrawled lettering. "The records here show that Elise's mother died during childbirth, leaving Elise as the last living Bastinda. They changed her name and sent her to Othaside to give her a chance at a normal life and to get rid of the last of the Bastindas."

"Why would Rumpelstiltskin need the last living Bastinda?" thought Lily out loud.

"The list of objects he was acquiring…," said the Historian.

"Yes?"

"Well, they're strange to begin with: horn of a bolgroc, scale of a dragon, urine of a dying Munchkin; it goes on and on. It seems like he was going to perform a ritual."

"Or a spell," said Lily, "but he's not a wizard; I wouldn't imagine he'd know where to start."

"Actually, he knew a wizard by the name of Niggle who now sits on the Wizards' Council. Maybe he was helping him. In fact, according to Jack's notes it was the wizard Niggle who performed the finding spell that allowed Rumpelstiltskin to find the girl in the first place."

"Why was he doing all that?" asked Robert.

"He must have been preparing to do something. Something big," said Lily.

"It certainly makes sense," agreed the Historian. "What you have to understand about Rumpelstiltskin is that he has immense power inside of him, but he can't access any of it for himself. He can grant someone any wish, to be famous, to be strong, to be rich, to be a bloody giraffe if that's your deepest desire. But he can never use his own magic on himself."

"Must be frustrating," Robert thought out loud.

"Veszico said that he was heading for the City of Oz. He might be going for the wizard."

The Historian sat himself down. "It's getting late, and if you've got all you wanted, I think it's time for you both to leave."

Lily quickly grabbed the list of objects that Rumpelstiltskin had been collecting and pocketed it while the Historian stared intently at the fire.

"Goodbye, Bzou."

"Nice to meet you, uh, sir," said Robert and half bowed awkwardly, realized he looked ridiculous, and stood up.

The Historian kept his eyes on the fire. "Feel free to visit again. And Lillian, enjoy the night air."

A foul-looking shadow danced above the door as Robert and Lily entered the hallway that would take them to the staircase.

"What did that mean?" asked Robert.

"He likes to play mind games. It doesn't matter; we got what we came for."

Robert couldn't tell in the dim light but it almost looked like Lily's skin was growing darker.

CHAPTER THIRTEEN

BIG BAD WOLF

The Historian waited until his guests had ascended the stairway before leaving his chair. He ran with great speed down the hallway toward the Archives, moving with such precision and force that he looked like a star athlete and not a nine-hundred-year-old werewolf. He turned down one hallway, then another, ascended a stairway, then bolted into a room with a large steel door. He pushed open the door with great effort, slipped inside, then slammed it shut and listened as the locks automatically slid into place on the outside of the door, locking him in. The room was narrow, high, empty, and made of thick stone. The only window was a large opening, with bars welded across it, set into the wall. The moonlight streamed in through the window, illuminating the narrow cell and spilling over the large body of the Historian as he ripped the clothes from his old body, felt his blood boil, his muscles tense. He began to feel the change flood through him.

Stiltskin

Robert held onto Lily's shoulder, as he could barely see his way up the stairs. The floor flattened out and he could see the outline of the high doors at the other end of the old hall.

The howl that echoed through the castle was one that Robert would never forget, partially because it was one of the singular, most chilling sounds he'd ever heard and partially because the events that immediately followed were nigh on unforgettable.

"That's not what I think it is, is it?" asked Robert, already pretty sure he knew the answer.

"Yes, he must've changed at will."

Robert banged on the ceiling high double doors. "Open up, we want out!"

Nothing.

"It's strange, though," said Lily. "Why would he change?"

"Can you open these doors?"

Lily pulled on one of the large circular door handles, and the door creaked open. The first thing Robert saw was the moonlight spilling through the doorway. The second thing he saw was the shocked expression that had affixed itself to Lily's face.

"What? What is it?" said Robert. He looked out through the doors and saw the full moon sitting comfortably above the castle walls. The Pixies lining the walls looked down at the doorway; their wings twitched with anticipation.

"Run, Robert!" shouted Lily and her voice dropped an octave at *ert*.

"What? Why?"

And then his common sense kicked him hard in the head.

"She's a werewolf," said the voice in his head calmly, "and it's a full moon."

"Oh. Shit."

Lily staggered out of the doorway and gripped her head with both hands.

"Oh shit, oh shit."

Lily's back bulged beneath her clothing; her hands widened and the fingers stretched; hair grew across the back of her hands.

She swung her head up toward the moon. He face was becoming longer, her eyes burned bright amber, and Robert watched in a frozen silence as her teeth grew pointier.

137

"Rugghhnn!" growled Lily.

"Sound advice," said the voice in Robert's head, "you should run."

Robert's feet were moving before the rest of his body clued in. He flew at the door, ignoring the growing chatter and shouts of the Pixies above, turned the handle of the door set into the castle wall and threw his weight against it. The last thing he saw before he slammed the door shut was Lily, or the beast that had been Lily, tearing the shredded clothes from its body with long claws. Its head was now a wolf's head, and it stood upright on long, muscular legs, its whole body covered in hair. Lily the werewolf let out a long howl.

Robert, running breathless, almost tripped over the Gnomes.

"General! Lily's... werewolf... full moon... big... really, really big," said Robert as he struggled for breath.

The Pixies shifted their eyes to the outside of the wall.

"Yes, moron," said Gnarly, "we know. I suggest you run."

"What are you two going to do?"

"We can take care of ourselves but we can't help you. We won't harm Lily and there's no way to get you out of here easily. Running is your best option right now."

Something heavy banged against the door.

"Moron, run!" shouted Gnick who had produced a dagger and threw it with complete accuracy at a particular pudgy-looking Pixie who plummeted dead to the ground in front of them. Four Pixies flew down to eat their fallen comrade, and then remembered what was trying to get through the door.

Robert now saw that General Gnarly and Gnick each had a length of thin rope. They both lassoed a Pixie and were dragged up into the air as the creatures shrieked and attempted to fly away.

"Run, moron!" shouted General Gnarly as he rose up and above the castle walls.

You don't need to tell me twice. Robert then realized that he had been told several times. He turned and sprinted off in no direction in particular.

Robert wasn't any sort of athlete. He'd failed at almost any sport he'd ever attempted. His physical education teachers in school had blamed it on him being gangly and uncoordinated and suggested he be thankful that he was able to put one foot in front of the other without hurting anyone. Robert wasn't a good runner because he could never find the correct motivation. It seemed pointless. On the flipside, he had always maintained that he could have made an excellent track star if there was someone chasing him with the intention of inflicting bodily harm.

It was that motivation of self-preservation that spurred Robert to run as if a massive, possibly hungry werewolf was chasing him. He could hear wood splinter somewhere in the distance behind him as, he assumed, Lily broke through the castle door. He held onto the fond hope that she wouldn't chase him. He then made the mistake of glancing back to see the girl he had once thought to be beautiful, now large, hairy, and drooling, running on all fours along the road after him.

"Oh shit, oh shit, oh shit," said Robert in between breathing.

He veered off the path and headed toward trees that led to the East, or was it West?

"East, I think," said the voice in Robert's head.

"Thanks," said Robert.

He glanced back again and wished he hadn't. The wolf was gaining ground.

"You should look for a door," said the voice.

"A door. Right. But won't that take me to Othaside?"

"Well, there are no werewolves there, are there?"

"Excellent point."

He reached the trees and looked back to see the werewolf skid to a halt fifty feet behind him. She was snarling.

"Lily, are you still in there?" shouted Robert with as little futility as possible.

The creature's eyes shone in the moonlight and she stood up on her hind legs.

"Shit," said Robert and fought to keep control of his bodily functions.

"Shit," agreed the voice.

The werewolf was at least seven feet tall, with dark hair and long, sharp-looking claws. Her knees were inverted, like a wolf's, and she sniffed the air.

"Lily, it's me, Robert. Remember?"

The wolf threw its head back and let out a long howl that was answered by a deeper howl coming from the direction of the castle. It occurred to Robert that the Historian must have been stalling, knowing the moon was coming. He felt a pang of sorrow for what the old man had done to Lily, but the thought was fleeting as the wolf dropped to all fours and charged at Robert who turned and ran into the trees.

The forest was dense, which Robert hoped would slow down the large creature. That small glimmer of hope was smashed into tiny pieces, burned, drowned, hung, drawn, quartered, and laid to rest in a quaint little area of Robert's mind as, seconds later, the sound of trees being literally pushed over could distinctly be heard behind him.

"A door, need a door, looking for a door," he panted.

Robert tripped on some sort of spiky shrubbery and tumbled out of the trees into a tiny clearing. And all was silent. This was not comforting. The sound of crashing trees had at least been a small reassurance that danger was behind him somewhere. He scrambled to his feet and listened intently to the silence. Moonlight shone through the treetops. He reached into his shirt and pulled out the vial of blood. Now seemed a good time to use the White Rabbit's gift to have a door take him anywhere he wished. He was almost certain that anywhere he wished would be better than here, or at least would offer the opportunity of not being torn to pieces. And then he heard it. Breathing. The sort of deep, heavy breathing often heard on the other end of creepy phone calls. And then he felt it. Warm drool dripped onto his face and down his left cheek. If his entire being wasn't overtaken by sheer unadulterated fear, Robert would have been disgusted that he was being drooled on. He didn't want to look up, but he'd long since lost control of what his body should or shouldn't be doing.

He looked up.

The werewolf was clinging to a tree, thirty feet off the ground, staring down at Robert.

"Nice doggy," was all Robert could think to say.

The werewolf dropped to the ground in front of Robert with the agile grace of a prima ballerina. Robert tried to picture the werewolf in a tutu. It didn't look funny.

The werewolf opened its mouth to reveal the kind of teeth no human ever wanted to be within fifty feet of without a good, sturdy, electric fence. The creature roared in Robert's face… or at least it would have, if Robert's face had still been there. Robert was already weaving through the trees with the grace and dexterity of a drunken spider monkey. The werewolf leaped into the trees, and Robert looked back just as she crashed down behind him and swiped out with one clawed hand.

Robert felt the cold tingly feeling of something slicing into his flesh and he pitched forward, felt a yank on his neck, and rolled to a stop. He looked up to see the werewolf looking down at him, something shiny hung from a bloody right claw. The vial of blood: Robert's passport. He could feel warmth spilling slowly onto his back and watched as the giant creature sniffed at the air.

"There!" screamed the voice in Robert's head.

Inexplicably, without any sort of reference other than *there*, Robert knew to look to his right and saw exactly what the voice was talking about. A distortion in space, a tear in the fabric of reality. A door.

Robert dived between the two trees to his right and could feel the werewolf's breath on his neck. He stood before the door and hesitated.

"What are you doing?" said the voice.

"I don't know where it'll take me."

"You can either go or stay but one of the options has your flesh being ripped from your bones. Just saying."

The doorway shrank to half the size.

Robert jumped headfirst through the doorway as the werewolf pushed itself through the trees with a crash. The world around him slid into a swirly sort of mass and for a moment, Robert thought he'd passed out. To his dismay, he found that he was wrong.

Rumpelstiltskin left the City of Oz as night fell and shadows overtook the city wall. He had the information he needed and now all he had to do was find a door to take him to Othaside. It took a lot of self-control not to bolt from the city, but with the City Guards patrolling the streets and the Agency on his tail, it made more sense to lay low and leave once it was dark.

The Dwarf followed the coastline to the West, hoping to avoid any foot traffic, as the coastline was treacherous at the best of times. Strong winds were always a hazard to those taking the coastline path; there was always the risk of being blown off the two-hundred-foot high cliffs that plummeted toward the ocean. The high cliffs ran from the City of Oz all the way to the borders of Munchkinland.

Two hours out of the city, Rumpelstiltskin found a door but was severely disappointed at its location. The door was situated floating in the air around six feet away from the cliff's edge, over the thrashing ocean. The moonlight illuminated the doorway nicely, and although ninety-nine percent of doors appeared close to the ground, there was always the tricky and rebellious one percent that chose to appear wherever the hell they wanted to.

The evil Dwarf stood with his hands on his hips, contemplating the distance to the door and whether he should just keep looking and find one that wasn't suspended two hundred feet above the thrashing ocean and sharp jagged rocks.

No, he'd already wasted enough time. This was it. He turned and walked ten feet away from the cliff edge, then turned back, braced himself, prepared to run, and then decided he should back up some more. This was it, one final piece and then he'd be able to finish what he started. He ran. It wasn't really as fast as he'd hoped. He tried moving faster; panic began to set in as he approached the edge. He changed his mind exactly 0.457 seconds too late and tried to skid to a stop. Failing miserably, he tripped over a rock and propelled off the edge of the cliff, through the air, and straight through the door.

As it turned out, Robert and Rumpelstiltskin were passing through doors at the exact same time in two completely different places. In the nether regions of the ethereal doors' transit system, they actually passed right by each other but never noticed. When someone experienced a feeling akin to their insides being rearranged and the concepts of up and down have vacated one's existence, it's often surprising how much people fail to notice.

Robert was spewed forth from a door somewhere else in Thiside. His exact location was around two hundred and fifty-three miles from where he'd entered the door. Doors didn't affect time; stepping through one door was much like stepping through a normal door, in that the traveller went in one side and instantly came out the other side. The only differences with the doors of Thiside were the physical disorientation symptoms that everyone experienced and never really got used to.

Robert pushed himself to his feet and winced at the pain in his back. Wherever he was, it was raining and cold, wind swirled from no distinct direction, and he thought he could hear screaming. As his eyes adjusted to the dark, he found he was standing on the top shoulder of a valley. The valley was all flowing grass, with stone pathways running here and there. The main focal point of the valley was undoubtedly the large, castle-like building sitting in the middle of a huge lake. A stone bridge that must have been at least a mile long was the only access to the castle.

"What is that place?" asked Robert to no one in particular.

"It's a prison," said the voice.

"And how do you know that?" Robert actually found it comforting to have someone to talk to, even if he was talking to himself, and even more so that he could talk openly without looking crazy to anyone else.

"I'm just assuming. One way in, one way out, dark castle, middle of a stormy valley. Do you hear screaming?"

"I thought I did but figured it was the wind. Look! There's someone on the bridge!" said Robert.

A short, fat person wrapped in what looked like a hooded cloak was walking along the bridge toward the castle. Lightning flashed across the sky.

"We should go," said the voice. "We'll need to get back to Lily and the Gnomes. Hopefully she'll have changed again before we get back there."

"And how do we go about doing that?"

"The doors. Just keep going through them and sooner or later, hopefully, we'll get close to the Archives again."

Robert's stomach lurched at the thought of going back through one door, let alone several of them.

"Do we have to?"

"Do you have a better idea?"

"Am I really going mad?"

"Do you think you're going mad?"

"Why must you answer everything with a question?"

"Why must you ask so many questions?"

"You know what?"

"What?"

Robert opened his mouth and then closed it again. "I don't know where I was going with that."

"Maybe you are going mad."

Robert turned to face the door; it was a lot smaller than it had been when he came through it. He took one last look at the valley and the figure on the bridge and pulled himself through the doorway.

Lightning flashed, because it thought it was an appropriate time to do so.

CHAPTER FOURTEEN

TWEEDLE

The short, pudgy individual who was slowly trekking his way across the stone bridge toward the Tower was extremely unhappy. The rain had soaked him to his skin but that wasn't what bothered him. He'd fallen into a bog around fifteen miles back and now smelled like something scraped off the bottom of a shoe, but that wasn't what bothered him either. It was the glorious meal that he'd had to leave in order to make this trip. *That's* what bothered him.

Agent Tweedle had been on assignment in the Kingdom of Hearts as a consultant to the Queen, who had to deal with constant treason from the Humanimal Lords who lived in her lands. The Agency was dispatched to handle the problem and in turn, chose Agent Tweedle for his negotiation skills and his knowledge of Northern politics. As it turned out, the blame for the problem fell solely with the Queen of Hearts, who was partial to enormous banquets and enjoyed demeaning her servants.

The main problem was that she believed in extremely high taxes and the indignant Lords who had to pay her those taxes did not. And to enforce this disbelief, they'd taken to causing riots, interrupting trade routes, and posting rude pictures of the Queen all over the kingdom.

Agent Tweedle had arrived almost ten months ago and had since been putting off starting negotiations, as he enjoyed the large banquets that the Queen arranged daily, but solving the current situation would probably put an end to them. As long as things stayed the way they were, the Queen was happy, because she continued to collect taxes. The Humanimal Lords continued to be enraged.

The Fairy Veszico had passed on the news from Lily, and now Tweedle found himself trudging across the bridge to the Tower on a dark and stormy night. Of course, it was always dark and stormy in the Valley of Storms.

He met the Troll at the end of the bridge and pulled off his hood. Tweedle stood just less than five feet high. His girth, which measured around four feet wide, severely offset his bulky frame. His legs were short and spindly and his face was wide and frog-like. His hair was shaggy and his eyes were small and beady and missed nothing.

"Evenin', Troll," said Tweedle in a high-pitched Cockney accent.

"Bloody ell you got fat," said the Troll.

"And you wonder why I never visit."

"Ere t see the Atter are ya?"

There was a shrill scream from the highest tower, and the lightning flashed for good measure.

"The Witch sounds unhappy."

"Aye. But really when es she eva appy?" chortled the Troll. "Camon," said the ugly little creature and slurched off toward the prison.

Agent Tweedle followed closely behind. He hated the Tower and did his best to avoid the place, but he understood why he had been chosen to be here on this night and it wasn't just because he was close by. Tweedle's past was a dark and twisted mess and it was always surprising to the Agency that Agent Tweedle turned out to be as well-adjusted and intelligent as he did. He was a mixed breed of witch and Dwarf, which was so rare as to be almost unheard of in Thiside. The result was a short, fat man with an unusually long life, which of course made him an excellent candidate for the Agency, who looked unfavourably on having to train new recruits. His unique personality and insatiable thirst for studying behaviour also made him an excellent negotiator and interrogator.

The inmates were mostly asleep, with the exception of a few insomniac individuals who stared at Tweedle through their barred windows with dark, hollow eyes. Tweedle knew most of the inmates, as he'd been responsible for interrogating at least half of them. The other half, the ones who needed a more physical approach, were interrogated by Jack. Both Jack and Tweedle were feared and/or hated by inmates of the Tower but for completely different reasons.

The Troll stopped at the last cell on the left and turned to the Agent.

"Ee's been in solitary since Jack left, no contact wi anyone so e might be a bit pent up."

The Troll swivelled back to the door and scratched a long, ugly fingernail down the centre of the door.

Tweedle heard several large locks slide away, and the door opened a crack. He grabbed a candlestick from a holder on the wall and pushed open the door.

"I'm lockin ya in," said the Troll. "Don't want ta risk nother scape."

Tweedle nodded to the ugly little creature as the door squeaked closed and the locks magically slid back into place.

The cell was dark except for the light filtering in through the small barred window set into the door. The cell had no other windows. Tweedle swung the candle around and illuminated one corner, with a thin straw mattress and pillow. The next corner had a small hole cut into the floor that unceremoniously acted as a toilet. He swung to the opposite corner; candlelight revealed the Mad Hatter sitting with his back against the wall.

The Hatter shielded his dark eyes from the candlelight. He looked more like a scarecrow than Tweedle had ever seen. His clothes were ragged and dirty, his face missing any trace of color; his hair, long and scraggly, hung about his skinny shoulders.

A spark of excitement shuddered through Tweedle. He'd always wanted to speak to the Mad Hatter and this was his chance. The Hatter was one of the most fascinating behavioural cases, second only to Tweedle's own past.

"Hello, Hatter," said Tweedle as he sat a few feet away and placed the candle between them.

The Hatter squinted in the dim light.

"Oh," said the Hatter with disdain, "it's you two."

"No, just me," said Tweedle.

"Delude yourself on your own time. If I have to tolerate your presence you can at least be honest with me. So who's in there these days? Tweedle Dee or Tweedle Dum?"

"You know very well that neither of them ever existed," said Tweedle unwaveringly.

"Such an unholy union your parents made, a witch and a Dwarf. Not surprising you ended up the way you did."

"We're not here to talk about me—"

"Us," interrupted the Hatter.

"What?"

"Us. You're not here to talk about us."

"Me."

"Us."

"Why don't you tell me about the Dwarf?" said Tweedle, trying to shift the gears of the conversation.

"I didn't know your father, you fat idiot," spat the Hatter and then burst into a fit of laughter, which ended abruptly. He leaned forward, looked from side to side to make sure there wasn't anyone else in the cell, and then whispered. "It's okay. I know your secret; it's okay to tell me. You see, I'm sitting on quite the secret myself."

The Hatter leaned back, folded his arms, and winked at Tweedle knowingly.

"Right," said Tweedle. "How about we talk about Rumpelstiltskin?"

The Hatter shook his head. "Avoiding the subject isn't going to make it any better, you know!"

"The Dwarf Rump—"

"Yes, yes. He escaped, I helped him, no big secrets here. Except the secret I'm not telling you. But the Dwarf has his own agenda, had it for a long time."

"Why did you send him to see your son?"

"Ah, my boy. How is he?"

"He's well."

"Is he... here?"

"Why would he be here?" asked Tweedle calmly.

"I just thought he might be inspired by the Dwarf to come visit his dear old dad."

"Your son was sent to Othaside as a safety precaution. He has a life there; I hardly see how a little Dwarf would convince him otherwise."

The Hatter looked sad for a moment before his face cracked into a grin.

"Well, back to matters at hand. I'll answer any questions you have, directly, mind you, as long as you tell me which of you I'm speaking to."

A bead of sweat formed on Tweedle's head. *It couldn't be. How would he know?* Tweedle was fortunate that his long life cycle allowed him to outlive a great many people and the details of his past were, for the most part, buried within the Agency or the Archives and a few others who also lived long lives.

The Hatter leaned forward. "A madman can't fool a madman and as you can see, I'm clearly very mad. I know your story, Tweedle Dee... and Tweedle Dum. But like I said, your secret's safe with me, I just want to know which one of you I'm currently talking to. That's all."

Tweedle tried to collect himself. And failed miserably. "Ah... eh... uh."

"That's not really English, is it? Look, I know you convinced everyone that your two personalities have been amalgamated into one and therefore you are completely normal and able to function as a regular member of society. But I know better. I know why you can retain so much information. I know why you deal so well with madmen and the criminals of Thiside. It's because you're just as mad. You simply hide it better. You're both traitors to yourselves. You're both still in there, it's plain and obvious to me. You're a charade, a fake, a counterfeit. You are a grand theatre production with two main actors but only one voice. Now," said the Hatter and unfolded his long spindly fingers in a questioning gesture, "tell me that I'm wrong."

Tweedle was sweating profusely. He'd been so careful. After his therapy, he'd been able to convince everyone that he'd developed being normal into a fine art.

"You... y-you're wrong."

"Am I?"

"I'm not here to talk about us." Tweedle clamped his hands over his mouth.

"Ahh, there you both are. You have to admit that taking a page out of my extensive book isn't a bad idea. It is better to be exactly who you are rather than exactly what you think people want you to be."

"B-but, you're mad."

The Hatter smiled broadly. "Then you, my friends, are in good company."

Tweedle twitched slightly and burst into tears.

The Hatter stood up to his full height. With the candlelight throwing shadows against the wall and the thunder rolling outside the Tower, the

Hatter looked truly ghastly, his hair hanging in thick greasy strands and his ragged clothes draped over his skeletal body.

In the Agent's mind, Tweedle Dum bawled incessantly while Tweedle Dee simply whimpered. The ropes of sanity that the split personality of Tweedle Dee and Tweedle Dum had perfected over time had been frayed in a matter of minutes. When he was a boy, Dum and Dee had been two personalities trapped in the young boy's body, not opposing personalities but more like conjoined twins. They had bickered and fought and agreed and loved and laughed. However, such weirdness can be tolerated for only so long and his options came down to severe therapy or time in the Tower before his madness hurt someone. The choice was natural.

"Troll!" shouted the Hatter.

There was a snarfling sound and the locks on the door slid aside. The door creaked open a few inches and the Troll poked his ugly little head through.

"What ya want?" drooled the Troll.

"Our dear friend here seems to have lost his mind. I don't suppose there's a spare cell where he might rest? I'll look for his mind while he's sleeping," explained the Hatter politely.

"What did ya do ta him?"

The Hatter adopted a look of pure surprise and innocence. "Me? We were just talking and he started... well, look at him."

The Troll opened the door. Candlelight skittered across the wall, illuminating the cell to reveal the large, round figure sitting cross-legged in the middle of the cell sobbing. The Troll looked at the Hatter, who shrugged.

"I didn't even get to tell him my secret," said the Hatter and shook his head disappointedly.

The Troll waddled over to Tweedle and took him by the hand. "C'mon, ther ther, s'aright, ee as that effect on a lot o people."

The Troll grabbed the candle, then pulled on Tweedle's hand to lead him out of the cell. Tweedle hoisted himself to his feet, head hung low, and the pair exited the cell, leaving the Hatter to himself.

The door swung shut and the light ceased to occupy the room. The Hatter stood in the middle of his cell and grinned maniacally at no one in particular.

CHAPTER FIFTEEN

FANDERWINKING

Robert had assumed that travelling through the intricate system of the doors would become easier the more he did it. He was wrong. He'd lost count of how many times he'd turned around and stepped back through the door, and the nauseating feeling that crept up his bowels and tickled his tonsils had yet to subside.

He stepped out of yet another door and as he did so, the world slipped back into focus. He was standing on a long beach with a vast blue ocean gently lapping up on the sand. The sun peeked over the horizon and the smell of sea air filled Robert's lungs. And then he saw them. He wasn't sure at first, but as the sun crested the horizon and then suddenly shot into the air, spilling morning sunlight over everything, he quickly became certain.

"Those are Mermaids!" he exclaimed.

Three female Mermaids were lying farther down the beach, sunning themselves. They were naked from the waist up. *I suppose they're naked from the waist down, too.* "They're beautiful!" he said.

"Yeah I suppose," said the voice.

"You suppose? You suppose? Look at them, they're beautiful!"

"Well, they're half fish aren't they?"

Robert looked at the Mermaids. "From the waist down, yes."

"I just don't see the appeal," said the voice.

"How can you possibly be me? Do you know how many times we've disagreed over the last several hours?"

"Well, I haven't been counting…"

"Twenty-six," said Robert.

"So you've been counting, then, have you?"

"Twenty-six disagreements!"

"Well, it's been a long night."

"I just don't understand how you can possibly be my mind or my conscience or whatever you are. I just don't—"

"Those Mermaids are getting closer," said the voice.

Robert opened his mouth to argue and then realized that the voice in his head was correct. The Mermaids were crawling along the beach toward Robert, dragging their long fish tails behind them. They were around thirty feet away. Their naked breasts looked large and perky and bounced seductively. Their long, dark hair blew in the sea breeze. The morning sun shone upon their bronzed skin. They made the most beautiful snarling sound and their fangs looked sharp…?

"What the hell?" asked Robert.

Twenty feet.

The Mermaids were beautiful but they were snarling and even spitting a little. Each had her mouth opened unnaturally wide, revealing long, snake-like fangs. One of them looked like she had bits of a dead creature hanging from her jowls. They were crawling faster and they looked distinctly hungry.

Ten feet.

"I hate to keep suggesting this," said the voice.

"I'm way ahead of you," said Robert and turned and ran. The door was still open, a shimmering hole on the beach. He could hear the snarling of the Mermaids behind him. He dived head first through the door—

—and rolled out onto hard green stone.

He looked back at the door to check the door's size. He'd learned that the doors shrank the closer they came to winking out of existence, and that the average life span of any given door was around fifteen minutes. This one was still large so he had some time.

He was standing in a courtyard. Or at least, he was standing in the remains of a courtyard. There were piles of green rubble everywhere. The green rock sparkled where the sunlight hit it.

"It looks like emeralds," said Robert who had gotten far too used to speaking out loud as he was now completely comfortable with the voice in his head speaking back to him.

"Pretty," said the voice.

"This must have been the Emerald City. From the Wizard of Oz. Or, well, I suppose the book was based on what this used to be," Robert corrected himself.

He still had a hard time getting his head around the fairy tales of Othaside being based on actual reality, even though they were only loosely based. The Mermaids had been a real eye-opener. Mermaids as bloodthirsty creatures were a far cry from beautiful creatures who helped people, sang songs all day, and hung out with fishes.

He must have travelled miles through Thiside during the last several hours trying to find a door that was remotely close to the Archives. Almost everywhere he went, there had been signs of life. He'd dropped into a colony of Fairies, he'd appeared in a dim mine shaft with slimy skulking things living in the dark, he'd walked close to the edge of a high cliff, and conversed with an old man living in a cave. Even the most remote areas of Thiside had someone or something living in it. But not here. This place was desolate; not even the air moved.

Robert climbed to the top of a pile of rubble made up of broken statues. He looked out over the landscape, which stretched all the way to a blackened harbour that looked like it had burned to pieces. Piles of rubble lay everywhere. More disturbing were the carcasses of giant man-like creatures that were scattered everywhere. It looked like someone or something waged an epic battle here. In the stillness that occupied this broken city, there was a sense of something that Robert couldn't place. It felt...

"Electric," said the voice.

"Yeah, I can feel it. There's a heaviness to it."

"Ohh, did you feel that?"

"Feel what?"

"Sorry, thought I felt a shiver. Felt good. This place has magic."

If the voice in Robert's head had been a person, he imagined that it would be staring off into the distance, thinking carefully about a faint memory stirred by the feeling it had just experienced. He wasn't sure why he suddenly thought of the voice as a different person, as it was firmly present in his mind, but the image seemed to fit, if only for a moment.

"We should keep going," said Robert and his stomach whimpered at the prospect of re-entering the doors.

Robert slid and crawled his way down the pile of rubble and stepped back through the doorway—

—and stepped out onto a grassy hill at the edge of a forest. Robert recognized this place. It was where he'd run into the forest the night before, to escape from Lily. That seemed like a lifetime ago. He'd been wandering through countless door after door all night, trying to get back here. But now he was here, he wasn't sure what he was supposed to do. Thankfully, fate had the situation well in hand.

"Robert," said Lily's voice from behind him.

He'd been looking down into the valley and turned now to see Lily walking out of the forest. She was completely naked and streaked with mud. Her hair was matted and she had deep circles under her eyes. She had what looked like blood around her mouth. Despite all this, and it could have been due to sleep exhaustion, Robert still found her beautiful. In her left hand hung something silver: Robert's necklace and vial of blood from the White Rabbit.

Of course, she'd tried to tear him to pieces last night, but now she was Lily again. Or Lillian Redcloak as the Historian had referred to her. *Redcloak.*

"Little Red Riding Hood," he said as the realization dawned on him.

Lily stood a few feet away, arms at her side.

"Yes, that's what I'm called in Othaside. A true bastardization of the real tale, as you saw last night." She looked ashamed.

"Yes, it's a bit different than what was read to us in elementary school. Although the real story would have scarred us for life, I imagine."

Lily smiled, and then tears began to flow, creating clean lines through the streaks of mud on her face.

"I'm so sorry, Robert. Even after all this time…" She collapsed to her knees and began to sob.

Robert knelt beside her, pulling off his sweater, then pulling it over her head to cover her up. A part of him, the very male part that purely enjoyed the naked female form in all its glory, said *awwww* in disappointment. But he knew it was the right thing to do.

Lily smeared the arm of the sweater across her eyes. "I can control it when I effect the change myself, by my own choice. But if it's the moon that triggers it, I have no control. I didn't mean to attack you."

"I think you were hunting me, actually."

"I can see everything that's going on but I can't do anything. I hate feeling that powerless, I hate it! It makes me feel the way I did when he first attacked me."

"He knew the moon had come up. He stalled us, didn't he?" asked Robert.

"Yes, he must've known; maybe he's so old he can sense it. The moon in Thiside ignores all lunar cycles, making it hard to predict when a full moon will rise, but usually there's at least a half moon the night before, so I know to be locked up." Lily looked at Robert then as if she'd realized something. "How did you get back here? I saw you go through the door."

"You told me there were doors everywhere all the time in different places. I just kept going through until I ended up back here. I've honestly lost count. I think I'm going madder. I've been talking to the voice in my head all night. And I'm beyond tired." Even as he said the words, he realized that he actually didn't feel that tired at all. If anything, he felt invigorated.

"You've been jumping doors all night?"

"Yeah, I saw some amazing sights. And creatures. Did you know Mermaids are bloodthirsty creatures? Scared the life out of me!"

Lily smiled a tired smile. "Do you know what happened to Gnick and the General?"

There was a buzzing sound from above and two pixies flew out from over the forest. One carried a bundle in its hands. Both of them were tied around the mouth and each had a Gnome on its back. The Pixies landed and Robert saw that the Gnomes had gagged the Pixies with the rope so they could steer them. The Pixies looked angry. The one with the bundle threw it at Robert as the Gnomes untied their transportation.

"Youze orrible lil Gnomesez!" spat one of the Pixies as they retreated into the air.

"Soddingz lil blanderzkitez," agreed the other. And they buzzed off, back toward the archives.

The Gnomes approached.

"I'm sorry," said Lily resolutely.

"It's forgotten," said General Gnarly and nodded slightly. "It seems my reports of you were true after all. That's a powerful creature you have inside of you."

"Nice to see you're still in one piece, moron," said Gnick.

"How did you get away from her?" asked the General.

"I've been door jumping all night, according to Lily."

"All night?" asked the General.

"Why is that so surprising to everyone? I just kept heading back through the doors and I kept coming out in different places in Thiside. Lily... uhh... the werewolf version took my passport when she attacked me."

Lily grabbed Robert's head and pushed it forward and pulled back his shirt. "You're not even marked? There's not even a scar!"

Robert had forgotten about the blood he'd felt on his back. He'd felt the burning, he knew she'd cut him. Not long after he'd been jumping through the doors, he'd forgotten all about it.

"That's a neat trick," said Gnick.

"The doors," explained General Gnarly, "you've noticed the discomfort when you're going through them?"

"You mean when it feels like someone's sticking a finger in your brain and swirling it around?"

"Not exactly as I would have put it, but yes. How many times did you go through?" asked Gnarly.

"Lots," said Robert and shrugged.

"Robert, door jumping is very rare," said Lily. "It takes an amazing amount of resilience and stamina to do it. There's a race of humans here called Fanderwinks who are like adrenaline junkies. They go door jumping for fun but even they can only make it maybe thirty or forty times before they start losing the feeling in their limbs, all sense of equilibrium, and in some cases, lose their minds completely. What you did is unheard of!"

"Well, yay me, I guess."

"We procured some clothes for you," said General Gnarly and handed the bundle to Lily. "We should really get going."

"Which brings up the question, where are we going?" added Gnick.

Lily stood and stripped off Robert's sweater, at which Robert did his best to avert his eyes.

"We're going to the City of Oz to see the wizard Niggle," said Lily.

"And as time is of the essence, how are we to get there?" said the General.

"I know it's not your favorite way to travel, General, but we'll need to use the doors to at least get close," said Lily. "Are you going to be okay, Robert?"

"I'll live."

"Then we should find one."

"Your Fairy's back," said Gnick as Veszico flew down from the sky. She landed in Lily's outstretched palm, stretched, and then she spoke. Robert had expected to hear the usual sound of a tiny bell that he normally heard when Veszico spoke, but instead he actually heard a voice.

"I delivered the message to Tweedle; he didn't seem happy about it," said the Fairy.

"I can hear you!" said Robert.

"I told you that you would. The more you become ingrained in this world, the more things will make sense," said Lily.

"I've been flying all night; do you mind if I rest?" asked Veszico.

"Not at all."

The Fairy crouched into a ball, wrapping her wings around her upper body, and curled up. The air shimmered and it looked like Lily was holding a rock, which she stuck in her pocket.

"There's a door over there," said the voice in Robert's head.

"There's a door over there," said Robert and pointed to the shimmering slice in reality.

"I just said that," said the voice.

"Sorry, I shouldn't take credit."

"It's okay, no need to apologize. We've been through a lot."

"Well, I don't want to take you for granted."

The two Gnomes and Lily were staring at him.

"Sorry," said Robert. "I've had no one to talk to all night."

Lily took Robert by the hand, which felt natural to him. This woman had led him into a completely new reality, introduced him to strange creatures and new lands, and then she'd turned into a giant wolf creature and tried to kill him. That was a special kind of bond that didn't happen every day.

The foursome headed toward the door. Lily stopped and pulled the silver chain with the vial from her pocket and put it around his neck. "You should have this back."

"Wait, what happens when I go through the door? With the passport on me, won't I just jump to a door in Othaside?" asked Robert, suddenly panicked.

Lily pulled up her sleeve to reveal the dragon tattoo. "This is my passport; the red eye is the blood of the White Rabbit. All Agents receive it. All you need to do is cover it with your hand, so hold the vial tightly. The passport reacts to the essence of the doorway. If the vial can't touch it, you'll remain in Thiside."

"Got it."

"Oh, you'll need to carry Gnick. We need to be touching so we don't end up in different places."

Gnick climbed up Robert's leg, across his back and up onto his shoulder. "Don't drop me, moron."

General Gnarly jumped onto Lily's shoulder while her left arm linked with Robert's. She covered her tattoo with her hand and Robert gripped the vial of blood around his neck tightly.

The group stepped forward and vanished through the door.

CHAPTER SIXTEEN

FOLLOW THAT DWARF

The wizard Niggle had barely slept. His night had been ruined by the events of the previous day. He could go for weeks on end without anyone showing up at his door. The Dwarf Rumpelstiltskin had been one thing, but the Agent Jack threatening him afterward had been enough to push Niggle's nerves over the edge. He'd tried mixing a potion normally used for calming livestock before slaughter, and drunk it with Flabber-juice, an alcoholic beverage much like vodka only three hundred and twenty times stronger. The concoction hadn't made a dent. He'd sat up on the edge of his bed all night, staring at the window, twitching spasmodically.

He looked at the same window now and the two Gnomes sitting on his window ledge stared back. One of them held a small dagger and was trimming his beard with it.

"Hello, wizard," said the one not performing personal grooming.

"H-h-hello. I... uh... who, er... who are you?" Niggle could feel his insides begin to recoil, and sweat broke out on his brow. The best-case scenario was that he was hallucinating. Oh, how he wished he was hallucinating.

"My name is General Gnarly of the Warrior Gnomes of the Grimm Mountains and this is my lieutenant, Gnick."

Not a hallucination, then.

"Uh, and why is he... uh... doing that?"

"Our beards grow an inch a day; they need trimming often."

The wizard was feeling more and more queasy. "And h-h-how can I h-help you?"

"You can start by answering your door."

There was a knock at the door, which caused the wizard to jump, knocking over one of his favorite tea sets.

Niggle made it halfway to the door and then turned back to the Gnomes. "It's not a Dwarf, is it?"

"No."

"Or an Agent?"

"One of them isn't."

Not really the answer he was hoping for. He twitched violently, opened the door and Lily pushed past him into the apartment. Robert smiled kindly and offered his hand to the wizard, who was so agitated that his pointy hat began to droop at an awkward angle. The wizard extended a shaky hand, realized he didn't know the gentleman in front of him and retracted it again quickly.

"P-please, come in."

"Greatly appreciated," said Robert and stepped into the wizard's home.

Lily had taken a seat by the fire, Robert stood by the window with the Gnomes, and Niggle stayed by the door, thinking that he should apply to move his chamber into a different tower.

"My name is Lillian Redcloak and I'm an Agent." To prove the point she pulled up her shirtsleeve to show the dragon tattoo. "My associate, Robert Darkly, is an Othasider assisting in the pursuit of the Dwarf Rumpelstiltskin who has escaped... yes, Robert?"

Robert had raised his hand.

"Haven't we already established that I'm originally from here? Or at least, my father is?"

"I don't see the point."

"Well, you keep introducing me as an Othasider but obviously I'm not. What?" asked Robert, apparently of no one. "Yes, I'll tell her that, too. Not to mention that I think I've earned the right to be here."

Niggle looked from the Othasider, or whoever he was, to the Agent. Obviously, this Darkly character was unhinged. Unhinged people were dangerous. Niggle began to mentally locate any sharp objects in his apartment and tried to map whether this Darkly character was anywhere near any of them.

"All right," agreed the Agent, "Robert is indeed from Thiside but has grown up in Othaside. He's now assisting us to track down the Dwarf Rumpelstiltskin who escaped from the Tower two nights ago. The Gnomes are here to protect us. We'd like to know if you've seen Rumpelstiltskin in the last twenty-four hours?"

"Yes," replied Niggle quickly.

"Well, that was easy," said Robert.

"L-l-look, I'll tell you everything you w-w-want to know if you'll just promise to leave right away. And have th-th-that Gnome put away the sharp th-thing."

"I agree to your terms," said the female Agent. "Now, tell us everything."

The voice in Robert's head had agreed it was a good point to make going forward. There seemed little doubt that he fit nicely into the world of Thiside. Better than he ever had in Othaside. And from the whispered conversation he'd heard, he knew his father was here somewhere, as they'd been talking about him in the present tense. A million other questions bounced around in his head. Why did he have a voice in his head? How did he heal from the attack by Lily's werewolf? How did he survive the night of door jumping? Who was the head of the Agency? Where was Jack? Where was Rumpelstiltskin? What happened to the cat he'd found back at the halfway house?

"All very good questions," said the voice, "but you should pay attention."

Niggle was recounting what he knew as quickly as possible to get the visitors out of his room. "The d-Dwarf was here yesterday afternoon and he a-a-a-a-asked me to perform a finder spell for the same girl he was looking for almost f-fifty years ago."

"Elise Bastinda?" asked Lily.

"Y-y-y-yes, how did you know that?"

"Doesn't matter. Why did you help him all that time ago and again yesterday?"

"I w-was indebted to him for s-s-s-saving my life and I was very young. Now I'm just t-terrified of him."

"So you performed the spell for him successfully?"

"Y-yes. I'll be happy t-t-to tell you the location, the same way I did to your other Agent."

"What other Agent?" said Lily.

"Jack. The G-G-Giant Killer."

"He's Jack from Jack and the Beanstalk?" said Robert, impressed.

Lily gave him a stern look.

"Sorry," said Robert.

"Jack was already here?" Lily asked Niggle.

"Y-yesterday afternoon, a c-c-c-couple of hours after the d-Dwarf left."

"Why does Rumpelstiltskin need the last Bastinda?"

Niggle looked down at his feet, apparently in the fond hope that he could spontaneously combust.

"Come on, Niggle," said Lily, "what's he doing? Why does he need the witch? She must be almost sixty years old."

The wizard sighed and looked at Lily with sad eyes. For a moment, he looked very old. "When he s-s-saved my life, the payment wasn't the finder spell. He w-wanted access to the Council archives."

"And you gave it to him."

"I was y-y-young and scared. He j-j-just wanted a few minutes in there and I didn't see the danger from j-j-just a few minutes. It wasn't until years later that the Council learned of the m-m-missing pages."

"Pages from what?"

"One of the archival spell b-books. Volume s-s-s-sixty-s-s-s-six. It chronicles the research into the doors and how the b-blood of the White Rabbit was incorporated into the system so it became regulated."

"And the missing pages?"

The wizard swallowed. "Th-they d-detailed how to remove those regulations."

"So Rumpelstiltskin has the knowledge to remove the need for passports. Anyone would be able to pass through the doors on either side."

"Yes."

Robert finally clued in. "To do this, he'd need something like a shopping list of items? Maybe working toward a ceremony?"

"N-n-not a ceremony, a s-spell. An extremely p-powerful spell. And yes, he'd n-n-need items."

"This is important, Niggle," said Lily, "do you know where he'll perform the spell once he has all the pieces?"

"I don't know. Somewhere with a strong magical field. The magic here isn't as s-strong as it used to be but there are s-s-still powerful pockets. It'll have to be in Thiside. This is where the original s-spell was created. To undo it, he'll have t-t-t-to return to Thiside."

"Wait a minute," said Robert, "he was collecting these items years ago, before he was caught. Where are the other items? Maybe he doesn't have all of them yet?"

"We can't assume that," said Lily. "We need to move if we're going to stop the Dwarf before he comes back to Thiside. Hopefully, Jack's already caught up to him, but we can't assume that, either. But we have to try, we have to stop him before he removes the regulators and opens up the two worlds. Niggle, we need to know where to find Elise Bastinda in Othaside."

"Of c-c-course."

"I imagine you're tired of being scared of the Dwarf, and if you help us, this will ensure that he's put away forever and you'll never have to worry about him again. There's one other favor I need to ask. It's a big one."

Niggle twitched slightly and then pulled himself together. The thought of being rid of Rumpelstiltskin was a comforting one. For the first time in a long time, the wizard stopped shaking.

"What do you need me to do?"

Niggle stumbled into the empty hall and dropped a couple of the items he had been carrying. Robert and Lily entered after him, followed by the Gnomes.

The Great Hall in the Wizards' Council building was completely empty. Large tapestries adorned the walls, and the floor was polished to the sort of gleam that an old lady would find suitable. The lamps had been extinguished to allow the early sunlight to enter the hall through the large floor-to-ceiling windows at the front of the building.

"Yes, this'll do," said Niggle and began drawing a large chalk circle on the ground.

"Do you do this sort of thing a lot?" asked Robert.

"Of course he does, he's a wizard," said Gnick.

"Actually I t-try and stay away from m-m-magic; nasty stuff."

"But you're a wizard," said Robert.

"D-doesn't mean I have to like it," said Niggle, who seemed to be feeling a lot less nervous now that he had a purpose in life.

Robert suspected that the prospect of removing Rumpelstiltskin from the wizard's life was a great motivator.

"The magical c-concentration," said the wizard, "is strongest here in the hall. If you listen carefully, you can hear the em-em-emerald stone humming."

Robert listened but heard nothing. He turned his attention to the Gnomes. "How are you two going to blend in once we're in Othaside?"

"We aren't stepping a beard's hair through that door," said General Gnarly.

"Not a chance!" agreed Gnick.

"Why not?" asked Robert.

"Gnomes aren't made to travel through doors to Othaside," explained Gnarly. "We turn to ceramic."

"Really?" said Robert. "What? And then people decorate their gardens with you?" Robert began to smile at his own joke and then stopped. "Bloody hell, is that where garden Gnomes come from?"

"Sadly, yes," said the General. "It's said we were once the largest group of creatures to exist in Thiside, before the passports were introduced and the regulators were installed into the doors. Before such limitations, Gnomes passed through doors all the time. Our numbers were greatly diminished."

Robert couldn't help but think of his adoptive parents, who'd kept a whole collection of garden Gnomes. He'd thrown a rock at one once and smashed it! That could have been Gnick's distant relative. Robert decided it'd be better if he kept the story to himself.

"Speaking of which," said Lily, "I don't know where we'll be coming back through to Thiside. I suggest you stay on the outskirts of the city near the Eastern gate; we'll send Veszico to find you as soon as we are back. She's small but can carry a human if necessary. She knocked Robert out with a frying pan once." Gnick stifled a laugh. "She'll have no problem carrying the two of you. If we fail to stop the Dwarf in Othaside, we may need you quickly."

The General nodded and Gnick bowed.

"I think I'm r-ready," said Niggle.

"Good luck, moron," said Gnick.

"You too, shorty," said Robert. The room went silent. Robert looked at Gnick; Gnick looked at Robert. And then they both laughed. Robert felt a kinship with the little men, one he assumed was mutual, which was why he risked being stabbed repeatedly with very short knives. He was relieved to find that it didn't happen.

"Risky," said the voice in Robert's head.

"Well, you've got to laugh, haven't you?" said Robert.

Robert and Lily walked over to where Niggle was standing in front of the circle he'd drawn. He'd also drawn some intricate symbols within the circle, and just for good measure, he'd lit some candles. The plan, as Robert understood it, was for Niggle to produce a door for them, which he would do his best to direct at the location they were aiming for in Othaside. This would save them firstly, having to find a door in Thiside and secondly, ending up in the nether regions of Scotland or elsewhere in Europe. The creation of doors was severely frowned upon by the Wizards' Council and most wizards didn't have the knowhow or the power. Having played with magic as little as possible, Niggle wasn't aware of the limitation that other wizards had when producing doors. He just assumed he would be able to do it. Not knowing one was the most powerful wizard in existence had its advantages.

"So what do we do now?" asked Robert.

"The door," explained the wizard, "will appear in the middle of the circle, but it'll be b-brief. You'll have only a short time and I'll do my b-best to direct it toward your d-d-destination, but I'll admit I've never done this before."

"Not totally reassuring," said the voice in Robert's head.

"Make sure your necklace is exposed," said Lily as she rolled up her shirt sleeves. Robert removed the vial from within his shirt.

"Are we ready?" asked Niggle.

"Yes," said Lily.

"I suppose," said Robert. "So what happens now, you whisper some sacred chants or say some magic words?"

"Nothing as e-elaborate as that, I'm afraid," said Niggle. He raised his right hand, concentrated, and snapped his fingers. A white spark flashed from his fingertips, and then blue flames shot up from within the circle all the way to the ceiling. Rushing wind filled the hall like a hurricane and the tapestries flapped and thrashed against the green stone walls.

Within the column of flame, Robert could see a pair of large dark eyes filled with flame and a wide mouth with lots of jagged teeth and...

"Oh," said the wizard and snapped his fingers again. The wind died down and the column of blue flame winked out. "Sorry, that wasn't the right spell."

"What the hell was that?" asked Robert.

"Truthfully, I'm not actually s-sure. L-l-l-looked angry, though, didn't it? Here we go," said Niggle, who raised his left hand and snapped his fingers.

Robert shielded his face. When he dared look, there was no wind, no blue flame, no scary creature. Just the usual strange distortion in the air that marked the doorway. It floated just above the circle that Niggle had drawn.

"Quickly n-now!"

Lily grabbed Robert's hand and pulled him into the circle and through the doorway. The door winked out of existence.

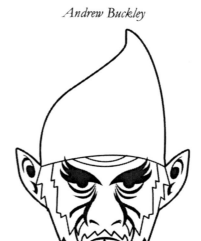

CHAPTER SEVENTEEN

A GRAVE SITUATION

R obert noticed there was a difference travelling between Thiside and Othaside as opposed to just travelling in Thiside. The feeling was worse. It felt like someone had grabbed his toes from the interior and pulled him inside out. Every nerve ending tingled uncomfortably. He looked around. They were at a bus stop.

"Where are we?" asked Robert.

"Judging by that big sign over there, it looks like we're outside Burnley."

Robert looked over to see a large sign that said, *You Are Now Leaving Burnley*.

The bus stop was located on a small country road in the middle of nowhere. Rock walls and large fields shrouded in thick mist could be seen in all directions. It always shocked Robert that no matter where a bus stop was located in England, some bastard always managed to graffiti it. All the fields were empty except one that held six depressed-looking sheep. Of course, anyone would be depressed if they were forced to stand in soggy grass for hours on end.

"So this is Yorkshire?" asked Robert.

"Western Yorkshire, actually. According to the wizard, Elise Bastinda is located in Hebden Bridge. It's about an hour's walk in that direction," said Lily, pointing away from the setting sun. She set off walking.

"Wasn't it morning when we left Thiside?" asked Robert, walking quickly to catch up.

"The two realities don't operate on the exact same time frame. It constantly fluctuates."

"And what about the doors? How come I've never seen a door in Othaside?"

"The same reason rain didn't touch me here when we first met. This reality doesn't believe in me, or us, or the doors, or anything else from Thiside. People don't see the doors because they don't believe they exist. Sometimes they see them out of their peripheral vision, but as soon as they look directly at it, they can't see it."

"Surely people have gone through them before. Don't they end up somewhere else in this reality?"

"No. The doors don't work the same way here. Go in one side and you'll come out the other."

"Everyone knows that," said the voice in Robert's head.

"Oh, you're still here," said Robert with a hint of happiness.

"I wish you'd stop doing that," said Lily.

"Sorry, it's become a hard habit to break."

The mist felt heavy and allowed for only limited visibility. Like any old country road, there was no traffic, and even if there was traffic, the road was only wide enough to accommodate one car. Robert was home. And yet, he felt as far from home as anyone could possibly feel. He'd always felt a disconnect with this world, but in Thiside everything felt normal. Or as normal as could be expected.

"Why do you think Rumpelstiltskin wants to break down the doors anyway, so to speak?" asked Robert.

"I don't know. To cause chaos, to end life as we know it, just for something to do on a boring Sunday afternoon? Who knows?"

Robert looked sideways at Lily. Her profile was beautiful, her features were more than pleasant, she bounced in all the right places, and her eyes always looked alive. Of course, she was less desirable when she was a large, hairy, carnivorous beast.

"Lily, what happens when all this is over? To me, I mean, what will happen to me?"

"I don't know, Robert," said Lily and there was a hint of sadness in there somewhere. "It's not for me to decide."

Rain began to fall through the mist and the sky grew dark. Thunder rolled somewhere in the distance. As they crested an especially steep part of the road, the lights from the village of Hebden Bridge illuminated the mist in the distance.

"There it is," said Lily. "Let's hope we're not too late."

Agent Tweedle had stopped sobbing and was now trying to reason with the Troll, who was promptly ignoring him. Tweedle had been placed into the cell across from the Mad Hatter, and he now stood on a makeshift pile of bedding, straw and some sort of small dead rodent so he could see through the barred window in his cell door.

"Come on, Troll," he said, "I just had a slight emotional…"

"Breakdown!" shouted the Hatter from his cell.

Tweedle couldn't see the Hatter but the mad man wasn't helping in any way.

"I was going to say *moment*. A slight emotional moment."

"Looked like a mental breakdown to me and you have to admit, I'd know."

Tweedle's voice no longer held the same confidence and authority it had less than an hour ago. He was no longer himself. The Hatter had undone it all. For years, he'd convinced people of his sanity while all the time hiding his insanity deep, deep down. His split personalities had stood in a united front, showing everyone that he was, physically and mentally, a well-rounded member of society. But now that he was exposed, the personalities didn't want to get along. Tweedle Dee wanted to stay in the cell but Tweedle Dum wanted out into the world. Tweedle Dee didn't want to touch the dead rodent creature in his cell but Tweedle Dum wanted to do nasty things to it and then eat it. Tweedle Dee wanted to talk nicely to the Troll but Tweedle Dum wanted to tear its limbs off. The years of maintaining balance between his personalities were lost.

"Look, Troll, I am still an Agent and I order you to let me out, plus, it'd be the nice thing to do," said Tweedle Dee and smiled through the bars.

"Or alternatively, you could come close enough and I'll be happy to rip your spleen out through your nose!" said Tweedle Dum.

"Oh, don't be like that, you silly little man," said Tweedle Dee.

"Blow it out your ass!" said Tweedle Dum.

The Hatter's pale face appeared in his own barred window.

"Gentleman, if you're making a case for insanity, I think you're doing a damn fine job, and I applaud you." And then he applauded them.

"There really is nothing creepier than an English graveyard," said Rumpelstiltskin to no one. It was over fifty years since he'd been here in Hebden Bridge, when the Agency had caught up with him and thrown him in the Tower to rot for all eternity. The night had grown dark quickly and the mist was so dense that the Dwarf was having trouble finding what he was looking for. He was so close to finishing what he started, so close to breaking down the doors that separated the two worlds. And then he'd have some fun! The Agency would be too busy herding people like sheep…

Smash!

"Bloody hell!" shouted the Dwarf. The shovel and flashlight he'd been carrying skittered off across a gravestone. He looked back to see what he'd tripped over and found a small sheep staring back at him.

"Ba-a-a-a!" said the sheep.

"Something you can say about Thiside, at least there's no damn sheep." He retrieved his flashlight to find the glass had cracked and the device wouldn't turn on. He picked up his shovel and turned to take his anger out on the sheep, but it had already run off. He made a guttural sort of shout and kicked at a stone vase that was apparently permanently attached to the gravestone upon which it sat. The Dwarf yelped in pain and swore so colourfully as to make a rainbow blush. He grabbed the shovel and stomped through the graveyard, checking the names on gravestones as he went.

The village of Hebden Bridge sat comfortably amongst the mist and the rain in much the same way that it had for centuries. Hebden Bridge's main attraction was the bridge close to the centre of town. It wasn't an especially large or impressive bridge. There was nothing amazing about its architecture or engineering. However, it did have a faded sign that had been posted there at the end of the eighteenth century warning anyone who was caught desecrating or marking the bridge that they would be deported to Australia. Most British people who had more than a few brain cells immediately saw the advantage of leaving cold, dark, and damp England for sunny, warm, and beautiful Australia and immediately took to painting the bridge with bright and sordid colors. In the middle of the day. In front of local law enforcement.

The county of Yorkshire was famous for its sheep and its vast countryside. If any English person felt the need to see a sheep or to wander through a lush green countryside complete with little rock walls and piles of sheep poop, all he had to do was head to Yorkshire and breathe it all in. Literally. It also had one of the best fish and chip shops in all of the United Kingdom. It was this fish and chip shop that Frank Norberton, a forty-seven-year-old ex-naval officer, staggered out of at the same time Lily and Robert entered the village.

Frank had recently staggered out of The White Lion pub after enduring several hours of fascinating conversation about the state of Lancashire and asking questions like, "Why would anyone live here?" and "What happened to the North West of England anyway?"

Most Yorkshire people believed that Lancashire people were below the average class of common, hardworking Englishman. They were often puzzled as to why they didn't just move to Yorkshire where people are generally better. Lancashire people held a similar point of view about Yorkshire people. And so the war raged on.

In his right hand, Frank held a bag of hot chips with gravy. His left hand was busy waving about trying to balance himself, as he was having trouble keeping his centre of gravity in the same place for more than a few seconds at a time. This was a common occurrence that happened every time he exited The White Lion.

Robert spotted Frank as he was trying to make it across the small cobbled street. A few other people ran here or there trying to get out of the rain, but Frank seemed not to care.

"We should ask directions," said Robert to Lily. Lily nodded and they headed for Frank, who immediately guarded his chips as if Robert meant to steal them. The smell of them was enough to remind Robert that he hadn't eaten since Mrs Goathead's supper, and his stomach complained accordingly.

"Hello," said Robert optimistically.

"Ello," said Frank with apprehension.

"Good evening," said Lily.

"Elloo," said Frank with a little more enthusiasm.

"I was wondering if you could give us directions," said Robert. "You see—"

"From London are ya?" said Frank and almost lost his balance.

"Well no, not really. But yes, I suppose I am. In a way. Or at least I was," replied Robert.

"Well you either is or you're not, lad, make up ya mind."

"Well, I wasn't born there. Although I thought I was until a couple of days ago but—"

"What my friend is trying to ask, rather inarticulately, is directions to—"

"Oh elloo," said Frank, suddenly remembering that Lily was there. "You're a pretty little thing, aren't ya?"

Frank leaned far too close to Robert, and then looked back to Lily.

"What are you doing with the likes of this fellah? Ya could do betta ya know?"

"Now hang on a minute—" protested Robert.

"We're not together," said Lily.

"Now we're not," agreed Robert, "but we could be, not to say we should be or I want to be." Lily and Frank both looked at him. "Well, it's not that I don't want to be, it's, well, it's complicated."

"Anyway," said Lily, "what we're looking for is directions to the graveyard at Slack Top. Would you be so kind as to give us directions?"

It looked like Frank had finally found his centre of gravity, at least for the time being, but he seemed to be having trouble focusing.

"It's night-time!" he said. "Why ya want t' go t' a graveyard at this time of night?"

"Not really any of your business," said Robert.

"I wasn't talkin t' you, ya Southern pillock."

"Now look here—" began Robert, but Lily placed a hand on his chest and smiled. Robert watched the true power of beautiful women everywhere unfold before his eyes. She arched her back ever so slightly to emphasize her bosom, smiled to show perfectly white teeth, flipped her dark hair back over one shoulder, and fixed her eyes on Frank.

"We have friends who live by the graveyard and it's the only landmark we know. Could you be so kind as to point us in the right direction?" Lily flashed those amber eyes, smiled coyly, and gently touched Frank's arm.

Frank dropped his chips.

"Please?" she added.

"Uh, yes, I uh, actually I'm just heading up there myself. You just head up Smithwell Lane over yonder." Frank pointed across the intersection where they were standing to a street that curved up over one of the surrounding hills. "Walk up there and you'll reach the graveyard on your right-hand side. Ya can't miss it. Looks just like a graveyard."

"Thank you so much," smiled Lily and, grabbing Robert's hand, took off at a fast walk toward Smithwell Lane.

Frank forgot he had feet and tripped over himself.

The Hatter hung one arm out through the bars set into his cell door and grinned and waved at Tweedle in his cell across the hallway.

"So, just to be clear," began the Hatter, "you were sent here to interrogate me?"

"Yeah so what of it?" shouted Tweedle Dum.

"No need to be rude."

"I do apologize," said Tweedle Dee, "he's very upset, as you can imagine."

"Don't apologize! He did this to us, you snivelling wretch," sneered Tweedle Dum.

"Keep it down back there!" shouted the Troll from somewhere down the hallway.

"What I was wondering," said the Hatter as he traced a finger along the wood of his cell door, "was what were you hoping to find out?"

Tweedle squinted suspiciously at the Hatter and in a brief moment of clarity said, "Well, it's unusual, isn't it? The Dwarf getting out like that. It would take a lot of planning. You're both smart enough to do something like this, but there's no gain for you. And then there's the hole in the wall. How would you or the Dwarf know where the other is, when you never leave your cells? The Tower has all the magical protection it can hold; there's no way you should have been able to put a hole through the wall to begin with."

"All good questions."

"You said you were keeping a secret."

"It's a doozy."

"You're going to tell us, aren't you?" Tweedle grinned as his sanity slipped ever so slightly.

"Well, it's far too big to keep to myself," said the Hatter and smiled a ghastly wide grin.

Tweedle turned away from the door and stood in the middle of his cell while his personalities conversed.

"Um, Tweedle Dum," whispered Tweedle Dee.

"What do you want?" said Tweedle Dum.

"I think there's a possibility we can get out of here."

"What are you going to do, snivel and whine your way out through the bars?"

"You obviously haven't been paying attention; you're always too busy being angry."

"Do you have a point to make, little brother?"

"Yes, I do, but we're going to need to work together. Now, listen carefully."

Rumpelstiltskin was thankful for the light rain that fell over the graveyard at Slack Top; it seemed to be making the ground softer. He had been digging for thirty minutes and was already making good headway. He looked up at the gravestone that loomed up above him. The name *Elise Marie Palmer* was inscribed in the stone, along with the words *Loving daughter, estranged mother, possibly a witch.*

When Rumpelstiltskin had first come to Elise Bastinda over fifty years ago, she had been a young girl, very confused, and very lost. She had no friends and no understanding of why strange things happened to her. *She was the last Bastinda!* Rumpelstiltskin spit in the grave. One of the most powerful races of witches and she was condemned here to Othaside by the Agency. *Meddling fools!*

Rumpelstiltskin was sad to discover from the wizard Niggle that she was now dead. Not that it mattered for his own plans, but he had wanted to meet her before having to murder her. The Dwarf was evil, but he had his principles.

What he really needed were her bones, which was why he now stood in a wet hole in a dark graveyard in Northern England.

After another fifteen minutes, the Dwarf's shovel hit something hard, and he scraped off the mud to reveal a simple casket. His glee and excitement almost overtook him; he was so happy, so close! He cleared off the rest of the casket and, using the shovel, pried open the lid.

He experienced a range of feelings before anger rose to the top and beat the crap out of all other feelings. Things were not as he had expected.

Robert was enjoying the night air as he and Lily walked up Smithwell Lane. Frank had begun to follow them and, every so often, he could be heard swearing somewhere far behind them.

"Do you like me, Robert?" said Lily.

"W-w-well," said Robert taken aback. "Yes, I suppose I do."

"You suppose? So you're not certain?" she said without taking her eyes off the road ahead.

"Well, it's been a heavy couple of days. I think you're an amazing person, you're beautiful and mysterious. Admittedly somewhat less mysterious after last night."

"So it's the werewolf, then."

"No, the werewolf doesn't bother me."

"Liar," said the voice in Robert's head.

"Well, okay, yes, it's the werewolf. That's a side of you that terrifies me."

"I see."

They walked on in an awkward silence for several minutes that felt like several lifetimes.

"So," said Robert, venturing carefully, "you like me?"

Lily stopped walking and turned to face Robert. "To be honest, I don't find you physically attractive, you're not bred from the best of stock, you're very gangly, you don't often say the right thing, and taking into account all the evidence, it seems like you're going mad."

"Oh, well..."

"I'm not finished."

"Right, sorry."

"I've never had the chance to have a proper relationship and I never will be able to. There's no cure for what I am. What you see now is what you'd have for the rest of your life. I don't age, I don't change, and every time there's a full moon I'll probably try to kill you. It's not a life anyone would wish for."

Robert thought about it for a second while Lily's beautiful amber eyes drilled a hole through his head. "I am gangly. And I don't often say the right thing. I've always felt out of place until yesterday morning, and by all rights, I might be going mad. That's not normal."

"No, it's not," said the voice.

"But what you see is what you'd have for the rest of your life. I probably won't change; if anything, I might get worse. But I know where I belong now and it's not here in this world. It's in Thiside. I'm a good person, Lillian Redcloak. What I'm trying to say is that I'm perfectly willing to accept your flaws if you're willing to accept mine. Although if you're not attracted to me in the slightest I suppose—"

Robert stopped talking as Lily had clamped her lips to his.

"Kiss back!" hissed the voice.

And so he did. It was a magnificent moment that filled Robert with the kind of joy that can only normally be felt by children on Christmas morning just before they open their presents.

Lily detached herself and smiled a whimsical smile.

"I'll think about it." And with that she turned and carried on walking.

Good enough for me! Robert grinned and then chased after her. "So Elise Bastinda is dead, then?"

"I'm going to assume so as we were told we'd find her in a graveyard. I doubt she's there for the fun of it."

"What do you think we're going to find there?"

"I don't know."

"Well, what are we going to do if the Dwarf is still there?"

"I'm not sure."

"So we don't really have a plan?"

"No."

"Oh good, as long as we're on the same page."

It was empty! She was gone! The body of the witch wasn't where it was supposed to be. Rumpelstiltskin scrambled out of the grave, covered in mud, and was now in the foulest of moods. He paced back and forth trying to figure out what to do next. He couldn't complete the spell without the final piece. He needed the bones!

Something moved behind him and he spun around to find nothing but a few hundred gravestones staring back at him.

"Who's there?"

A sheep trotted out from behind a nearby stone and scowled at the Dwarf. Scowling was exceptionally hard for sheep. They sometimes managed a smile, but scowling took all the wrong muscles and they didn't have the concentration to do it very often. The average sheep could only manage maybe two, possibly three good scowls in an entire lifetime.

"Oh, it's just you," said the Dwarf and turned back to the grave.

Jack was leaning casually against the gravestone, looking angry. He had a large garbage bag sitting on the ground next to him.

"You!" said the Dwarf.

"Me," said Jack.

Lightning flashed as a storm began to organize itself in the skies above Hebden Bridge.

A similar storm, albeit with more personality, raged above the Valley of Storms. Lightning flashed, thunder rolled, and the rain threw itself out of the sky toward the ground with the distinct intention of making everything wet.

Inside the Tower, rain dripped down through the hallways as it always did when the rain was heavy. The rain snuffed out some of the flaming torches that illuminated the interior of the Tower and the Troll was having a hard time keeping them all lit. He slouched his way up and down the hallway holding a stick with a candle on the end and relit the lamps every time one went out.

"You're an ugly little bastard," shouted Tweedle Dum.

"Sharrap," said the Troll as another lamp fizzled out.

"He doesn't really mean it," yelled Tweedle Dee.

The Hatter clapped his hands enthusiastically.

"What are you so happy about?" said Tweedle Dum.

"I'm just so honoured to be in the presence of the pair of you. It's been so long since you've been your true self. It's glorious to behold!"

"We don't talk to madmen!" shouted Tweedle Dum.

"Well, *he* doesn't," said Tweedle Dee, "I'll talk to anyone."

"And that's why mother liked me best!" retorted Tweedle Dum.

"That's ridiculous and you know it."

"That's why she always paid more attention to me and ignored your tubby, whining ass!"

"You're lying!" shrieked Tweedle Dee.

"Gentleman, gentleman, no need to fight," said the Hatter soothingly.

Tweedle was doing his best to scowl at himself.

"In fact, we can change subjects altogether. We could talk about the secret that I'm not telling you."

Tweedle's eyes narrowed. "You keep talking about this secret but you're not telling us what it is. That can only lead us to think that you're lying."

"Oh, I don't lie. Ask anyone."

"You've got to admit that our choice of witnesses is limited."

"You could ask the Troll?"

"He's a snivelling toad!" shouted Tweedle Dum.

"You've been wondering about how the Dwarf got out of here when no one has ever escaped before."

"Obviously."

"But suurreeleee, you have some idea?"

Tweedle stared back at the Hatter with a blank look on his face.

"Oh come, come, you must know! Or at least have some concept? An inkling? An idea?"

Tweedle continued the blank stare.

"The hole in the wall could only be made with a compact magical spell. Which means someone brought it in. Who are the only people who can come in and out of the Tower at will?"

Tweedle screwed up his forehead as if thinking very hard.

"You're smarter than this," said the Hatter. "If you're not going to play along then I won't play, either!"

The Hatter turned his back to his cell door and a slight smile played at the corners of Tweedle's mouth.

"People like me?" said Tweedle Dee.

The Hatter swung around and gripped the bars of his cell. "Yes, go on!"

"An Agent. It would have to be an Agent. But it would have to be an Agent who had something to gain. But the only way they would have something to gain would be if they knew all about Rumpelstiltskin."

The Hatter was literally shaking the bars on his cell door with excitement. "Yes, yes! Keep going!"

"And the only way any Agent would know anything about an inmate is by interrogation."

"And who interrogated the Dwarf? Who?" shouted the Hatter.

"Jack. It was Jack!"

"You took your damn time getting here. The bones are gone!" said the Dwarf.

Jack was still leaning against the gravestone, his features as chiselled as the stone tablets lying around the graveyard.

"I was already here! I dug up the bones earlier today. If you'd kept to the plan and met me outside of the City of Oz like you were supposed to do, this never would have happened!" said Jack.

"Outside the city? We weren't supposed to meet outside the city. We were supposed to meet along the coastal path. You weren't there!" shouted the Dwarf, losing his patience.

"Who told you that?"

"The Hatter, of course."

Jack's face tightened. "I knew we couldn't trust that skinny idiot. I assumed I'd find you back here."

Rumpelstiltskin laughed. "That skinny idiot very nearly ruined our plan."

"Your plan, not ours. I'm just helping you make life more interesting," said Jack.

"What?" said Lily's startled voice from the edge of the graveyard.

"You can let me out now, Troll," said Tweedle.

The Troll shuffled in front of the Agent's cell door.

"What ya mean?"

"Well, of course you know I was just putting on an act so I could get the information I needed out of the Hatter?" explained Tweedle.

"Uh, wellz, no, didn't occur t' me really."

"And now I have it. I need to report back to my associates as soon as possible. So like I said, you can let me out now."

"So uh, you'z not really crazy then, eh?"

"Just an act, and a good one, I might add. Even fooled you, I see."

The Troll scratched his head. "Well I s'pose."

"Oh, come on!" said the Hatter, "you're not really buying this, are you? He was arguing with himself a minute ago!"

"Sharrap, Hatter," said the Troll and dragged a long nail down Tweedle's cell door.

The locks slid aside and Tweedle stepped from the cell and straightened his clothing.

"I just need a quick word with the Hatter." Tweedle waddled over to the Hatter's door and moved his face close to the barred window and whispered, "Thank you so much for releasing us, we won't forget what you've done for us today."

Tweedle smiled a wide grin and then walked away down the hallway, followed closely by the Troll.

"You'll never be able to hide it in the real world again, you know!" shouted the Hatter after them. "Everyone will know who and what you are! Just wait and see!"

Tweedle left the Troll standing at the gate to the Tower and began his journey across the bridge. He had much more of a spring in his step than when he'd first arrived. The storm raged all around him, but it was nothing compared to the storm that was raging in his head.

"Never be able to hide it. That's what the Hatter said," said Tweedle Dee nervously.

"He's right, you know, and I have no intention of hiding it. Why should we hide our true selves when people like Rumpelstiltskin are free to be exactly who they are? We won't hide anymore, everyone will know exactly who and what we are!" Tweedle Dum let loose a chilling laugh.

"I'm scared," said Tweedle Dee.

"You should be!" said Tweedle Dum. "They all should be!"

Lightning flashed across the sky and a shrill scream rang out from the Tower, hiding the giddy laughter coming from the small, fat figure waddling his way across the bridge.

Robert and Lily had cut across one of the fields to get to the graveyard quicker. The sheep in the fields posed no problem. As soon as they caught a whiff of Lily's scent, they all headed for the farthest corner of the field and huddled there, silently hoping the wolf in women's clothing wouldn't bother them.

Robert didn't have Lily's natural ability to see in the dark and he was having trouble avoiding the hundred or so piles of sheep crap that littered the field. After a while, he just gave up.

They reached the edge of the field and climbed over the short wall into the graveyard. Lily suddenly grabbed Robert and pulled him down behind a gravestone and put a finger to her lips.

"There's someone here already," she whispered.

"Is it the Dwarf?"

"It doesn't sound like the Dwarf," she whispered. Her eyes suddenly grew large in surprise. "What?" said Lily and stood up and strode off toward the voices.

Robert hurried to keep up.

What he saw, once they were close enough, was the same Dwarf that he'd found in his bathtub almost an eternity ago, covered in mud, holding a shovel, the Agent whom he knew as Jack, and a very full-looking garbage bag.

Lily marched right up to Jack, who was no longer leaning against the gravestone but standing at his full height.

"What do you think you're doing, Jack?" asked Lily.

"Hello again, Darkly," said the Dwarf with a sneer.

"Stiltskin," said Robert.

"Find your daddy yet?"

"Actually no, been a little busy chasing you around."

"I won't ask again, Jack. What are you doing with the Dwarf?" asked Lily, stabbing a finger at his chest.

"It doesn't concern you, Lily, go home," said Jack matter-of-factly.

"Go home? Are you out of your mind? I'm not going anywhere until you tell me exactly what's going on!"

"Go on, tell her, Jack, she's going to figure it out anyway," said the Dwarf.

"Shut up!" said Jack.

Robert eyed the garbage bag that was resting on the ground next to Jack.

"I wonder if that's the body of the last Bastinda?" said the voice in Robert's head.

"Excuse me," said Robert, "but I don't suppose that's the remains of Elise Bastinda in that garbage bag, is it?"

"Good guess, Darkly. You might just be as smart as your father," said the Dwarf.

"Aren't you curious who your father is?" asked the voice.

"Well, of course I am," replied Robert.

"Modest, too," said the Dwarf.

"Will you two shut up?" snapped Jack.

"Enough!" said Lily, grabbing a handful of Jack's shirt and lifting him clear off the ground. The tall man wriggled, but her grip was obviously too strong.

"Don't make me do this, Lily," growled Jack.

"Do what?" she asked.

"Lily, I wish you were unconscious," said Jack.

"Granted," said the Dwarf.

Jack landed on his feet as Lily's body slid to the ground.

"Lily!" shouted Robert.

Jack rolled Lily's body into the open grave of the last Bastinda and she slid unceremoniously into the open casket.

"No!" said Robert and punched Jack in the face. Every bone in his hand hurt. "Shit, that hurt."

"This'll hurt more," said the Dwarf from behind him.

Robert's first impulse was to ask *what will hurt more* but before he had a chance the back of his head was greeted by the flat side of the shovel and all he managed to get out was, "What wurrlll...?"

His body must have been getting used to being rendered unconscious. As he collapsed to the floor, he could still hear what was going on. For example, he knew that the tingly feeling on his side was his body sliding down into the grave. The thump he heard was his body rolling into the casket on top of Lily. He heard the Dwarf laugh. There was a creak, which he assumed was the casket lid closing. What followed were several deep thumps, which Robert knew to be the sound of Jack and the Dwarf burying them alive.

"Hold it together, Robert," said the voice in his head. And the voice sounded calm.

That should mean I'm calm, thought Robert, slowly regaining consciousness. And then madness and fear overtook him and he began to scream like a six-year-old girl.

CHAPTER EIGHTEEN

DOUBLE CROSSES & AWKWARD SITUATIONS

Robert had never suffered from claustrophobia; however, being buried alive really made him reprioritize his top five fears. He'd finally given up on screaming when he realized how pointless it was. He could hear thunder outside and assumed the storm must be raging in the skies. Lily was still unconscious. One had to assume that Elise Bastinda was a large lady, as Robert and Lily both fit into the casket and still had some room to spare. He wondered how long it would take to run out of oxygen. Everything was so dark.

"Of course it's dark," said the voice in Robert's head, "you're in a grave. Not exactly going to be flood-lit, is it?"

"Well, at least you're still here."

"You should try waking her up."

"I wouldn't know where to start."

"You could throw water on her?" suggested the voice.

"Where am I going to get water? I'm in a coffin."

"You could spit on her?"

"I'm not spitting on her. That's just rude."

"That's a good point. Try pinching her?"

"Worth a try. Where do I pinch her?"

"Well, I'd suggest maybe her neck?"

"Her neck?"

"Well, you don't want to pinch anywhere private. That's just rude."

"Right." Robert fumbled around in the dark, struggled to bring his arms up closer to his head, and felt around what must have been the back of Lily's head. He noted that her hair was very smooth, like a Labrador's.

"Are you actually comparing her to a dog?" said the voice.

"Well, you have to admit it's not a long stretch."

He brushed her hair aside and felt down to her neck and pinched hard.

Several things happened. Lily swore colourfully as her hand came up extremely fast and smacked Robert in the nose, who also swore, only with less colour.

"What the hell are you doing?" said Lily.

"Shnorry," said Robert, whose hand was cupped over his nose.

"Where are we?"

"We've been buried alive."

"That bastard. Wait until I get hold of them. How's your nose?"

"I don't think it's broken. Maybe I missed something up there but I thought that Jack was on our side?"

"It was Jack. That's how the Dwarf escaped in the first place. Jack must have helped him."

"But what does Jack have to gain from the doors being unregulated?"

"I don't suppose we could talk about this once we're out of the grave?"

"How are we going to get out of here? We've been buried alive. In fact, why aren't you panicking?"

"Why aren't you?"

"I did all my screaming already," said Robert.

"The grave wasn't too deep, it's just a matter of leverage."

"You're strong enough to get us out of here?"

"I'm not. But what's inside of me is."

The statement floated through Robert's brain looking for something to connect to. A few short yet disturbing flashbacks later, Robert hit a wall of realization.

"You're going to turn into that thing, into a werewolf! Forget it; I'm beginning to like it down here."

"Don't be silly, Robert."

"Silly? Who's being silly? The smell of pine wood and rotting flesh is blissful to me."

"You are being silly," agreed the voice.

"I'm not being silly!"

"This won't be like last time. When the moon forces me to change, I have no control, the creature bursts out of me as if it's breaking out of a cage. When I change myself, it's like I'm letting it out through the front door on a leash. I can control it."

"You're sure?"

"Robert, I'm over three hundred years old, I know what I'm doing. Trust me."

"Okay," he said solemnly. And he realized that he did actually trust her with his life. Ironic, being that she had been trying so hard to kill him less than twenty-four hours ago. "How do we do this?"

"I need to be naked."

"Come again?" said Robert.

"I'll need the clothes afterwards and I don't want them ripped when I change. Help me get undressed."

"Uh-ah," was all Robert could come up with for an argument.

Lily kicked off her shoes. The casket was around six and a half feet in length, around two and a half feet high, and three feet wide, which didn't lend itself to too much wiggle room. Lily struggled with getting the sweater off over her head while Robert fumbled with the zipper on her pants. Robert pondered on what a highly erotic moment this could have been, had it not been for the whole *we're buried alive* thing.

Robert pushed her pants down using his feet, then she kicked them off. He hadn't realized that all she was wearing was a sweater, pants, shoes and nothing else.

Lily finally succeeded in getting her sweater off.

"What now?" said Robert, who sounded nervous and was probably sweating more than he should have been.

"Relax, Robert, I realize this is awkward…"

"Noo… well just a bit, yes."

"But it's going to get a little worse."

"What?" said Robert.

"How could this be any more awkward?" said the voice.

"I need to climb on top of you," said Lily.

184

"Oh, that's how it's going to be more awkward," said the voice.

"Uh… wha… why?" said Robert.

"I don't want to crush you when I change and I don't want to bury you under the dirt. The only way to do that is to straddle you, change, and as I do so, I'll push upward out of the coffin and break through the earth."

"And there's no other way? You see, I'm a man, I have urges…"

"We're in a life-threatening situation. How can you be thinking of those urges at a time like this?" said Lily.

"Well, it's been a while," said Robert. He was thinking about how to protest but it was too late as Lily was already manoeuvring herself on top of him. He could feel her pressed up against him.

"Think of something else!" shouted the voice in his head.

So Robert did. He thought about tractors, and garden Gnomes, sheep, antique bathtubs, Lily in a bathtub…

"Not that!" said the voice.

"Okay, I'm ready," said Lily. "Your heart is racing. Are you all right?"

"I'll live."

"This might be horrifying for you but I suppose you've already seen it once."

Robert was about to apologize for his male urges when all of a sudden it was no longer an issue. He heard the cracking of bones first and in such a small space, it was truly ghastly to listen to. Her body expanded above him, and he felt hair grow from her face as her nose began to stretch and protrude into a wolf's snout. He could sense her tense up as she pushed with both arms so as not to crush him. Her whole body radiated heat, and her muscles writhed against him as they stretched and transformed. He heard splintering as her nails grew, then broke through the bottom of the casket as the overall size of her body expanded and the lid cracked open. Mud and dirt began to pour in on all sides. She began to growl a low guttural growl and drooled on Robert's face. For a moment, she didn't move too much more and Robert began to fear that she'd overestimated her strength. The growling grew louder and she pushed herself upward. In retrospect, Robert considered that particular moment to be one of those moments that he never actually expected to find himself in. In fact, it probably made the top of the list. Buried alive, trapped in a casket with a beautiful naked woman, who then transformed into a werewolf while straddling him.

"Definitely top of the list," agreed the voice.

The lid cracked completely and the earth began to shift.

It had taken Frank a long time to make it up Smithwell Lane as his keen sense of direction, heavily influenced by alcohol, had become about as sharp as a plastic spoon. To his credit, he'd actually managed to stay on the road for the most part, except when he stopped to relieve his bladder, during which time he detoured to one of the fields and ended up falling into a ditch. He hadn't noticed at the time, but the sheep in the field had enjoyed a good laugh at Frank's expense. Laughing and grinning came much easier to sheep than scowling.

He'd finally reached the graveyard at Slack Top as the rain began to pour and lightning lit up the skies. For a moment, he'd thought that he'd seen a man and a child holding a big garbage bag standing in the graveyard, but then they were gone and Frank chalked it up to being really, really drunk. Frank lived not much farther up the lane, but something else in the graveyard caught his eye. Like any good Yorkshire man, he was profoundly superstitious and fully believed that banshees roamed graveyards at night to guard the dead. He could hear something over the sound of the rain. It was like a growl or a roar, and there was creaking, and then thunder.

Frank was not brave by any stretch of the imagination, but he enjoyed telling a good story as much as anyone. If he actually managed to see a banshee, then that would make a spectacular story to tell the lads down at the pub and so his drunken brain encouraged his jelly-like legs to propel him forward into the graveyard to investigate further. He tripped over the one sheep, who was no longer scowling but continued to be lost in the graveyard.

"Ba-a-a-a!" said the sheep.

"Bugger off wit ya!" said Frank as he scrambled to his feet.

He staggered up the overgrown path that ran through the middle of the graveyard. The lightning lit up his surroundings on a regular basis and Frank found that he'd begun to shake.

"What are you doing, Frankie old boy, this is no place for you," he said to himself.

And then he saw the earth move over to his right. He stared intently through the darkness at where he'd seen the movement, and as his eyes adjusted, he saw it move again. It was like the grave was breathing.

He squinted at the headstone, which read *Elise Marie Palmer*. Frank remembered Elise. She was a large woman with eternally messy hair and a general hatred for pretty much everyone. She'd really gone off the deep end when her son had been killed in a tragic farming accident. She'd taken to dancing naked on the moors whenever there was a full moon, and when confronted about it, she hadn't even known what she was doing or why.

"It just felt like the right thing to do," she would say.

The earth heaved again in front of him and there was that growling sound again. Frank's natural reflex urged him to back away from the grave. He did so as it heaved again. And then again. And then the earth exploded, along with splintered wood, just as lightning flashed across the sky.

Frank let out a squeal that sounded like someone had stepped on a guinea pig. A large, wolf-like creature clawed its way up and out of the grave, stood in the mud and the rain, and howled at the sky victoriously.

Frank was instantaneously sober. He screamed again and sprinted away, not down the path, but through the graveyard, up over one of the walls, and disappeared into the darkness. He was found the next day curled up in the corner of a field surrounded by grinning sheep, half out of his mind. Later in the week, he resolved to move to Lancashire where everything that had once seemed boring now seemed much more safe and normal.

Robert climbed and wriggled his way out of the grave, then lay on his back in the mud and tried to catch his breath. He had Lily's clothes stuffed under his own sweater so they wouldn't get buried in the grave. He looked up at the werewolf, who was looking back down at him. Its tongue hung out the side of its mouth and it was panting.

The werewolf knelt down beside Robert and licked his cheek. The creature began to shrink before Robert's eyes. The claws retracted, the bones cracked as they realigned, the muscles shrank, long, black hair grew from its head while the wolf hair shed away. Breasts protruded from its chest and Lily knelt beside him, looking exhausted. She lay down in the mud next to him and put an arm across his chest.

"I need to rest a moment," she said, and he put an arm around her and pulled her close.

As they lay there together in the mud, the rain falling toward them, lightning flashing above them, an empty grave beside them, Robert was thankful that they had escaped. He was even more thankful that they were together and with that in mind, he smiled contently as thunder resounded across the sky.

Rumpelstiltskin and Jack exited a door in Thiside and found they were on a mountaintop. It was still daytime in Thiside and the sun was only just beginning its fall toward the horizon.

"Where are we?" growled Jack.

"How should I know? You didn't wish to go anywhere, you just wished for a door!" shouted the Dwarf.

"Why didn't you tell me that at the time?"

"I wasn't thinking about it at the time, I just wanted to get out of the damn rain and that wretched graveyard."

"Then we should go back through the door until we're closer."

"You know, you've never told me, Jack, exactly why it is you freed me to finish the thing that you originally arrested me for."

"I don't need to tell you!"

"True, but it would sure help me understand things better. You have to admit it's hard for me to trust you without knowing your motives."

Jack grabbed the Dwarf by the shirt and picked him up so they were face to face.

"Look here, you little twerp! You should be thankful that I arranged for you to escape from the Tower. You're lucky the Hatter is a gullible idiot who agreed to accept a smuggled-in spell to create a hole between your two cells! Most of all, you should be thankful that I haven't changed my mind and killed you yet. I don't like you, Dwarf. And I don't need to tell you anything."

He dropped the Dwarf in a heap and hoisted the garbage bag containing the remains of Elise Bastinda over his shoulder.

The Dwarf's eyes narrowed as a nefarious scheme entered his devious little mind.

"Fair enough," said the Dwarf from the ground, "I suggest you wish for another door, or even better, wish where it is you want to go."

"Where is it we're going, anyway?"

"To perform this spell, I need a strong magical field. The strongest there is."

"And where would that be?"

The Dwarf smiled. Jack was big, he was old, he was an excellent interrogator, he was amazing when it came to hurting people. But first and foremost, Jack was an idiot.

"The Great Hall in the Wizards' Council building, of course," smiled the Dwarf.

"Fine. Let's get this over with so you can work your spell. I wish for a door to take us—"

"Ah, ah, ah," said the Dwarf. "Not us. You have to wish *me*. Any reference to yours truly will render the wish null and void."

"I wish for a door to take *me* to the Great Hall in the Wizards' Council building."

"Granted," said the Dwarf and a door opened before them. "I'll take the bag; there may be wizards waiting on the other side and your authority will certainly be more effective against them than mine would be."

Jack handed over the bag.

"Okay," said Rumpelstiltskin, "let's go."

And with that the Dwarf jumped through the door. Jack dived after him...

...and rolled out into the Great Hall in the City of Oz. The wizards were having lunch and were surprised by the appearance of an Agent. Jack was equally surprised to see that there was no sign of Rumpelstiltskin anywhere in the vast hall.

"Excuse me," said Jack, "did any of you see a Dwarf come through here?"

An elderly wizard with a pointy nose and long, flowing, white hair, part of which was sitting in his soup, said, "No, I'm afraid not."

"This is rather inappropriate," said another wizard. "Just because you're an Agent doesn't give you the right to disturb our lunch. We'll have to speak to the Agency Director about this."

"My apologies, I'll look elsewhere." Jack strode from the hall with his fists clenched. He waited until he was out of the hall and in a stairwell before he punched a hole through the wall.

"That damn Dwarf tricked me!"

The Dwarf in question stepped out of a different doorway that appeared to be in a lush field next to a small cottage. The smell of bread floated through the air. Rumpelstiltskin let out a chilling laugh in celebration of his own brilliance. *What a fool, Jack is. He wished for him to go to the Great Hall, not me! He even believed that there was a miscommunication that caused us not to meet up outside the city. He'll believe anything. Although I can't help but wonder what he has to gain from me completing my little project? Either way, he doesn't know the true location of the spell and therefore he will no longer be an issue. Now, on with the show!*

Rumpelstiltskin stole a few bread rolls from the ledge of the cottage, which he assumed must be the house of the Muffin Man and, carrying his garbage bag, ran away down the Yellow Brick Road in search of a door to take him to his final destination.

Soaked to the skin and freezing cold, Robert couldn't be happier. They lay together for around half an hour, during which time Lily had fallen asleep. Robert had discovered that she had a cute snore. Sort of like a puppy. Although he still found it hard to look at her without seeing a giant snarling monster, he couldn't help but find her to be the best thing in the entire world that had ever happened to him.

Lily began to wake up, and Robert couldn't resist asking something that had been bothering him. "Lily, who is Jack?"

"You mean in relation to the fairy tales of Othaside?"

Robert didn't want to offend Lily, as he now knew that Thisiders who had been replicated as characters in fairy tale stories in Othaside often found the comparison insulting.

"I know you don't like to talk about Thiside in those terms, but yes. The Agency seems to employ particular kinds of people."

"The kind with a long life span," said Lily.

"So where does Jack fit?"

Lily snuggled closer to Robert. The rain had subsided to a light drizzle. "Jack was just a man. A farmer. He belonged to one of the few human families that lived in Thiside over a thousand years ago."

"He's over a thousand years old?"

"Doesn't look bad, does he?"

"I suppose, if you like that tall, blond, muscled type with striking features. Of course it's not everyone's cup of tea."

"Certainly not mine," said Lily.

"You two never... you know... got together?" said Robert with a certain amount of hesitation.

"Absolutely, lots of times."

"Really?" said Robert with obvious disappointment.

"No, I'm just playing with you," said Lily and laughed. "Jack is a very distant person. He doesn't relate well to anyone."

"I could see that."

"When he was around thirty years old, he lived in a village that fell under the rule of the Evil Queen."

"She was actually called the Evil Queen?"

"Don't interrupt."

"Sorry."

"The kingdom was attacked by a Giant who destroyed almost everything and was responsible for over a hundred deaths. Jack killed him."

"That's it?"

"Do you have any idea how hard it would be for a human to kill a Giant?"

"Actually, I have no idea."

"Even being a werewolf, I doubt I could take down a Giant. No one knows how Jack did it. The archives don't have any information on the event other than what was passed down by word of mouth."

"If he's just human, how is he still alive?"

"The Evil Queen was a powerful sorceress. As a thank you for saving her lands, she granted Jack and his family the gift of immortality. He can't die."

"Ever?"

"Ever. He can't be killed, he can't even be injured."

Robert thought about it. "Jack and the Beanstalk."

"Yes. Only without the beanstalk or the magic beans."

"Remarkable."

Lily slipped back into her clothing, which was also soaked and covered with mud, but there were now more important things at hand than the state of their clothing. There was the state of reality to think about. Lily had assumed that Jack had wished for a door and that the pair was probably back in Thiside already. Not knowing where Rumpelstiltskin was going to perform the spell left them at a bit of a loss.

"What about the wizard? Niggle? Couldn't he tell us where the magical fields are located?" said Robert.

Lily looked thoughtful. "He's probably the best chance we have. We'll need to find a door first, though, and who knows how long that'll take."

"There's a door over there," said the voice in Robert's head and Robert instinctively looked to his left. Hovering twenty feet away next to an ornately carved sculpture of an angel was the telltale distortion in the air.

"That's amazing," said Robert, "how do I know these things?"

"Know what?" said Lily as she tried to scrape some of the mud from her sweater.

"There's a door over there," said Robert, pointing to the door.

Lily looked at Robert. "That is amazing. How did you know that?"

"The voice in my head told me."

Lily looked troubled as she always did when Robert referred to the voice in his head. "Has this happened before?"

"The voice? All the time, damn thing never shuts up."

"No, I mean a door appearing when you needed it to?"

"Just one other time, in the forest where you were about to ki... ehh... attack me. Or maybe you were just trying to hump my leg. It was hard to tell at the time, what with the snarling and growling and such."

"Funny. You door jumped for hours and didn't get any stranger than you already are. And doors appear when you most need them."

"What does that mean?"

"I have no idea. But let's not waste it." She grabbed Robert's hand and led him toward the door. "They've got a head start. We're going to need to door jump fast and get as close to the City of Oz as we can, and hopefully Niggle's nerves are still holding up. Ready?"

"Ready!" he said with more confidence than he actually felt.

Lily took a deep breath. "Here's hoping we can find them fast." And they stepped through the doorway and stepped out...

...into the apartment of the wizard Niggle who screamed and spilled hot tea all over himself and then screamed some more.

"Well," said Robert, "that worked out nicely."

Lily looked surprised. Robert was proud of himself although he didn't really know why, and the wizard Niggle continued screaming. At that exact moment, the front door was kicked open and in the doorway stood a very angry-looking Jack.

Lily dived at Jack, knocking him back into the hallway. The wizard Niggle waved his hand and the door slammed shut.

"Lily!" said Robert. He turned to the nervous wizard. "Open the door!"

"N-n-no way," said the wizard. "What are y-y-you doing back here?"

There was a crash in the hallway. Robert ran over to the door and pulled on the handle but the door wouldn't budge. "Open the damn door!"

"N-n-no," said the wizard resolutely. He was clutching a now-empty tea pot to his chest as if it was his security blanket.

Robert didn't have a temper. He was rarely angry. He often wished he did have some small smidgen of rage in him, but he'd never had the right motivation. Until today. He stalked up to the wizard, grabbed his tea pot and threw it against the wall.

"Open the door now!" he said directly into the wizard's face.

The wizard looked terrified. He pointed at the door and it swung open by itself to reveal Lily carrying an unconscious Jack over her shoulder.

"See," said Robert, "now was that so hard? Sorry about the tea pot."

Lily kicked the door closed behind her and dropped Jack into a chair. "Rope won't hold him. Wizard, I need you to bind him."

Niggle sighed. He looked at Jack and muttered a few nonsensical words. Jack's arms pulled tight to his side and his head snapped up. Lily walked up to him and slapped him a few times. Jack's eyes opened slowly and he began to struggle, but the invisible bonds wouldn't budge.

"Forget it, Jack, you're bound to the chair."

"Let me go, Lily."

"Not until you tell us where the Dwarf is going."

"Us?" said Jack. "There's an us? You mean you and Darkly?" Jack laughed out loud.

Robert had known Jack only as a surly, angry individual. He now decided that watching him laugh was far more disturbing than his usual self.

"Are you just going to stand there and take that?" said the voice in Robert's head.

"Shut up!" said Robert.

"Ohh, the Othasider's grown a backbone. A couple nights with Lily here must have really loosened you up," smiled Jack.

Robert walked closer to Jack. "I've heard of you."

Jack laughed. "Going to interrogate me, Darkly?"

"Didn't you have a beanstalk?"

Jack stopped laughing.

Robert continued, "And a cow. I seem to remember that you had a cow and you traded it for magic beans. Pretty dumb choice, when you really think about it."

Jack was turning a pastel red colour. "I'll get out of here eventually, you know."

"Hit him with a hard one," said the voice.

Robert bent over so he was inches from Jack's face. "It's a real honour to meet a fairy tale character such as yourself."

Jack strained against the invisible bonds that held him. "I'll kill you when I get out of here, Darkly. I'll kill you! You're just like your father and you'll end up exactly like him! You'll probably even share a cell!"

The wizard had been busy unpacking a new teapot, which Lily grabbed from him and smashed up the side of Jack's head.

"Try and focus, Jack. We need to know where the Dwarf is going!"

Jack didn't take his eyes off Robert, who was leaning casually against the fireplace staring back at Jack.

"Why does it matter?"

"Because we know what he's doing. We know he's going to remove the blood regulation from the door. It'll break down the barrier between Thiside and Othaside. It'll be just like it was before. Othasiders will pour into Thiside."

Niggle twitched at the thought.

"Would that be so bad?" said Jack. "At least we'd have a purpose again."

Lily moved in between Jack and Robert's staring contest. "Is that why you did it? Because you're bored?"

"Aren't you?"

"No. I'm happy with who I am."

Jack barked a laugh. "If there's anyone who's not happy with who they are it's you, Lillian Redcloak. I've been alive for centuries. Centuries! I'm sick of living this existence. In my day, Giants roamed the land, Ogres burned villages, Goblins ravaged entire Kingdoms! I want those days back, Lily, I want them back! And the Dwarf can do that. If he breaks down the doors, it'll cause chaos. We'll have something to do again. The Agency will have real assignments again instead of spending all our time negotiating between Humanimals or catching thieves. We'll live between both worlds!"

"You're an idiot, Jack, and we're going to stop the Dwarf."

"You'll never find him. There are magical fields everywhere and he just needs one strong one to finish the spell."

"A-a-a-a magical field?" said Niggle.

"Where's the strongest magical field?" Robert asked Niggle.

"The r-r-remains of the Emerald City. It's the strongest magical field in Thiside. It's also abandoned. It'd be the p-p-perfect place to p-perform the spell."

Jack rocked himself forward and stood up, the chair still attached to his body. He charged at Lily, knocking her over, then ran as fast as anyone with a chair attached to their rear end could and threw himself out of the open window of the wizard's apartment.

Robert ran to the window in time to see Jack hit the ground a hundred feet below. The chair smashed upon impact and the stone pavement cracked.

Lily joined Robert at the window.

"Is he dead?" asked Robert.

"No," said Lily.

Jack picked himself up and brushed himself off. He cast a glance up at the window, then turned and ran through the crowd that had begun to gather.

"Should we chase him?" asked Robert.

"No, we need to get to Rumpelstiltskin." They turned away from the window to find Niggle clutching another teapot to his chest. "We need to get to the Emerald City. Can you produce us another door?"

"N-n-no. The Great Hall is the only place we can perform it and there's currently training in session."

"Robert, can you open a door?"

Robert thought about it. "I wouldn't even know where to start. We could door jump?"

"It won't get us there fast enough."

"Horses?" said Robert.

"What's a horse," asked Niggle.

"You haven't noticed that there aren't any horses here?" asked Lily.

"That's a good point," said Robert. "There has to be some form of transportation?"

Niggle twitched and almost dropped his teapot. "One of the younger wizards has a pair of S-s-s-screech Demons. They'd get you there f-fast."

"Take us to them," said Lily.

Robert's perception of right and wrong, up and down, reality and fantasy, black and white had all been completely skewed, then shredded, then burned, then drowned over the last two days. Robert heard the words *Screech Demon* and the first thing that came to mind wasn't something warm and fuzzy. He hated to ask the question, but as he followed the wizard and Lily out the door he felt he had no choice.

"What's a Screech Demon?" he asked.

After hearing the answer, he wished he'd just left the question alone.

CHAPTER NINETEEN

SCRAACCHHHHHHAAKKK!

O h," said Robert. "That's a Screech Demon."

Lily had explained on their way toward the stables located in the rear of the Wizards' Council building exactly what a Screech Demon was.

"It's a demon," she had said matter-of-factly.

"As in, it came from hell?" asked Robert.

"Not exactly. You interpret it as heaven and hell with a god and a devil. In Thiside, there isn't a strong perception of an afterlife, but there is a Pit."

"Which is… like hell?"

"I suppose. But it's literal rather than figurative."

"You mean it's an actual pit?"

"Yes. It's located very far North of here. It's a twenty by twenty shaft that goes down to an immeasurable depth."

"Well, how deep is it?"

"Immeasurably deep," said Lily in all seriousness.

"So this Pit just sits open and…?"

"No, not open. It's since been covered with a large trapdoor that can be opened only by magic. Once the first few creatures crawled out of it, the

Wizards' Council had it covered. Every so often something breaks through the trapdoor and it has to be resealed. A pair of Screech Demons broke through around three hundred years ago. Aside from the screeching and the occasional mauling, they were found to be quite amicable and trainable creatures."

"Mauling?"

"Only when they smell fear."

"Oh, good, then," said Robert, the blood slowly draining out of what most would consider to be an already very pale complexion.

They were heading through the wizard's kitchen where a variety of green, skinny, bald creatures with long fingernails, pointy ears, and vicious-looking teeth were preparing a soufflé.

"Lily," he whispered. "What are they?"

"Goblins."

"What are they doing?"

"Looks like they're making a soufflé."

"Goblins can make soufflés?"

"Robert, seriously, we have to get rid of those perceptions you've grown up with. Goblins are renowned as the best chefs. They look scary but they're literally born with recipes and culinary concepts running through their heads. You should try some of their cooking; it's to die for."

A particularly nasty-looking Goblin with bright eyes and a set of wicked-looking fangs grinned at Robert and nodded politely before it resumed piping decorative icing onto a four-layer cake.

"Weird," was all Robert could manage. And then they arrived at the stables.

"Oh," said Robert. "*That's* a Screech Demon."

A young wizard with rosy cheeks and a large scar down one side of his face was petting the head of one of the beasts. The Screech Demons were bright yellow in color, with smooth, oily skin and bright red eyes. They looked like a dragon but were the same size as a really large horse. They had a set of wings that they kept furled up on their backs, four strong-looking legs, a long tail on one end and a long neck on the other tipped with a small, spiny head. They looked like something out of a nightmare.

"We're going to ride those?" asked Robert with clear scepticism, in case anyone missed it.

"This is the ap-ap-ap-prentice wizard Arfund," said Niggle. "He's agreed to lend you his S-s-s-screech Demons as long as you p-promise not to d-damage them."

"They're sensitive, you see," said Arfund. "And I've raised them since they were eggs. They're part of the family, really."

"We'll take good care of them," said Lily.

"We're going to ride those?" said Robert again, because apparently everyone missed it the first time.

"They look quite nice," said the voice in Robert's head.

"You shut up."

"Oh don't be such a baby."

"Nothing to do with being a baby, it's to do with flying on a Screech Demon or, more accurately, falling from a Screech Demon while it's flying."

"You'll be fine," said Arfund. "We have saddles for them."

"Oh good!" said Robert abandoning the scepticism and attempting sarcasm, which was also unanimously ignored.

Lily pulled the rock that was Veszico out of her pocket. The rock unfolded itself and a sleepy-looking Fairy stretched herself out in the palm of Lily's hand.

"Veszico, I need you to find General Gnarly and Gnick. They should be close to the City Gate. Bring them to the ruined Emerald City as fast as possible and be on the lookout for Jack. I don't have time to explain to you but he's betrayed us and can't be trusted, stay away from him!"

The Fairy looked shocked and then angry. She placed her tiny hands on her tiny hips. "I don't believe it."

"I don't have time to argue, I know you liked Jack—"

"You're lying!"

"We can talk about it later. Go and fetch the Gnomes."

Veszico took off from Lily's hand and began to glow bright blue with a hint of red and flew off.

"Angry little thing," said Robert.

"She's going to be heartbroken," said Lily. "She's always loved Jack."

"Because they share the same size brain?" said Robert.

Lily smiled and kissed Robert on the cheek.

"I'm happy you're here, Robert."

"Scraacchhhhhhaakkk," screeched the Screech Demon and the sound was piercing. It felt to Robert like a hundred nails on a hundred chalkboards.

"Do they always do that?"

Arfund secured the saddles to his pets. "Only when they're excited. Or angry, or hungry, or horny."

"So if it does that at me it's either really happy to see me, really pissed off to see me, wants to eat more, or wants to hump me?"

"Sounds like you've got a solid understanding of Screech Demons, my friend," said Arfund.

Robert's nerves were beginning to fray at the prospect of having to mount one of these creatures, and he dearly wished he had a tea pot to hug. Niggle had vanished back to his apartment and Lily was petting the Screech Demon that was already saddled. Its head, which was covered with spikes, swung back and forth as if it couldn't wait to get off the ground. She climbed onto its back and slid into the saddle. The creature unfurled its wings and flapped excitedly.

"Sccreacchhhhackkkk," said the Screech Demon and Robert wondered if there was blood coming out of his ears.

"All right," said Arfund, securing the last strap, "your chariot awaits. Remember, be gentle with the reins and try not to be scared because they'll just play around with you."

"Doesn't sound that horrible," said Robert.

"And then they'll eat you."

"I'll try and keep the fear in check, then, shall I?"

"That'd be best."

Robert approached the creature, which stared at him with burning red eyes. It looked unimpressed.

"Just grab the reins here and swing yourself up. They're mildly telepathic, so they'll understand what it is you want them to do so try and think nice thoughts."

Robert was trying not to shake as he swung himself into the saddle. "Nice thoughts, right, got it."

"Ready?" said Lily.

"Are you kidding?"

"It's now or never. This is the fastest way to the Emerald City."

"Okay, okay, I'll be fine," said Robert without a shred of confidence.

"Remember," said Arfund, "nice thoughts!"

"How do I make it go?" asked Robert.

"Just think *up* and hold on."

"Just think up and—"

"Scraffaaccckkk," screamed the Demon and launched itself into the air with the most amazing amount of speed. It went up like a firework. The only thing louder than the screeching of the Screech Demon was the screaming of Robert Darkly.

The sun slid itself across the mountains, performing the occasional flip and sometimes a hop before beginning to dip its way toward the horizon. The magic could be heard skittering across the vast green desolation that was the remains of the Emerald City.

The petrified carcass of an Ogre began to shift and jostle and was thrown to the side by a massive Humanimal with a man's body and the head of a rhino.

Rumpelstiltskin had been door jumping for well over an hour before he got close enough to the ruins that he could walk the rest of the way. On his way, he'd picked up three henchmen whose services he'd bought in trade for wishes. With the Agency so close on his heels, he felt the need for some protection. The rhino Humanimal was named Barflunder and he'd come as a pair with his best friend Crushnut, who was a less distinct Humanimal with a man's body, legs and arms as thick as tree trunks, but he had the brain of a hamster. Such Humanimals were extremely rare and almost never recognized as Humanimals and were just considered to be slow. The third henchmen, who Rumpelstiltskin now realized to be a bad choice, was a Humanimal who from the waist up was human but from the waist down was an ostrich. His name was Ian and he was always in a hurry.

"So what's all this about anyway?" growled Barflunder menacingly, as he knew no other way to growl.

"None of your business!" said Rumpelstiltskin.

"Buuhhhh," began Crushnut and then lost his train of thought.

"You'll have to excuse Crushnut," said Barflunder, "he has trouble keeping track of his thoughts."

"Come on, you lot!" shouted Ian, who was jumping over rubble and prancing ahead with the grace of an over-happy gazelle.

"What's in the sack then?" asked Barflunder.

"None of your business," snapped the Dwarf.

"Rouuuuuu," said Crushnut.

"That's right, Crushnut, smells funny, doesn't it?" said Barflunder and snorted.

"It's a dead witch. Happy now?" snapped the Dwarf and stormed past the oversized pair.

"Blarrrr," said Crushnut.

"He is touchy, isn't he?" said Blarfunder.

The group stopped somewhere around the middle of the ruined city in the same courtyard that Robert had stood in earlier that day. Ian had overshot the courtyard by at least a mile and Rumpelstiltskin was content just to let him go.

"All right, you two, keep a look out."

"Look out for what?" asked Blarfunder.

"For Agents."

"You never said anything about Agents. Agents are dangerous!"

"Nalgggg," agreed Crushnut, who was idly crushing rocks using his forehead.

"Big fellahs like you, scared of Agents?" said Rumpelstiltskin with feigned surprise.

"Well no, not scared, just, ya know, wary. I met the Director of the Agency once. Bloody scary, that one. Not someone to trifle with."

"I highly doubt anyone is going to come here, but you two—"

"Three!" shouted Ian as he ran over a pile of rubble and skidded to a halt in the courtyard. "What are we doing now?"

"Like I was saying, you three keep guard on the edges of the courtyard."

"Why on the edges? You're not going to do anything funny with that dead witch, are you?" asked Blarfunder.

"Dead witch? Who has a dead witch?" said Ian.

"That what he's got in the bag, a dead witch, told us so himself."

Rumpelstiltskin rubbed his temples. He remembered henchmen being much simpler back in the day. They followed orders without question. Now they wanted to know everything.

The Dwarf walked over to what looked like a ruined storage shed and struggled with the door, which stubbornly refused to move an inch.

"You, Rhino head, come over here," said Rumpelstiltskin. When there was no sign of movement, the Dwarf looked over to see Blarfunder standing with his large arms firmly crossed.

"I don't appreciate the derogatory term," said Blarfunder, sounding insulted.

"But you have the head of a rhino."

"Maybe I'm a rhino but have the body of a human. Ever thought of that?"

"Well..."

"It's insulting, is what it is. It's not like you'd say *you, human body, come over here.*"

"I didn't mean anything by it."

"You humans are all racists against us Humanimals."

"But I'm not a human either. I'm a Dwarf!"

"Hardly a minority, though, are you?"

"What?"

"Well, there's thousands of you Dwarves, only a few hundred Humanimals, though."

"Look, I'm in a bit of a hurry," said the Dwarf. "How do I make this up to you?"

"You could start by apologizing."

"I'm very sorry for calling you rhino head. Now come and move this door."

"Wouldn't hurt you to say please."

Rumpelstiltskin began jumping up and down in frustration. "Will you please come and move this damn door!"

"All right, all right, no need to shout."

Blarfunder picked up the door as if it weighed nothing and threw it like a Frisbee across the landscape. Under the door were several cloth bags, which the Dwarf dragged out into the middle of the courtyard.

"Now go back to..." began the Dwarf and then realized that Blarfunder had raised a questioning eyebrow, which was not the easiest thing for a rhino's head to do. "I mean, please go back to keeping lookout."

"Happy to," said Blarfunder and returned to his post. Ian was running laps around the courtyard while Crushnut was standing at one end of the courtyard using less than one percent of his brain. Blarfunder assumed his position at the other end of the courtyard and proceeded to look mean.

Rumpelstiltskin felt a shimmer of excitement creep up his spine and tickle his brain. This was it. What he'd started all that time ago was finally going to be finished. The stupid blood of the White Rabbit would mean nothing and there'd be a whole new world to terrorize without being hindered by the Agency. After the regulators were removed from the doors, they'd be far too busy dealing with the hundreds of people falling through doors to worry about little old Rumpelstiltskin.

He began to unpack the necessary ingredients for the spell with a maniacal grin pasted across his face.

Robert couldn't determine if it was the warm-blooded nature of the creature he was straddling or if he'd wet himself. In his opinion, it could go either way. He'd come extremely close to passing out after initial take-off as the Demon had carried him up and up through the clouds, high above the Earth until his head spun. He couldn't be certain but he almost thought he could hear the voice in his head laughing with excitement, and that simple fact made him certain that the voice was not a part of him.

He'd wished with all sincerity that the creature would stop climbing and glide back down to a reasonable height. Which it did. After that, it all seemed so easy. It took the simplest thoughtful urge to tell the Demon what to do and which way to go and even how to do it. Every so often, the Demon would let out a *skkrraccchha* or a *sccraaahtatatata,* but even that had ceased to irritate Robert as he fully began to appreciate the feeling of flying. Forty-eight hours ago, he was an accountant working in a cubicle, sitting comfortably in a one-sided relationship with a nice girl, he had an apartment and a landlady; he visited his adoptive mother every other weekend. He was boring. Now he was racing above the world of Thiside on the back of Screech Demon in pursuit of an evil wish-granting Dwarf who threatened to twist reality inexplicably. He was in the company of a beautiful werewolf. He'd been attacked by bandits and Mermaids. He'd met a giant White Rabbit and a wizard. He'd jumped through reality as if it was an everyday chore. He'd been injured and healed, buried alive, and almost burned to death. He'd very briefly owned a cat. And most importantly, he now knew this was his home. This was where he was born. And no matter what the outcome, this was where he was determined to stay.

"That's if you make it out of all this alive," said the voice.

"What do you mean?" shouted Robert over the wind that was rushing by.

"You don't have to shout, I'm in your head."

"Sorry."

"I mean that this is where you'll stay as long as you survive whatever it is Rumpelstiltskin's going to do to you."

"Well, yes, I suppose so."

"Sorry, I broke your train of thought."

"No, it's okay. Good to be brought back to reality, thanks," said Robert, but didn't mean it.

Lily finally caught up to him.

"You're going in the wrong direction!" she shouted.

"Oh," said Robert, "Sorry!" he shouted back and thought to the Demon to turn itself around, which it did with grace and finesse and shot itself forward with powerful wings. Lily flew above and to his left.

"You're very good at this," she yelled.

"What can I say? I'm a natural," he shouted back.

Lily looked beautiful. Her hair, which was still filthy from the graveyard, whipped around her head and her amber eyes blazed as the sun set and twilight swept across the land.

"How long until we get there?" he shouted.

Lily pointed ahead. Rushing toward them in the distance across the darkening horizon was a line of shimmering green.

Villages and settlements flew by beneath them as the Demons propelled themselves over the land. It felt to Robert as if the Demons barely used their wings but flew under their own volition and only used their wings for an occasional burst of speed. He looked at Lily again.

"You should tell her," said the voice in his head.

"Tell her what?" said Robert.

"How you feel."

"What do you mean?"

"Do I seriously need to spell it out for you?"

"You want me to tell her now?"

"Why not?"

"We're flying hundreds of feet above the ground, racing toward the ruins of the Emerald City and who knows what else."

"Can you think of a better time?"

Robert couldn't.

"Lily!" shouted Robert.

Lily looked over as the last remnant of sunlight slipped across her features before the sun nosedived beneath the horizon.

"I think I love you!" shouted Robert.

The look she gave him was not what he expected. It looked like she was about to smile but then she instantly looked worried and then screamed, "Look out!" which wasn't exactly the combination of words he was hoping for.

A chunk of green masonry the size of a garbage can flew between them, clipping one wing of Lily's Screech Demon, which screamed and plummeted toward the ground.

"Lily!" shouted Robert but didn't have time to see if she was okay as another piece of masonry was thrown from somewhere on the ground, causing Robert's Demon to flip sideways. Robert flailed at the reins as he slid from the saddle and fell from the creature.

Oshitoshitoshitoshit! was the mantra that flew smoothly through his mind. It was probably just a play of light, or maybe the adrenaline, or possibly the feeling of absolute horror, but it felt less like falling to Robert and more like the world was rushing toward him to smash him into little pieces. *So this is how it ends.* He fondly hoped that Lily was okay, and then, in a glimmer of hope, he thought that maybe his Demon would come and retrieve him. That same balloon of hope was quickly popped when he saw his Screech Demon falling unconscious out of the sky not far away from him. Thoughts, questions, and memories jumbled quickly through his mind as the world rushed to meet him: *Who is my father? Am I dating a werewolf?* A Dwarf in his bathtub. Lily's eyes. A hippopotamus in a tutu. Buried in a coffin. The halfway house burning around him and the kitten appearing in the fireplace. *Shit!* And then he hit the ground.

The courtyard was decorated with intricate symbols that looked like they'd been drawn in blood. The air crackled like arcing electricity as the magical field began to stir and the spell was woven. It was a complex spell with no room for mistakes. The Dwarf knew that such a powerful spell posed a danger when performed in such a large magical field, but it was the magical field that powered the spell. As it turned out, magic had a strong sense of irony.

Rumpelstiltskin was reading incantations from the scraps of paper he'd stolen from the Wizards' Council library when Crushnut grunted in surprise.

"Wotz that?" said Blarfunder, and Ian skidded to a stop next to him.

"Looks like a couple of dragons," said Ian.

Rumpelstiltskin finished the incantation he was reading and looked up into the sky where his idiot henchmen were staring.

"Those are too small for dragons," said the Dwarf, squinting. A sense of panic kicked him in the frontal lobe. "Those are Agents!"

"That's silly," said Blarfunder, "Agents don't have wings."

"They're riding Screech Demons!" screamed the Dwarf, jumping up and down. "Kill them!"

"Now, where's your manners?" said Blarfunder, wagging his finger.

"What?" sputtered the Dwarf.

"What's the magic word?"

The Dwarf made a quick mental note to kill his henchmen at the first available opportunity.

"Please kill them!" he shrieked.

"Yes, sir!" said Blarfunder and picked up a massive piece of masonry and threw it at the approaching pair of Demons as if it were a pebble. Crushnut began searching through the rubble to find his own rock to throw.

Blarfunder's throw hit one of the Demon's wings and it plummeted toward the ground over a hundred feet away. Crushnut found a piece of rock he liked and with one hand threw it with the dexterity of an Olympian at the second Demon, which dodged it, but lost its rider in the process. Blarfunder's second chunk of masonry hit the creature square in the chest and it fell to the ground.

Not bad. Maybe he wouldn't kill them after all. *Maybe I'll just maim them a little.*

"You, with the legs," said Rumpelstiltskin to Ian, "run off and make sure they're both dead."

Ian nodded and ran off.

The Dwarf returned to his incantations. Thanks to the greenish glow of the emerald stones and the forceful magical field, the ruins were never completely black, even as twilight began to slip away and the sky turned dark. Everything shone with a luminescent green.

As he read the incantations, the symbols he'd drawn on the courtyard began to glow. The dragon's tooth, the other items he'd procured before being incarcerated in the Tower, and the remains of the last Bastinda sat in the middle of the courtyard.

The air began to feel heavy and the wind began to pick up. Rumpelstiltskin danced around the symbols as he continued reading. Something snapped at the edge of the courtyard, and the Dwarf looked up to see a doorway appear. It shimmered and floated and represented everything about Thiside that the Dwarf hated. He was about to dismiss it with a sneer when Jack stepped out the door. He looked angry.

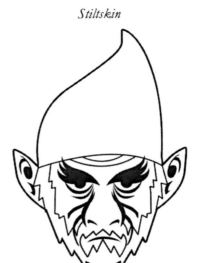

CHAPTER TWENTY

THE CHESHIRE CAT

So this is what it's like to be dead," said Robert as he floated in an infinite sea of nothingness. "I'm actually disappointed."

"It's phenomenal, really," said the voice in his head.

"How is this phenomenal?"

"Well, you're floating around in your own subconscious; you're actually inside your own head. That's not something that happens every day, you know?"

"You've lost me," said Robert, floating upside down. At least he assumed it was upside down. As everything was nothing but an inky blackness, it was impossible to tell which way was up and which way was down.

"Isn't it obvious?"

"Would I look this confused if it was obvious to me?"

"I don't know, I can't see you, it's too dark."

Although he was dead and floating in infinite space, Robert suddenly felt as if he wasn't alone. It was a creepy feeling and he'd feel better if he had something to look at, but he couldn't even make out his own hand in front of his face.

"So you're here with me?"

"Of course," said the voice.

Robert suddenly realized that the voice was no longer in his head. He could actually hear it.

"Who are you?"

"I go by many names."

"Am I dead?"

"Not in the slightest. But like I said, you're in your own subconscious, which is amazing when you think about it. It's like you're a person inside a person inside a person inside a person inside a person inside a person inside a per—"

"All right, all right I get it! I hope you don't take this the wrong way but are you mad?"

"Probably. It's hard to make it through life without being thoroughly mad, which is why you're so good at it."

"And I'm in my own brain?"

"Your subconscious. Where all your deep dark memories are sitting. Your only memory of your father is in here somewhere."

Robert was beginning to think that death would be a better option than being trapped in the dark with the voice that had been speaking to him in his brain and was now telling him that he was actually in his mind somewhere.

"Why didn't I die?"

"You fell through a door just before you hit the ground. I saved you."

"Why?"

"Some people are worth saving. And being that I recently took up residence in your subconscious I thought it was a better option that you lived."

"Who are you?" Robert asked again.

"I'm the Cat," said the Cat.

"The kitten I found?"

"Yes, that was me, too."

Robert thought about it for a moment. "Then you *are* the Cheshire Cat?"

"That's ridiculous, I've never even been to Cheshire."

"But you are the Cat. *The* Cat? The one that was powerful and then vanished."

"Self-important wizards thought they should control me. Ridiculous. They tried to bind me and hold me and failed miserably. The fun had gone out of this world and everything was so strict and orderly. Everything that your writers in Othaside had seen that made this place magical was slowly slipping away. And so I slipped away, too."

"Where did you go?" asked Robert.

"Wherever I pleased. I removed myself from Thiside completely. I floated through space as far as I could go and then I went further. I dropped into Othaside occasionally. I've always favoured Cannock Chase woods in England and appeared there many times as a large cat. I believe it made the news a few times," said the Cat.

"Why are you back now?"

"I felt a pull. A tugging. As if something had been introduced into Thiside, a catalyst that felt like it would bring change, and it drew me back."

"What was it?"

"It was you, Robert Darkly."

"Me?" said Robert. "I really don't think I'm the catalyst type."

"You're shaking things up and you don't even know it. Just by existing, you allowed the Dwarf to escape. Jack put his plan into action. Your father will probably get what he wants out of the deal. Lily found a connection with you. Things are changing. You're bringing the magic back to this world."

"Lily told me that you were a source of magic."

"And it's because of you that I came back. You are a bringer of change and chaos, my friend."

"Why haven't you shown yourself before now? And why not explain all this while you were the voice in my head?"

"I tried to become corporeal but there wasn't enough magic left in this world to allow me to remain. The best I could manage was a kitten, which in turn started a most unfortunate fire. But even the corporeality of the kitten began to slip away, so I chose to be incorporeal again, but instead of floating in nothingness I decided to float in your subconscious; that way I could stay in touch with you. And let's face it, you needed my help."

"You healed me after the werewolf attacked me," said Robert as pieces began to fit together. "You created the doors! When I needed them, it was you!"

"I don't create doors, silly boy. But sometimes I can move them where I need them to be."

"I was beginning to think I was going mad! Why not tell me you were the Cat all along?"

The Cat let out a light laugh. "Well, it was funny, wasn't it? Your lineage lends to being a little off the deep end, so those around you almost expected it of you."

"My lineage?"

"All in good time. We have more pressing matters at hand."

"So what now?"

"We're in the remains of the Emerald City and Rumpelstiltskin is casting a spell that will make the magical field churn and expand. I believe that if you can get me close enough, I'll be able to become corporeal."

"And if you're corporeal, you'll be able to help us stop him?"

"There are great things ahead of you, Robert Darkly, and I don't see any advantage to the Dwarf completing his spell."

"So how do I get out of here?"

"This might hurt a little."

"What will hurt?" asked Robert, who was becoming accustomed to painful experiences.

"This," said the Cat.

A door appeared next to Robert and he was instantly sucked into it—

—and was thrown up into the air twenty feet before crashing down on a patch of grass amongst the ruins of the Emerald City.

"Oourgg," groaned Robert.

"I did warn you," said the Cat, now back in Robert's head.

Robert stood up and looked around. The Emerald ruins glowed and in the distance he could see people moving around.

"Robert!"

Robert turned to the voice to find Lily just as he'd left her. She was carrying an unconscious man who looked like he had the legs of an ostrich. She dropped the man and ran to Robert, throwing her arms around him. They embraced and Robert was happy that he wasn't a smear on the ground somewhere.

"You're welcome," said the Cat.

"I saw you fall," said Lily, "I thought you were dead."

212

"Nahh," said Robert, "takes more than a fall from a Screech Demon to kill Robert Darkly."

Lily pulled back and Robert was surprised to see tears in her eyes. "How did you survive?"

"It's a long story and we don't have time. We need to get to Rumpelstiltskin. Who's that?" asked Robert pointing to the unconscious Humanimal.

"I think he's a henchman."

"He has ostrich legs."

"Nothing slips by you, does it? Come on."

Lily took Robert's hand and together they weaved a path through the rubble and dead creatures toward the courtyard that became more and more illuminated, as if the luminescence from the ruins was being concentrated toward it.

Jack held Rumpelstiltskin by the front of his shirt. "You're a double-crossing little weasel!"

"I just thought by tricking you," said the Dwarf, "that it'd throw the Agency off my tail and relieve you of any suspicion. After all this is said and done, you still want to be an Agent, don't you? I thought that was the whole point. Bring back the good ol' days! I assume you want to appreciate those days from anywhere other than the inside of the Tower. It adds to the charade; I'm the fugitive, you're the brilliant Agent on my tail."

"Just finish the spell," said Jack and released the Dwarf.

"How did you get here, anyway?" asked the Dwarf.

"Special order of the Director. She used emergency orders to send me through a door created by the Wizards' Council to get me here and take control of the situation."

"But that means…"

"That there'll be more Agents coming soon. And the Emerald Guard."

Rumpelstiltskin's blood pressure shot to its peak and he turned a lovely mauve colour. "Why did you do that?"

Jack shrugged. "Like you said, it adds to the charade. When they get here, I'll tell them you'd already completed the spell and got away. So finish fast and then get out of here."

"It's not that easy!" shouted Rumpelstiltskin. "It's intricate, it takes time, you idiot!"

"Then get on with it," said Jack matter-of-factly and went to stand next to Blarfunder, who was polishing the horn on the end of his rhino's snout.

Rumpelstiltskin resumed his incantations and a ball of green fire appeared in the courtyard above the gathered objects. The glow from the surrounding ruins crept toward the courtyard, making the surrounding rock and masonry brighter and more distinct.

"I wonder what happened to Ian?" said Blarfunder to Crushnut.

"Mehh," said Crushnut.

Robert crouched next to Lily behind a large piece of masonry thirty feet from the courtyard. The air had taken to crackling and snapping and sometimes swirling. Thanks to the green ball of flame currently floating in the courtyard, it had been easy to find Rumpelstiltskin. Robert had noticed Lily bristle at the sight of Jack.

"How did he get here?" she growled.

It looked like the Dwarf had employed two other henchmen and one of them had a large rhino's head on its shoulders. The other was picking its nose and aside from looking like he could rip entire telephone companies in half, let alone a telephone book, he didn't seem like much of an immediate threat.

"Now what do we do?" asked Robert.

"Get us as close as you can to the emerald flame in the middle of the courtyard," urged the Cat in Robert's head.

"I don't know. I think I can take the two henchmen. But we need to stop the spell," said Lily. "And I don't know how to do that."

"Destroy the papers he's reading from," said the Cat.

"We have to destroy the papers," said Robert.

"How do you know?"

"I just know."

"Know what?" said an unfamiliar voice. Blarfunder lifted the piece of masonry they were hiding behind over his head and grinned at the pair. There were few things in life more disturbing than the grin of a rhino.

"Kill them!" shrieked Rumpelstiltskin and continued reading from the spell pages.

"Sorry," said Blarfunder. "Nothing personal, just business."

He swung the piece of masonry down but Lily caught it and threw it backward over her head.

"Time to move," said the Cat. Robert's legs realized they should be doing something and he sprinted toward the courtyard. He made it an entire five steps before Jack tackled him, knocking him to the ground, driving the air from his lungs.

"You are very strong," said Blarfunder to Lily. "I'm going to enjoy this."

"Rrreeaaaaa," agreed Crushnut, joining his friend.

Lily squared off with them as Jack reared up to pummel Robert. He raised a fist and Robert tensed for the blow... but it never came. Jack was thrown from his place atop Robert and flung across the courtyard. A glowing red ball buzzed around him.

"Veszico!" said Robert. He looked toward Lily, who was backing into a corner.

Blarfunder and Crushnut were completely shocked when two Gnomes landed on their shoulders. They were equally shocked when, much to their dismay, the Gnomes swiftly slit their throats.

Blarfunder's last thoughts were about how he had not expected to die today and how a little heads-up would have been appreciated.

Crushnut's last thoughts were less coherent and lacked anything prolific. His last thought was *Wwaarrgg.*

Robert sat up and felt the press of cold steel against his throat. Rumpelstiltskin held a clump of his hair in one hand and a knife to his throat in the other.

"All right, that's quite enough of that," said the Dwarf. "Any more swift movements will result in our friend Mr. Darkly's untimely demise."

"I'd rather no one moved," said Robert.

"Shut up!" said the Dwarf.

"Sorry."

Veszico landed on Lily's shoulder and the Dwarves stood to either side of her. Jack took his place behind Rumpelstiltskin.

The air crackled and snapped, causing the occasional spark, and the green ball of fire slowly began to grow.

"How do you expect to finish your spell while holding Robert?" said Lily.

"You're saying I should kill him now and be done with it?" replied the Dwarf.

"I really don't think that was what she was saying," said Robert.

"This doesn't concern you," said the Dwarf.

"It bloody does," said Robert. "It's my neck that's at risk here."

The Dwarf quickly moved aside as Jack hauled back and hit Robert square in the jaw.

Robert hadn't taken a punch to the face since he was twelve years old when the school bully had decided Robert had looked at him funny. He didn't recall it hurting this much. Blood trickled from his lip.

Robert could see Gnick tense up and he felt a wave of appreciation for the Gnome.

"The spell is all but done," said Rumpelstiltskin.

Robert spit blood. "Obviously. If it's not done then it has to be all but done, then, doesn't it?"

"You... never... shut up!" said Jack and punched Robert again.

"Dammit, Jack!" said Lily.

"All of you stop. Mr. Darkly here can help me finish the spell." Rumpelstiltskin dragged Robert by the hair, all the while holding the blade to his throat, into the courtyard to kneel ten feet from the ball of fire.

"Don't move!" Jack shouted at the others and Robert, although he couldn't see them, assumed they had begun to move to help him. He felt warm and happy that his companions cared for his life.

"They might not care for you, they might just care for the good of civilization," said the Cat.

"You have to ruin everything, don't you?" said Robert.

"Well, it's about time things changed," replied the Dwarf, believing that Robert had been addressing him. "And it's not ruining anything, it's fixing everything. It's putting things back to normal!"

"You must be crazier than I am if you think anything in this world is normal. I grew up in what would be considered to be a normal world and even *that* is not normal."

Rumpelstiltskin released Robert's hair and pulled the papers out of his pocket and handed them to him. "Read the last page."

"What happens when I read it?"

"Why does it matter?" asked the Dwarf, becoming red in the face again.

"I'm just curious as to what will happen. After all, I'm a part of it now."

"You'll finish off the last incantation which will release the spell from the glowing ball of fire you see before you and it will abolish all regulations on the doors. Everyone will be free to move about whenever and wherever they want."

"Can I move a bit closer to the big fireball thing?" said Robert.

"Why?"

"Well, I think I've been fighting a cold, my throat's been hoarse. I'd hate for the big ball of flame not to hear me."

"Crawl up to it and hug it if you want. Just read the words or the last thing you'll feel is cold steel cutting your spine in half." To iterate the point, the Dwarf nudged him in the back with the knife.

Robert crawled forward on all fours until he was within reaching distance of the green fire. Robert was surprised to find that it wasn't warm at all. If anything, the fire was giving off intense cold.

"Don't do it, Robert!" said Lily.

"Shut up!" spat Jack.

"Is this close enough?" said Robert loudly.

"Yes, this'll do," said the Cat in Robert's head.

"Yes, that's perfect," agreed Rumpelstiltskin.

Robert stood up and turned to face the Dwarf and everyone else.

"Don't need these anymore," said Robert. He screwed the papers up into a ball and threw them backwards over his shoulder into the now pulsating ball of flame. The papers vanished into nothingness, and Rumpelstiltskin stood in a shocked silence with his mouth open.

"You bastard!" shouted Jack.

"I'll kill you!" screamed the Dwarf, finally remembering he had a voice.

"I don't think so, gentleman," said Robert. "You see, I've been carrying a secret weapon, one that I didn't even know I had. That's how secret it was."

And Robert laughed.

"Oh no, he's lost his mind," said Lily.

"I have this voice in my head. It's been talking to me a lot lately."

The green ball of fire shifted awkwardly behind him.

"Uh, Robert," said Lily and took a step back.

"I've never really understood myself, I've always had weird things happen to me, and then I discover there's this whole other world right here that I belong to. My father's from here, did you know that, Rumpelstiltskin?"

The Dwarf had also seen that the ball was no longer a ball and was also backing away. "Actually yes, I know your father well and I hope he rots in hell!"

"Oh." Robert hadn't expected that.

"Robert, look behind you!" said Lily.

Robert turned and found the ball of flame was now oblong, and then a triangle, and then an intricate symbol, and it was continually getting bigger.

"Advice, please?" Robert asked the Cat but there was no answer.

"Run!" shouted Lily.

Robert turned to run and saw that everyone else had already scattered.

The full force of the explosion hit him in the back and he felt a piece of him dislodge. He sincerely hoped it was the Cat he felt and not his spleen rupturing. He was thrown several feet across the courtyard and slammed into a chunk of emerald rock. He was comforted by the thought that the rock probably hadn't felt a thing so at the very least he didn't have that on his conscience.

Waves of extremely cold green flame washed over him, plastering him to the hard surface. Out of the corner of his eye, he could see the luminescence spread out across the ruins, delivering the green glow back to the landscape. A moment later and it was all over. Robert slid roughly to the ground and slipped into sweet unconsciousness.

What most people failed to realize was that spells had a life span. Aside from the Cat, a few of the more senior wizards of Oz, the exiled Evil Queen, and the wizard Niggle, no one else in Thiside or Othaside knew this. The actual successful execution of a spell came when the spell died. In its death, a spell caused a massive release of magic that completed the objective of the spell.

As soon as Rumpelstiltskin began reading the incantations, the spell was thrust into existence and the further along the spell casting went, the stronger and more developed it became. Having no mouth, it had no external way of projecting its opinions. Internally, though, it could chat up a storm. From conception to destruction, the spell's timeless thoughts had gone something like this:

"Well then," said the Spell, "this is a turn-up for the books. What have we got here, then? Looks like a Dwarf. Ugly Dwarf, at that. I bet he smells funny. And there's a couple of big fellas over there. They don't look overly smart, do they? Heyy, a door! I haven't seen one of those in… well… ever. Well, that *is* a large woman. No, wait, it's a man with long hair. He should cut that, he looks like a woman. I wonder if he gets comments about his hair, it is quite nice. I bet he uses some sort of special plant extract to keep it that shiny. Wow! Those look like dragons! Why are they throwing rocks at them? That's not very nice. I see the Dwarf is reading again. It feels good when he reads, makes me feel all tingly. Hey, there are two people sneaking behind that rock over there. Oh never mind, the big one found them. Something very strange about that tall gangly-looking one. He's got something inside of him that's very unusual, I wonder if anyone else can see it? Aww, the Dwarf's stopped reading. That's a very shiny knife, looks like he's going to shave that tall gentleman with the thing inside him. That's awfully nice. Oh, they're coming closer."

"Hello," said the Cat to the Spell.

"Hello," said the Spell.

"Please don't take this the wrong way but I'm going to burst forth from this human and use you as a springboard to launch myself back into the world."

"I don't think that's what I'm meant for."

"No, that's true, but I'd certainly appreciate the effort," said the Cat.

"Well, I don't personally have any problem with it."

"And please allow me to offer my most sincere condolences in regards to your impending death."

"That's awfully nice of you," said the Spell appreciatively. "It's really no big deal, it's life."

"If you say so."

"So what happens now?"

"Well, you're going to become unstable and explode."

"And then you'll use the explosion to birth yourself into existence?"

"Well, yes. If you don't mind me saying so, you have a fantastic grasp on all of this."

"Thank you. I like to think I'm a very intuitive Spell. Whoa, that didn't feel good. What was that?"

"That was you becoming unstable. This next bit is going to hurt a little bit but please be assured that I hold the utmost respect for you."

"Well, thank you, I really appreciate the sentiment… oh… that doesn't feel goo—"

And the Spell exploded, ending its life instantly.

Rumpelstiltskin was sprinting as fast as his little legs could carry him. While sprinting, he was cursing. He cursed the spell for becoming unstable. He cursed Robert Darkly for his interference. He cursed the Mad Hatter for ever setting him on this path in the first place. He cursed Jack because he was an idiot. He even cursed several chunks of masonry and rotting Ogre remains that blocked his path as he tried to move as swiftly away from the explosion as possible.

The last thing the evil Dwarf ever heard was *scraachachcachacha!* as an injured and extremely pissed-off Screech Demon ripped his head from his shoulders. The part of a Screech Demon's brain that dealt with recall and memory was exceptionally small but there were certain things that stuck out in a creature's mind. Thanks to highly enhanced eyesight and hearing, the thing that stuck out in the minds of the two Screech Demons was the order of, "Kill them," issued by the Dwarf they were now eating. Chances were, he wouldn't be making that mistake again.

Robert woke up lying on his back. His head was resting in Lily's lap while a massive black panther licked the side of his face.

"Am I dreaming?"

"No, silly," said Lily. "You had me scared. I thought you were dead."

"I'm happy I'm not dead," said Robert.

"So am I," said Lily and smiled.

"Really?"

"Yes. Really."

For a while, Robert lay still as happiness and exhaustion washed over him. The panther continued licking his face. It was a big cat, very regal looking. It also had a large mouth with sharp teeth and Robert thought asking it to stop would be rude and possibly hazardous to his health.

"What happened?"

"The spell became unstable and exploded. Rumpelstiltskin failed. The doors are still intact."

"Where is everyone?"

"General Gnarly took a nasty hit to the head, he's not doing very well. Gnick's wrapping him as best he can. Jack was knocked unconscious."

"And the Dwarf?"

"Dead."

"In the explosion?"

"No."

"You killed him?"

"No."

"Gnick killed him?"

"No."

"You know, you could just tell me."

"Rumpelstiltskin fled from the scene when he realized what was happening. I pursued him and almost caught him but I wasn't fast enough. The Screech Demons survived their fall and caught Rumpelstiltskin running from the explosion. Apparently, Screech Demons hold a grudge."

"So we won?"

"It seems that way."

"Lily."

"Yes, Robert?"

"Can I ask you something?"

"Of course."

"Why is there a giant panther licking my face?"

"You should ask him that."

The panther backed off and stretched its large muscular body while Robert sat himself up with Lily's assistance. His back felt like it had been slammed into a large rock and he was convinced that his entire backside would be bruised for many years to come. The giant Cat sat in front of him and tilted its head. Robert felt it looked familiar.

"I should look familiar," said the Cat. "I've lived in your head for the last twenty-four hours. You should really clean up in there; it's quite the mess."

"You're the Cheshi... I mean, you're the Cat."

"I am indeed. And thanks to you, I'm back in Thiside, for a while at least. For that, and for allowing me to reside in your head, I owe you a great deal of thanks. Walk with me."

Robert struggled to his feet and walked beside the Cat. They left the courtyard and rather than climbing over the ruins, a path unfolded before them; the broken pieces of buildings slid together to form a flat surface.

"That's amazing," said Robert.

"It's really nothing," said the Cat. "After a while, you grow tired of floating and climbing and just feel the need for a good stretch of the legs.

"In stories, you're always a regular house cat. I wasn't really expecting a panther."

"When you've lived as long as I have, you sometimes get bored with your appearance. Between you and me, I don't actually look like anything. I've always liked cats, though, and so in one form or another I've always assumed the image of one. They're amazing creatures. You can never tell what they're thinking; makes them very mysterious."

"What will you do now?"

"I don't know. I've spent so much time existing as nothing. It'll be nice to be something for a while. I think I'll travel between Thiside and Othaside, maybe learn a new language. Who knows?"

"At least you have some idea what to do. I don't know what the future holds for me."

The Cat stopped, turned to Robert, and sat down. "Robert Darkly, son of a mad man, exiled from his home as a baby. Your life is about to begin."

"So I will go mad, like everyone thinks?"

"To be honest, a little madness isn't necessarily a bad thing. I know what you desire most of all."

"I want to see my father."

"As you should. When you choose the time, I'll make sure there's a door there for you to use." The Cat sighed. "You should get back to the courtyard. Your Gnome friend isn't going to last much longer and the Director of the Agency will be here soon, which means it's time for me to make myself scarce."

"Will I see you again?"

"I'll be around."

Robert looked back toward the courtyard to see that a door had opened there. "Thank you for everything," he said.

But the Cat was gone.

When Robert returned to the courtyard, Lily and Gnick were crouching next to General Gnarly. The Gnome was pale; his right arm and the majority of his body had been bandaged. Robert could see spots of blood seeping through. Tears glistened in Gnick's eyes.

"Don't be upset," said General Gnarly in his gruff voice. "The road ends for all of us eventually."

"Thank you for everything, General," said Lily. "It's been an honour to fight by your side."

"I'll see you on the other side," said Gnick.

"General, I don't know what to say," said Robert.

"It's okay, moron," said the General and choked out a laugh. The tiny man fell silent and the life slipped from his eyes.

"Agent Redcloak!" snapped a sharp voice from the middle of the courtyard. "Care to tell me what happened here?"

Lily and Robert turned and came face to face with a short, old woman dressed in a dark suit. Her hair was pulled back tight in a bun and her eyes were small and beady. She was smoking a cigarette and the smoke danced around her. To Robert, she gave off the distinct impression that if he angered her in any way, she'd remove one of his limbs without giving it a second thought.

"Robert, this is Madeline Goose, the Director of the Agency. Director, this is—"

"Robert Darkly," croaked the old woman. "I know who you are, Mr. Darkly."

"Rumpelstiltskin is dead," said Lily, "Robert stopped the spell before it could be completed. Jack betrayed us."

"I know that already," snapped the Director. "Agent Tweedle reached me after I sent Jack ahead. The Hatter informed him that Jack was behind the escape. The City Guards will be here shortly to escort him to the Tower."

"But…"

"No exceptions, Lillian. I'm as much a slave to the rules as anyone else."

"Yes, Director," said Lily obediently.

A group of twenty guards arrived at the ruins through the same door that the Director must have come through. They were dressed in full black armour, with red plumes complete with helmets that covered their faces. They were all well built and could probably snap Robert like a twig. Two of them picked Jack up off the ground and slapped him a few times until he regained consciousness.

"Wh… here… the Dwarf," said Jack, making as much sense as a drunken Scotsman.

"Jackson Rutherford Goose," began the Director through a cloud of smoke, "you are hereby charged with aiding and abetting the known criminal Rumpelstiltskin with his escape from incarceration and attempting to destroy the regulators that are placed upon the doors. You are to be transported to the Tower immediately by the City Guards. Agent Tweedle will meet you at the border to the Northern Territory to make sure you are successfully delivered to the Tower. On a personal note, I can't imagine under what circumstances I could be more disappointed in you, my son."

Robert leaned toward Lily. "Her son?"

"Take him out of my sight!" commanded the Director.

The guards escorted him from the courtyard. Jack struggled with great futility against their grip and screamed back over his shoulder.

"I was trying to make it better, Mother! I wanted to give us purpose again!"

The Director lit another cigarette as she watched Jack get dragged away.

"The Director is Jack's mother. She's been the Director of the Agency for several hundred years," said Lily.

"Mother Goose? The woman who reads stories to children?"

"When the Evil Queen granted Jack and his family immortality, it was his mother that took the most advantage of it. She was a simple woman, a seamstress, I believe. She found new purpose in the Agency and was eventually appointed Director. Jack was recruited not long after."

"She's sending her only son to prison."

"Not an easy thing to do, I imagine."

"It's not!" snapped the Director, and Robert actually jumped as the tiny woman stalked back toward them.

"Agent Redcloak, I want you to take the General's body back to his people and for goodness' sake, get cleaned up." The Director turned to Robert and the smoke surrounding her turned with her, as if it was attached.

Robert wanted to point it out, but for once thought it better to keep his thoughts on the inside.

"And what do we do with you Mr. Darkly?"

"I—" began Robert.

"It was rhetorical, Darkly, shut up."

"Yes, ma'am."

"Our usual procedure is to have your memory wiped clean and dump you back into Othaside with no recollection of what you've seen or done."

"I…" protested Robert but was silenced with a dark look from the Director, who continued.

"As you are, in fact, a born resident of Thiside and not completely human either, I see no issue with you remaining here, if you so choose."

Robert's eyes lit up. "Yes. I do want to stay here. This has been the most at home I've felt in a long time. Wait, what do you mean, not completely human?"

"You were exiled from Thiside when you were a baby. Your mother died in childbirth from injuries that were inflicted by your father. It was amazing that you survived. Your father was imprisoned and you were sent to Othaside to be given a chance at a normal life."

"A normal life!" said Robert. "I've never known who I truly was. I've been walking around in that world my whole life feeling completely out of place, like my body didn't fit my skin properly. Weird things kept happening to me and it's because you people were trying to give me a chance?"

"Don't snap at me, Darkly! We make decisions all the time without knowing the outcome. It's why the Agency exists. We make the hard calls. We make sure everything runs as it should. You're back now and I'm giving you leave to stay. It's an opportunity given to few, so you'd better damn well appreciate it!"

Robert flushed with embarrassment. "My apologies, ma'am… um… Director. I didn't mean any insult by it and I appreciate the opportunity, I really do."

"At least you know when to apologize. And no, you're not human. No one knows what you are. Maybe you'll live a normal lifespan and maybe you won't. Time will tell that story. It appears I'm down one Agent. You're rough around the edges and look like you couldn't find your own feet with a map; however, due to your unusual lineage and now that you want to remain here, I'd like to offer you the opportunity to become an Agent."

Robert looked from the Director to Lily and back again. A smile played on the edges of Lily's lips and her hand found his and gave it a squeeze.

"I don't know what to say," said Robert, which was ridiculous because he knew exactly what to say. "Yes, of course, I'd love the opportu—"

"A simple yes will suffice," said the Director. "You'll report to the City of Oz for training as soon as you are able."

"Thank you, thank you so much," said Robert and stuck out his hand to shake with the Director. She observed the gesture as if Robert was trying to give her something dead, smelly, and dripping, before turning and stalking away.

Robert turned to Lily, who was now beaming. "You're going to stay here."

"Yes," said Robert happily.

"I'm done thinking."

"What?" said Robert.

"Back in Othaside, before we were buried alive, I said I'd think about it. Us, I mean."

"Oh. Okay. And?"

"I do like you, Robert Darkly. I might even love you."

Robert gave it a moment's thought. "That's good enough for me."

He grabbed Lily and pulled her to him and kissed her with more passion than anyone had ever kissed anyone before in the entire history of the world. Or at least in the last five minutes of the history of the world.

"Something just occurred to me," said Robert.

"What's that?"

"You never told the Director about the Cat."

"What cat?" said Lily.

"The Cat," said Robert. "Don't tell me you don't remember the Cat?"

"Robert, I haven't the faintest idea what you're talking about. Maybe you are going mad."

Robert shook his head.

"To be honest," he said with a smile, "a little madness isn't necessarily a bad thing."

EPILOGUE

R obert flew swiftly through the air and crashed heavily into the wall. He quickly rolled to his left in case there was a follow-up attack. His opponent was smirking. He hated people smirking at him almost as much as he hated crashing into walls.

"Come on, Darkly," said the smirking Goblin. "I have fifty bakewell tarts to make before dinner and I don't have time for you to keep bleeding on me."

Robert had begun training a month ago, and out of all the classes he was required to undertake, hand to hand combat was his least favorite. He wasn't built for it. He was gangly and uncoordinated, which he blamed on his tallness. If something happened to his lower half, there was no chance of the message reaching his upper half in time for him to do something about it. To make matters worse, all hand-to-hand combat classes were taught by Bastian the Goblin, who was also a chef at the Inn where Robert had taken up residence.

The Agency had hired Bastian to train Robert in self-defence and fighting skills, as the Goblin, aside from being a splendid chef, was also one of the best fighters in Thiside.

"I don't suppose we could call it a day, could we?" said Robert to the tall, slender figure who was still smirking.

"One more time," said Bastian and assumed a fighting stance.

Robert took off at a run as his brain cycled through what he'd been taught. He feinted to the left and struck out with his heel. He caught nothing but air as the Goblin slipped underneath his kick, then jabbed him in the groin, causing him to crumple into a disorganized pile on the courtyard floor.

"Now we can call it a day," said the Goblin, still smirking. He scratched one of his long pointy ears, grabbed a towel from a nearby rack, and sauntered off out of the courtyard.

Robert nursed his testicles and hoped they were still operable. The sun had randomly been changing its position in the sky all day and had now settled itself in the West. A figure appeared above Robert, blocking the sun.

"That looked like it hurt," said Lily.

Robert got to his feet and tried to ignore the pain between his legs. And his shoulder. And his knuckle where he'd almost succeeded in punching Bastian but missed and hit a wall instead.

"Not really, I'm much tougher than I look. Or so I keep telling myself."

Lily was dressed in the suit that Agents in Thiside generally wore on a day-to-day basis: black shoes, trousers, with a suit jacket, and white shirt. The uniform looked completely out of place in a world where everything looked and felt medieval, but it served its purpose. That purpose being to identify exactly who was an Agent and who was not. It also didn't require a costume change every time an Agent had to cross over to Othaside. As usual, Lily looked fantastic. Her hair shone and her eyes gleamed.

They had kept their fondness for each other low key, but spent most of their free time together when Lily wasn't on assignment. Robert was to apprentice with her once his training was complete. Until then, he spent his days at the Agency Castle on the outskirts of the City of Oz learning the history of Thiside and some unexpected history of Othaside. He learned about politics and how to negotiate peaceful settlements. He was taught strategy and hand-to-hand combat. The thing he'd excelled at the most was interrogation techniques. It appeared he had a knack for talking his way around, through, and over things. He found he could get into people's heads very quickly. This pleased the Director, who was never actually pleased but often disliked certain things less, as she needed a good interrogator to replace Jack.

"How was your session today?" said Lily.

"As painful as usual. Bastian doesn't pull his punches like he did when we started. I miss those days."

"You'll get the hang of it. You could practice with me, if you like?"

"No," said Robert, "I wouldn't want to hurt you."

"Very thoughtful of you," said Lily and gave him a hug.

"How come you're here so early? I thought we weren't meeting until later."

"You're not happy to see me?" she asked coyly.

"Don't be ridiculous. Every moment I see you, I can't help but be happy," said Robert.

And it was true. He hadn't been back to Othaside since the night at the graveyard. Whatever life he had back there was gone. And he didn't miss it. Somewhere in the back of his mind, he was fairly certain that it didn't miss him, either, as he had never belonged there in the first place.

Lily held him at arm's length. "Listen, Robert…"

"You're being sent on assignment."

"How did you know that?"

"You're very easy to read."

Their relationship hadn't progressed past sharing each other's company and some fairly heavy make-out sessions. They both had a strong determination to take this slowly. This way of life and being in a co-dependent relationship was as new to Lily as it was to Robert. Spending so much time together had given Robert a keen insight into Lily's mannerisms and facial expressions that, coupled with his interrogation training, allowed him to read her fairly easily most of the time.

"I miss those days when I could surprise you," said Lily.

"I think you being a werewolf was surprise enough for me, I'm not sure I could handle anything that big again."

There had been only one full moon during the last month, preceded by a crescent moon the night before, giving Lily and Robert the warning that a change was coming. On the night of the full moon, Lily locked herself in the dungeon of the Agency Castle to allow for a safe change. She had asked Robert to stay away, which he had. Loving a werewolf had its challenges, but Robert was trying his best to be understanding and helpful.

"I'm being sent to the Grimm Mountains," said Lily. "The Warrior Gnomes are bordering on a civil war since the death of General Gnarly and we've been asked to step in to help find a resolution."

"How long will you be gone for?"

"No more than a week, hopefully. I look forward to you coming with me one day soon."

"The Director tells me it'll be two more months."

"And then I'll have to put up with you day in and day out."

"Sounds horrible."

"I guess I'll have to learn to live with it." She punched him playfully in the shoulder.

Robert smiled and bent slightly to kiss her goodbye. They walked to the castle gates and said their farewells. He watched her walk away until she was out of sight. He'd miss her, but at least this gave him the opportunity to do something he'd been itching to do for the last few weeks.

When he'd begun his training, he was expressly told that he would not be informed about who his father was or where he was being held until his training was complete. The reasons cited were that it would cloud his judgment and slow his training. But Robert had other ideas. He wanted desperately to meet his father. To confront him. To find out who he was and, in turn, find out about himself. He only knew what snippets he'd heard during his journey with Lily and the Gnomes. Bits and pieces he'd picked up from his teachers, who skirted the issue. Most people seemed in awe of who Robert was and where he had come from. Many eyed him suspiciously, as if they expected him to snap at any moment. He knew his father was incarcerated and he knew the main facility for incarceration was simply called the Tower. During his night of door jumping, he'd seen a Tower in a valley and every one of his natural instincts told him that was where his father was held.

With Lily gone, this presented the perfect opportunity. She would never approve of what he was going to do, but she didn't, couldn't, understand.

Hand to hand combat was his last class of the day, and he took the hour-long walk back to the City of Oz. He had found that there really were no horses in Thiside; there were many other creatures that were for transportation, but they required money and Robert had little. He didn't mind the walk.

The sun was descending in a slow and lazy arc when Robert entered the Inn of the Massacred Goat; an unfortunate name, but all the good ones were taken, or so the Innkeeper claimed. He headed upstairs to his small but cosy room and stripped off before wrapping a towel around himself.

He walked down the narrow hallway into the shared bathroom and locked the door. The bathtub was set into the wooden flooring and always seemed full of hot water. He was pleased to find that showering was as uncommon as horses in Thiside. Everyone took baths or simply didn't wash themselves.

Robert soaked himself until he began to turn wrinkly before returning to his bedroom.

"Hello, Robert," said the Cat when Robert opened the door.

"Bloody hell! You almost gave me a heart attack!" said Robert, clutching his chest.

The Cat, still in the form of a panther, was sitting contentedly on the bedroom's large feather mattress.

"Tonight's the night, then?" said the Cat.

"What do you mean?" said Robert, pulling on a pair of jeans he'd purchased at the local market. "What are you doing here? I mean, I assumed I'd see you again, but some sort of forewarning wouldn't hurt, you know."

"My deepest apologies. I'm very used to just appearing. I often forget that people aren't used to that sort of behaviour. I'm here because I told you that I knew your deepest desire and that when you were ready, I'd provide you with a door."

The Cat swished his long tail back and forth while Robert finished getting dressed.

"I had just planned to look for one outside of the city," said Robert.

"I'm here to save you the trouble."

"It would have been no trouble," said Robert, too quickly.

"Ah," said the Cat tilting its head, "you're having second thoughts. You want to delay the actual act to give you time to possibly change your mind."

Robert sat down on the bed next to the Cat. "It's daunting."

"I understand," said the Cat.

"I want to know so badly, but the thought of meeting whoever man this is terrifies me at the same time."

"Would you like me to come back another time, then?" said the Cat with a purr.

Robert took a deep breath and stood up. He reached into his bedside drawer and pulled out the silver chain with the vial of blood that the White Rabbit had given him.

"No, I want to do it now."

"As you wish. I still feel I owe you a great debt. Should you ever need me, simply call and I'll find you. Best of luck, Robert Darkly."

The Cat looked to the corner and the room began to distort as the fabric of space and time frayed at the edges and a door opened. It floated in the corner of the room, and Robert approached it with as much confidence as he could muster. He hadn't been through a door since his last return from Othaside in pursuit of Rumpelstiltskin, which now seemed like an eternity ago. He placed the chain around his neck and held the vial of blood in front of him.

"I wish to go to the Tower," he said in a clear voice and then stepped through the doorway, which disappeared in a flash along with the Cat.

Robert stepped out of a door and stumbled onto the cobblestone bridge. Rain bounced off the stone and dark clouds blanketed the sky. Robert looked down the long bridge to the Tower. It rose ominously, and somewhere high above, a shrill scream rang out. The last time Robert had seen the Tower, he had been at a distance. Up close, it looked far more terrifying: dark, sinister, creepy, and a variety of other words describing bad things.

"It's times like this that I wish I had a voice in my head to speak to," said Robert.

Lightning flashed across the sky.

That was appropriately timed, he thought and began his walk across the bridge. He was halfway across when he stopped and approached the edge of the bridge to look at the vast moat. He remembered seeing something in there when he was here last. And sure enough, there they were. The moat creatures moved beneath the surface, massive worm-like creatures writhing and turning, churning the waters above. One swam beneath the bridge and Robert could see the eyeless face, large mouth, and rows upon rows of teeth as it yawned and swam endlessly on through the water. Robert staggered back and hoped he never had to see one up close as long as he lived.

Eventually, he reached the end of the bridge and stood before the massive stone gate. He wasn't entirely sure what to do from here. Truthfully, he'd been expecting guards and maybe even a locked gate, but as no one was immediately available and the gate was wide open, Robert decided to just walk in.

Inside the gate, he stood in an open courtyard that led to the entrance to the Tower, the door to which was also wide open. Firelight flickered inside.

"What you doin ere?" squidged a voice somewhere beneath Robert's waistline.

Robert looked down to see something brown and nasty staring back at him.

"Who are you?" said Robert.

"I'm the Guard Troll, ain't I?" said the Guard Troll. "Who arr you then?"

"I'm Robert Darkly. I'm an Agent, well, not a full Agent, I'm in training."

"'Course you is," said the Troll. "What you want then?"

"I'm here to see my father."

The Troll began to snicker in a guttural sort of way and then stopped abruptly. He squinted his dark little eyes at Robert and scratched a long fingernail across what was probably meant to be his chin.

"You're the one ee talks about all tha time. Always blabrin bout his boy."

"So he is here?"

"Oh aye! Couldn't tell at first, mind you. Bit dark out ere and yur muther no doubt muddied the waters, so t' speak. But no mistakin the resemble... the relsembla... the sim-lar-it-ies." The Troll stared at him. "Come wi me then."

Robert followed the Troll as he slouched his way across the courtyard, through the entrance, and into the Tower. The Troll took a right and headed down a long, wide hallway lined on either side with cell doors. Sinister, dark, and in certain cases, inhuman faces stared out from behind their bars. The ugly creature stopped at the last door on the left and hesitated.

"You sure you allowed t' be ere?" asked the Troll.

"Of course," said Robert calmly. "Why would I be here otherwise?"

"S'true," agreed the Troll, nodding to himself. "U gots a visitor!" shouted the Troll at the cell door and raked a long fingernail across its surface.

Robert heard bolts slide back and the door creaked open.

"Take yerself some light," said the Troll pointing to one of the candles mounted on the wall.

Robert took down the candle, took a deep breath, and entered the cell.

The door creaked closed behind him and the locks slid back into place.

The cell smelled funny, and as Robert turned, he felt a stab of sympathy for the inmates here.

"Whhoo arree yyouuu?" asked a voice from the dark.

"My name is Robert Darkly. I'm here looking for my father."

There was a quick intake of breath from the darkness and Robert swung the candle around to illuminate a thin, pale figure sitting perfectly still on a straw bed. His dark hair hung in dribs and drabs around his shoulders and his skin looked stretched across the bones of his face. His eyes were dark and he snapped his head up to look at Robert, who jumped. The man laughed hysterically and slapped his knees.

"Well, well, well. My son, my son."

"You're my father?"

The Hatter made a sad face. "Aww, you were expecting something grander, maybe? Sorry, sonny boy, what you see is what you get. Unless, of course, you're blind."

"Who… who are you?"

The Hatter sprang to his feet and in two strides had his arms around Robert in a hug.

Robert dropped the candle, instinctively broke the hug, and pushed the Hatter back. *I guess I did learn something in training.*

"Aww, no hugsy wugsy for daddy? Heartbreaker!" said the Hatter and giggled.

"Who are you?" said Robert again.

The Hatter bowed low. "My name is Marmaduke Ethel Seidfried Hatteracus but you, like all others, will know me better as the Mad Hatter."

Robert took a step back and retrieved his candle. "You're the Mad Hatter? My father, the Mad Hatter?" he said. "That actually makes a lot of sense."

"Not totally sane yourself, are you, my lad?" said the Hatter with a raised eyebrow.

"I wouldn't say I'm mad. I was hearing a voice for a while, but it turned out I just had a Cat in my head."

The Hatter stared at him blankly.

"I'm not mad," said Robert again.

"Well, I am, and here I am, and here you are." The Hatter sat cross-legged on the stone floor and looked up at Robert through sunken eyes. "I imagine you have questions, so please feel free to ask. It's the least I can do after missing every single birthday you've ever had."

Robert felt an intense discomfort being here. It wasn't the cell, it wasn't the stench, it wasn't even the thought that he'd probably get in trouble for being here. It was he: his father, sitting cross-legged on the floor like a kindergarten student waiting to be read a story.

"I had four questions. One was to ask who you are, but you've already answered that. Why did you send me the message through Rumpelstiltskin?"

The Hatter clapped his hands excitedly. "The answer to that question is the best and most glorious and it should be left until last. Ask me something else."

"Okay. I've been told a couple of times that I'm not human. As you can imagine, this comes as a bit of a shock. I also heard that you've lived an incredibly long life. So my question is; what are you?"

The Hatter made a sad face. "That's not a very interesting question Robert. I was hoping for something more creative." He sighed. "I am exactly what you see before you. Nothing more and nothing less and I'll always be this way."

"But how have you lived so long?"

"Because I can."

"That's it? That's your explanation?"

"If you want more interesting answers, then ask more interesting questions."

"All right. What happened to my mother?" The question had been bothering Robert ever since he'd been told that his mother had died during childbirth because of what his father had done to her.

The Hatter clapped his hands. "Much more interesting! Bravo, Robert. Bravo! Your mother never really understood me. But she constantly tortured me. She loved me, but then again, she couldn't stand me. She adored me but terrified me. She was beautiful and hideous all rolled into one. She was the love of my life and my darkest enemy. In the end, she did not want me." The Hatter looked at his hands lost in a memory. "But I still desired her, so I took her."

"You... you took her by force?" Robert forced the words out.

"Depends on your point of view," said the Mad Hatter, and Robert could feel the malice in the tiny cell.

"You're sick."

"And then, by hereditary inheritance, so are you. Maybe not now, maybe not tomorrow, could be years and years and years but mark my words, boy, you'll turn into me eventually."

"You're wrong. I'm my own person. I'm training to be an Agent."

The Hatter spit on the floor. "Agents! That ridiculous Agency and their rules. Look how easily their world would have collapsed if the Dwarf had succeeded with his plan."

"But he didn't. I stopped him. I stopped Rumpelstiltskin."

"And now you're going to become one of them." He spat again, this time closer to Robert. "Obviously, you're no son of mine."

"Under the circumstances, that doesn't sound like a bad option." Robert walked to the door and shouted for the Troll to let him out. He could hear the creature slapping along the stone floor somewhere down the hallway.

"Am comin! Am comin!"

Robert turned back to the cell and came face to face with the Hatter, who had moved silently from his sitting position. He smelled like the bottom of a hamster cage, and Robert had a slight gag reflex. The Hatter's eyes were wide and unblinking.

"Don't you want to know the answer to the ultimate question?"

"Would you mind backing up a little?" said Robert.

"Why did I send you a message through the Dwarf?"

"Anytime now would be good, Troll," said Robert, over his shoulder.

Another inmate seemed to be screaming, and Robert could hear the Troll trying to calm him/her/it down.

The Hatter leaned in and spoke quickly. "It's all about the blood, you see. Everything here runs on blood. Your blood, my blood, the blood of the White Rabbit. Everyone's blood!"

"It's a commodity," said Robert remembering the White Rabbit's words.

"Yes!" shouted the Hatter. "Priceless! And like any commodity, it can be traded. Working with the Dwarf was easy. He was such a twisted little soul that he just wanted the chance to get out, but it would have been impossible without Jack's help. He acted his part well, but then, he always did enjoy hitting me. That muscle-bound moron served as the perfect catalyst. So old and so bored, he jumped at the chance to cause some chaos and in doing so, he made the ultimate mistake. He entered into my world! My beautiful, pretty world of chaos."

"You're not making sense."

The Hatter gripped Robert's sweater. "I knew you'd come. All this, the Dwarf, Jack, the plan to ruin the doors! It was all for this moment, right now!"

Robert heard the Troll scratch his nail down the cell door and the locks slid away. The door cracked open.

"You wanted me to come here," said Robert as realization gripped him.

The door opened and the world fell to chaos. The Hatter smashed his forehead into Robert's nose, snatched the silver vial from around his neck, and bodily threw his son back into the cell.

"Whatz th—" began the Troll but was quickly silenced as the Hatter kicked him hard in the throat, throwing the creature back into the hallway. The Hatter leaped out of his cell and slammed the door behind him.

Robert threw himself at the door and pushed his face up the bars as the Hatter laughed uncontrollably. Blood trickled from Robert's nose and his head felt like it was splitting in two.

"What are you doing?" said Robert.

The Hatter kicked the Troll again. "It's a commodity, my son, a commodity. It all comes down to a simple trade. You for me and me for you. Enjoy your stay in the Tower, I'm sure we'll meet again one day. Hopefully, you'll have edged more toward madness by then. Ta ta!"

The realization flooded into Robert's mind. *This was why Rumpelstiltskin escaped. He thought he was supposed to finish his plan and open the doors for everyone, but that wasn't it at all. The Hatter just needed someone to deliver a message to me.* Everything else from then on just led him one step closer to the cell he was now occupying. His father had tricked everyone to get what he wanted. He'd moved people around like pawns and now he was free.

Robert wished he hadn't come here. He wished that Lily was here with him. He wished that his father was not the Mad Hatter; portrayed in the stories of Othaside as a fun, tea-party-throwing, crazy person but in reality, a sadistic, murderous psychopath.

The inmates were shouting and screaming, no doubt riled up by the Hatter's escape and the injury of the Troll. Robert couldn't take it anymore. He'd been tricked by a master trickster, he'd been offered a new life and now it was all at risk, along with his relationship with Lily. He banged on the door as his own blood dripped to the filthy floor, and as desperation overtook him, he began to cry.

The Hatter had dragged the Troll down the hallway, waving to inmates as he went, causing screams and shouts and pleas of freedom, all of which he happily acknowledged with a grin on his face and a hop in his step. His gaunt figure was almost stick-like and his face, cracked by his massive grin, looked ghastly and unnatural.

It took only a few minutes for the Troll to tell the Hatter what he wanted to know and where in the Tower he could find it.

Twenty minutes later, the Mad Hatter stepped out into the courtyard dressed in a dark blue suit complete with ruffles and lace. In one hand, he held a cane, and in the other, a black top hat, which he placed precariously atop his narrow head. Robert's silver chain with the Rabbit's blood dangled around his scrawny neck. He'd left the Troll spluttering for breath and choking on his own blood after the Hatter had slit the little creature's throat back in the hallway.

His plan had worked. The very essence of chaos began with the tiniest of actions. The slightest of movements. He'd only had to make a suggestion to Jack and the events were set in motion to bring Robert to the Tower. His son had not disappointed him.

The Hatter strode across the courtyard and emerged from the gateway at the foot of the long cobblestone bridge.

"The moment of truth," said the Hatter to no one in particular. Blood was the most powerful commodity in Thiside and if he was right, his son had just taken his place as a permanent resident of the Tower. The Hatter closed his eyes and took one long step onto the bridge.

Nothing happened. Lightning flashed overhead and thunder rolled.

He opened one eye to find that the moat creatures had not moved. He took another step, and could see one of the enormous monsters roll itself over just beneath the surface of the water. He stepped again, and again, and again. He then jumped up and down on the bridge. He skipped from one side of the bridge to the other.

He burst into the sort of laughter that only a mad man can make.

Over the sound of rolling thunder, over the Hatter's laughter, over the screeching of the witch in the Tower, over the shrieking of the various inmates, only one thing rang out louder than any other: the desperate screams of Robert Darkly.

The Mad Hatter; prisoner, father, trickster, murderer, and now one of the most dangerous people in Thiside, tipped his hat to one side and danced his way across the bridge away from the Tower.

...and no one lived happily ever after...

THE END (SORT OF)

A TASTE OF...

Prologue.

The gentleman stepped up to the podium and straightened his tie. He looked out at the several hundred students whose eyes all rested upon the gentleman's athletic build. An athletic build he was quite proud of, at that. He was a renowned gentleman, scholar, professional assumptionist and part-time religious expert. His theories and social experiments were famous the world over, and as a result, he was invited to the best parties and most prestigious events. He was happy. New theories were getting harder to come up with, and it had been at least a year and a half since his last lecture at Oxford University, but here he stood, once again on the brink of high expectations, with not one but three new theories to present.

The students were honored to have him as a guest speaker, and the other professors had waited for this lecture for several months, many of them having abandoned their families, moved across the country, and re-shuffled their schedules to make time to listen to what was expected to be a world-shaking lecture. Members of the national and international press arrived two hours earlier to get the pre-lecture buzz from the students and faculty. Things like *profoundly excited* and *would trade my left testicle to see that man speak* were uttered.

The auditorium sat in silence, poised on the edge of their seats, notebooks at the ready, recording devices fully loaded, their studious brains humming, fully prepared to be inspired.

The gentleman shuffled his notes and got right to the point.

"Ladies and gentlemen," he said, "I realize that I need no introduction and so, I will get right to the point."

Several students quickly wrote that down in case there was some hidden meaning to be uncovered later.

"Today, I have three new theories for you and they will be presented here for the first time."

Thunderous applause roared throughout the auditorium. Several people lucky enough to get a seat stood up and applauded harder.

The gentleman breathed in his last breath of true success.

"My first is a modern proposal of sorts; at first glance it may seem absurd, but as we all know, first impressions can be deceiving."

A few respectful chuckles arose from the audience.

"I believe that this modern proposal will benefit the world if taken seriously and pondered to the utmost." The gentleman cleared his throat, shuffled his papers once more, and launched into it with hasty abandon. "I present to you A Proposal for Global Public Nudity!"

When expectations had been so high that people reorganized their entire lives in the fond hope that their anticipations would be more than met, it came as quite a disappointment when not only were those not met. But instead, those expectations were drugged, tied, gagged, placed in a bag, driven out to the middle of God knows where, and buried in a twenty-foot-deep hole which was then covered with concrete.

Almost everyone in the room stopped breathing, and only a few people remembered to blink.

The gentleman mistook the looks of shock and awe as surprise and delight and continued enthusiastically.

"Firstly, designer labels and fashion have ruled our lives for long enough. The re-introduction of the tube-top should have been a clear signal that the industry can now manipulate us to wear whatever they feel is necessary for daily living. And furthermore, can charge whatever ludicrous prices they deem suitable. How many girls have come home from school crying because their best friend has the new designer label? It is a ploy. A well-thought-out ploy to separate us from our hard-earned wage. If we instigate global nudity, then the war over who is cool and who is not according to fashion becomes obsolete. No one needs to buy *skin*. We are all born with it; it's waterproof, durable, and available in a wide range of colours."

No one wrote anything down; everyone had enough trouble concentrating as the once renowned gentleman on stage quickly and carefully fed his career to the sharks.

"How many people hide their true self and figure behind the many shades of fabric that hang in the millions of department stores around the world? Like the army, that is mere camouflage. Fat people pretend to be thin. Females with a self-perception of less-than-adequate bosoms dress themselves up to appear a little more well-endowed than they actually are. Thin, ugly, small, repellent males are simply handed the ability to cover their true selves with designer shoes, shirts, pants, and so on, only to be later discovered by some poor unsuspecting female, or male, that he is less than he appears. The inhibitions that have clouded the minds of the general populace for so long would be stripped down to reveal the truth, and only the truth.

"What follows is a short list of some of the absolute advantages of Global Public Nudity.

"Parents will no longer have to endure the hassle of teaching their children the delicate art of tying their shoelaces. There will be no shoelaces to tie.

"Breastfeeding will become a communally shared experience, much like asking for directions or helping an elderly lady across the busy street. There will always be a wide number of *portable milk outlets* available, especially in busy places like malls or Starbucks.

"Global public nudity holds a great deal of advantages for men, also. No longer will a suffering male have to wait for a celibate fiancée to display the goods. *Playboy* will become a thing of the past, therefore cutting down on the clutter of magazines that shroud the bathrooms of many homes.

"The ever-present zipper problem will be abolished, as there will no longer be a vicious cutting device hanging around the groin section of the male body. But the greatest advantage to males will be the decrease in time that taken for women to get ready for work, a date, dinner, a movie, etc., etc.

"There will be a sharp decrease in the amount of emotional stress caused by elderly people exposing themselves in public places. The act of exposing oneself will no longer be an issue, as everyone will be totally stark naked.

"In conclusion, I realize that some of these points may initially appear as nothing more than barefaced cheek, an insult to society. But I assure you, these points are logical and viable and would instantly solve many of the problems that plague the world as we know it today. So I propose that we *strip* away our inhibitions and bare to the world our true selves," he finished with a flourish.

There was no applause, no standing ovation. If the university had allowed crickets to be present at the lecture, they would have been the only sound heard.

The gentleman mistook the looks of pity and disappointment as eager interest and spellbound curiosity, and so he quickly launched into his second theory, which involved aliens not only building the pyramids, but also inventing the mango chutney-curried chicken-mayo-dried cranberry sandwich. He managed to get through the majority of the theory before the Oxford security guards intervened. The mango chutney-curried chicken-mayo-dried cranberry sandwich theory was the last nail in the coffin of his career. As the security guards dragged the gentleman off stage, his last words were, "No, wait, I also have a theory about the devil, the dead not dying, Santa Claus, his elves, and a penguin!"

But no one heard him. They were all too busy laughing.

In many ways, he was wrong. Global public nudity would be amusing, somewhat entertaining, and probably really disgusting, not to mention completely absurd. Aliens did not build the pyramids. Slaves built the pyramids while under the overpowering influence of large men holding even larger whips. But on certain points he was absolutely correct. Had anyone bothered to listen to his theory about the devil, the dead not dying, Santa Claus, his elves, and a penguin, they would have eventually found out that he was right on the money.

One.

There were deals, and then there were deals. And this was a deal. The signature sat, burning comfortably, on the dotted line. Then, while the Prince of Darkness gleefully packed his clothes, the document was on its way to the administration office via the Underworld Postal System for filing. He didn't really like the demons in the administration office; they were low even by his standards.

Decisions, decisions. Whether to take the blue underwear or the orange?

It had been so long since he'd been allowed to get away from it all and really commit to some good old-fashioned deceiving. And to walk on the Earth again, that would be truly fabulous. The last time he'd possessed a body must have been at least three thousand years ago. Reflectively, though, he really hadn't had the best of luck with possessing people.

He shuddered as he packed his knitted doilies and remembered the whole Adam and Eve fiasco. That had been his first real possession. He'd been aiming for Eve but missed by a few feet and ended up in that stupid snake. He'd had to slither round for a good few hours before he got the hang of how to move, and then had to deal with the constant compulsion to eat eggs. It almost wasn't worth the hassle. Everything turned out okay in the end, introducing sin to the Earth and all, but he'd found the whole episode a rather trying ordeal.

No matter how many times he steeped in a bubble bath, it still took him weeks to shake that slimy, scaly feeling.

The Devil looked in a mirror and stared at the grim, distorted figure before him. *Sad. I really have to start getting more sleep.* Maybe he'd take up a relaxation program when he got back from the Earth, something to

245

improve his quality of life. Tai Chi: that's what he'd do. He'd go down to the dungeons and find some ancient Chinese souls who could teach him Tai Chi. After he'd tortured them for a while.

I'm forgetting something. The Devil picked up his going-away checklist and a pen.

-Pack clothes... check!

-Clean bathroom... check!

-Turn off coffee maker... check!

-Send Deal made with God stating Devil may walk the Earth for One Week document down to the administration department... check!

-Give bone-chilling speech to the new arrivals... check!

-Leave instructions with one of the demons on how to feed the fish...

That's it. He'd forgotten about his fish, Percy. The Devil walked out of his apartment onto the high rocky precipice that served as a sort of porch and looked down at his rather overly warm kingdom.

Demons wandered hither and thither, dragging tortured souls around with them. The Devil grimaced; it was so hot down here, and it wasn't even a nice dry heat, the humidity was unbearable. Soon enough, he'd be able to breathe the lovely fresh air that the human race so easily took for granted. The thought cooled him ever so slightly, and a small cloud of steam rose from his body. He stretched out his black, tattered, leathery wings and shouted out over the cavernous kingdom, his dark voice bouncing off the jagged rocks.

"Listen to me, all you inhabitants of Hell. For those of you who are new, there will be a public flaying of lawyers at six tonight. Make sure you bring something for the potluck dinner or you will not be allowed to enjoy the festivities. And if anyone's seen Azeal, could they please tell him I'd like to see him immediately in my quarters? That is all!"

The Devil re-folded his wings and stalked back into his home. He playfully tapped on the fishbowl where Percy the goldfish swam happily around without a care in the world, except that he could never understand why his water always stayed so warm.

There came a sharp rap at the door, to which the door grimly responded by swinging open to reveal a short, stumpy, egg-shaped demon with only one leg and half a wing. Even his horns looked like something created by using a toilet paper roll and lots of sticky tape. His yellowy-green eyes darted suspiciously around the room.

"Ahh, Azeal, do come in," motioned the Devil as he made kissy faces at Percy, who felt somewhat confused as to why this large, ugly, black mass kept making faces at him.

Azeal hopped in, started to lose his balance, flapped furiously with his half a wing in order to straighten himself and then proceeded to fall over. The Devil shook his head sadly and made a *tsk tsk* kind of sound with his forked tongue.

"I really have no idea how you ever survived through the Crusades. Maybe survived is a bit of a strong word. You did lose your leg and the vast majority of your wingspan."

Azeal, not possessing the ability to speak, simply made a rude noise and pushed himself back up on his one leg.

"Now listen carefully, Azeal. Percy is very special to me, and if you should accidentally kill him, I'll have you flogged 'til the rest of your wing falls off. Understood?"

Azeal burped loudly and grinned a maliciously stupid grin.

The Devil rolled his eyes.

"His feeding instructions are next to his bowl, along with his food. I'll be back in a week. If any pressing matters arise, the Second Coming, that kind of thing, you'll be able to reach me on my cell. Got it?"

Azeal farted and left it at that.

"Good," said the Devil. It suddenly became very clear to him that the clock on the wall was trying to tell him something.

"Oh my, is that the time? I'll be late." And with a great flapping of wings he ranout the door, knocking Azeal over in the process. The Devil popped his head back through the doorway.

"Azeal, did I mention that I'd have you flogged if you messed up?"

Azeal jumped to his foot and bounced up and down a couple of times while making distressed choking noises.

"Good." The Devil grabbed his suitcase and took off at a sprint.

The Gates of Hell looked dark as ever as the Devil ran up to them. The excitement was really getting to him and he could hardly stop himself hopping from one foot to the other.

One of the two large guards at the gates of Hell stepped up to the Devil.

"Pass, please."

"What?" said the Devil, brimming over with disbelief.

"I said pass, please. Bit deaf, are you?" replied the guard.

Fire began to burn in the Devil's eyes. "Do you know who I am?"

The other guard suddenly came running forward and pushed the first guard back. "I'm so sorry, boss," said the second demon guard. "You see, that's Stan, he's new here. Won't happen again."

The Devil raised himself up to his full height and spread his wings in a terrifying arc. Then he folded them up again and burst out in a fit of laughter.

"I really can't be mad at you today. Going to Earth, you see, approved by God Himself. Ha! Idiot. Do be a good boy and let me out."

The two demons pulled open the unbelievably large, iron gates to reveal a long line of people waiting to get in. Part of Hell's policy clearly stated that everyone had to stand in line for at least five years before entering.

These pitiful fools, and they thought standing in line at the supermarket was bad. The Devil grinned an evil grin and sprinted off toward the end of the line, which disappeared into a set of double doors marked with a large pink neon sign that said *Exit.* And then underneath, in smaller, less bright neon letters: *Fat chance.*

The Devil ran through the doors without a care for the poor dead people on either side of him.

"Move it, coming through, get out of the way you insolent fools!"

The way out of Hell was a little more difficult than getting in. Getting in required that a person be ignorant, redundant, or evil, and preferably dead, or so unbelievably cursed by God that there wouldn't ever be a chance of being redeemed. The Devil's situation was that of the latter. But by the recent agreement with God Himself, the Devil had been granted a temporary pass to get out of the Fiery Inferno and walk around for a whole week. During which he would wreak unspeakable havoc and attempt to add to the growing line of people waiting to get into Hell.

The passage into the world consisted of a long, dark tunnel that stretched endlessly up into seemingly nothingness. People generally fell down the tunnel. It was an extremely rare occasion that anyone went back up it. However, the Devil had done this before; he knew the drill.

He unfurled his dark wings and prepared for the flight up. Oh, he couldn't wait to see the body he would possess. He'd had a nice one picked out for quite a while now, a reclusive millionaire, young and healthy. The contract stated that he would have to inhabit a body the moment he reached the Earth, and the Devil knew it was just a matter of throwing himself into the right person. He flapped his wings, kicking up dust and debris, focused, then prepared for takeoff. He was pumped. He was ready. And so it came as a complete surprise at that point when a three-hundred-pound man in a white vest and boxer shorts with little hearts on them fell from the tunnel above and landed on the Devil's face.

The fat gentleman got to his feet. "Bloody hell! Where am I?"

The Devil arose from the ground and folded his arms.

"Well, you're dead, aren't you? And I'm assuming that in life you were somewhat of an asshole and consequently, here you are. Torture for eternity," the Devil pointed a long, bony finger toward the end of the line, "that way!"

The fat man, somewhat confused, replied, "Uhh, yeah, thanks," and waddled off toward the line.

The Devil shook his head, unfurled his wings once again, and with a great big flap worthy of an American Bald Eagle, flew up the portal. Everything always went a bit blurry around this part; going from one reality to the next was never easy. It always gave him the kind of feeling that his insides were turning outside. The Devil loved the feeling. And as he rose higher and higher, going faster and faster, heading for the end of the tunnel, he smiled at how easy he'd found it to strike such a simple deal that would allow him to take human form and destroy lives.

The end of the tunnel was nigh as he rushed toward a bright blue light. Then, nothing but frantic oblivion. All was dark.

The Devil opened his eyes and took a deep breath. *Ahh, fresh air.* It would appear he was on the floor. He tried to stand up but, as he did so, he didn't really move all that much higher. What was the problem here? His surroundings were simple: a couch, a TV, a lovely coffee table with some fine bone china.

The Devil stretched as his senses came into play.

A door opened off to his side and a pair of legs in badly wrinkled stockings appeared and dropped a plate of food in front of him.

The Devil looked down at the plate of brown mush and then up to see a little old lady grinning down at him.

She opened her mouth and cooed.

"Aww, who's a cute puddycat, Fuzzbucket?"

The Devil mustered all his strength and cried, "What?"

What actually came out was *meow*.

I don't believe it. I'm in a cat! How the hell did I end up in a cat?

The Devil didn't know what to do. The Devil, the Prince of Darkness, Beelzebub, the Deceiver himself, trapped in a cat for an entire week. And not just any cat: a cat called Fuzzbucket. He suddenly had a strong urge to systematically clean himself, and being in complete shock and not knowing what else to do, went ahead and did so.

Down in the depths of Hell's Administration office, a lowly demon examined the contract she'd just received to file. She made a *tsk tsk* sort of noise and shook her head as she read the fine print through a magnifying glass.

Please Note: If by any chance the above noted chosen body is unavailable due to death, dismemberment, or divine intervention, the party of the second part (being Lucifer, the Prince of Darkness) will waive all possession rights and will be deposited into a body of the party of the first part's (being God) choosing.

The demon lifted a large metal stamp and branded the word *received* into the contract with a satisfying *hisssss*.

The evening air was close and the heat, relentless. It beat at every passerby in the small town of Obidos, located somewhere in the west of Portugal.

Sweat escaped from every available pore on the body of Raymond Miller as he wandered down tight, quaint streets.

He loved Obidos at this time of year. Not so much for the heat, as no one really loved the town for its heat. But because Obidos was so quiet, hardly anyone around, no tourists, just the locals. The locals left him alone; they didn't like the strange visitor who appeared out of nowhere for a few weeks every year and then vanished without a trace. It became a favorite pastime of the locals to stand completely still with a fixed frown whenever Raymond would appear on the street. They would watch him walk down the street, moving only their heads until he disappeared into a shop or around a corner. Shopkeepers wouldn't talk to him except to tell him how much he owed them. They would answer any pleasantries or questions with a severe *umph*, all the time frowning like their lives depended on it.

They didn't like Raymond because he didn't follow the tourist trend. He always turned up out of season, and he kept himself to himself, not to mention he'd built a ghastly, great big mansion on the outskirts of town.

Raymond was in fact a billionaire who had quite methodically worked out when the off-season occurred for every beautiful place on Earth. He would travel round all year to these places, then build a house where he could stay for a couple of weeks, and that was his life, day in and day out. All he ever wanted was a quiet life, and when his one-hundred-fourteen-year-old grandmother died, she left Raymond, her only living relative, all her money. Although on the surface a quiet and very innocent-looking lady, she had made her money by running drugs from the United States to Japan. She was a little old lady with too much time on her hands, and she liked traveling to the Orient. Or that's what all the security people at the airports thought as they helped her off the plane and even carried her drug-filled luggage for her. Her drug-running name was *Silent Grasshopper.* Raymond had no knowledge of this, as she told him that she won all her money on the lottery, and so he remained blissfully unaware.

Raymond had been an Olympic swimmer before the inheritance, and although he remained in good physical condition, he no longer swam. When he got the money from his grandmother, he decided to follow up on his high school dream to do absolutely nothing. He traveled around the world, spending the vast amount of money he'd acquired. He partied occasionally, hired women to satisfy his carnal pleasures, hired people to cook for him, but really did nothing of any importance. If he vanished off the face of the Earth, the only person who would miss him would be his bank manager, who talked to him every few days and who could have been considered to be Raymond's only friend.

As Raymond walked out onto the bridge that crossed the local river, he stopped and admired the sunset. He could see a couple of children playing soccer at the other end of the bridge, a little too close to the road, he thought. There really wasn't that much traffic in the town, so there was probably nothing to worry about. At least, that's what Raymond thought right up until he saw the bus.

The bus driver's name was Dante and he was on the last route of the evening. He was, however, currently preoccupied with the sudden appearance of what appeared to be an orange object descending from the sky. Dante was so enamored with the strange object that he failed to see the young boy who ran out into the road after his run-away ball.

Raymond started sprinting before he even knew why. The urge hit him in the form of one simple word that felt very strangely as if someone had spoken it directly into his head. *Run!*

Everything happened very quickly. Raymond reached the boy just in time to push him out of the way; he looked up at the last minute to see an orange swirly thing plummeting toward him.

The orange swirly thing, consequently, was the last thing Raymond Miller saw in his life, as a millisecond later he was hit by the bus that killed him.

Moments later, the soul of Raymond Miller came face to face with a disgruntled-looking man dressed in a black robe standing next to a large neon sign that pointed *up*.

WANT MORE? MORE? MORE?!

WELL, SAY NO MORE, FRIEND!

AVAILABLE WHEREVER WORKS OF GENIUS ARE SOLD

Andrew Buckley

ACKNOWLEDGEMENTS

A various amount of blood, sweat, tears, and a number of other fluids (including Mountain Dew… shameless product placement, send money) went into writing this book.

Most of all I want to thank my family for being supportive of my insane writing endeavors, especially my wife who is, above all else, a constant inspiration to me.

I'd also like to thank Ricky Gunawan for his amazing cover art, Lisa and Eugene at Curiosity Quills Press for continuing to accept bribes in order to publish my work, and my amazing editor, Mary Harris.

Without Mary, every single word in this book would be in a different order, separated by a comma, and preceded by an inappropriately placed ellipsis…

THANK YOU FOR READING

Curiosity Quills Press
http://curiosityquills.com

Please visit http://curiosityquills.com/reader-survey/ to share your reading experience with the author of this book!

ABOUT THE AUTHOR

Andrew Buckley (born 1980 in Lees, Manchester, UK) is a contemporary Canadian novelist (an author of satirical fiction), marketing professional, freelance writer, and podcaster.

Buckley attended the Vancouver Film School's Writing for Film & Television program where he graduated with Excellence. After pitching and developing several screenplay projects for film and television he worked in marketing and public relations for several years before venturing into a number of content writing contracts. During this time he abandoned screenwriting altogether and began writing his first novel, *Death, the Devil, and the Goldfish*, which was published in December 2012 by Curiosity Quills Press.

Andrew lives in the Okanagan Valley, BC with his wife, 3 children, two evil cats, and a very needy dog. Fueled only by Pop Tarts and Tetley Tea he spends his time writing, working, and podcasting for more hours than are actually contained in a day.

Death, the Devil, and the Goldfish, by Andrew Buckley

From the Bahamas to Heathrow airport, to the rain soaked streets of London the dead have ceased dying. This is inconvenient for a number of reasons but what's the real reason behind the chaos?

In London we find Nigel Reinhardt to be a disgraced, confused, and gifted London police constable who owns a prophetic goldfish. When the Devil hatches a nefarious plot to take over the world by possessing a cute little kitty and seizing a factory of robotic Christmas elves, it's up to Nigel and a group of unlikely companions to save the world or die trying... or both.

Quite Contrary, by Richard Roberts

The secret of having an adventure is getting lost. Well, Mary is lost. She is lost in the story of Little Red Riding Hood, and that is a cruel story. She's put on the red hood and met the Wolf. When she gives in to her Wolf's temptations, she will die. That's how the story goes, after all.

Unfortunately for the story—and the Wolf—this Little Red Riding Hood is Mary Stuart, and she is the most stubborn and contrary twelve year old the world has ever known. Forget the Wolf's temptations, forget the advice of the talking rat trying to save her, she will kick her way through every myth and fairy tale ever told until she finds a way to get out of this alive.

257

The Last Condo Board of the Apocalypse, by Nina Post

Kelly Driscoll tracks down monsters for a living, but the job isn't what it used to be. When a reclusive client hires her to locate a rival angel, Kelly's search takes her to a downtown highrise that has become home to hundreds of fallen angels and dimension-hopping monsters.

As the fallen angels take over the condo board, argue over who's handling pizza delivery, and begin planning for a little shindig otherwise known as the apocalypse, Kelly must team up with an unlikely group of allies to find her target and keep the fallen angels at bay.

Sharcano, by Jose Prendes

A half-eaten megalodon shark corpse is found beached. A priest commits suicide. A previously unknown volcano rises from the China Sea and brings about a tsunami that destroys Shanghai. Yellowstone erupts after 640,000 years of silence. A pit in Nicaragua known as the "mouth of hell" begins violently erupting.

When Reporter Mick Cathcart and Marine Biologist Agnes Brach set out looking for answers, they never expected to stumble upon the biblical end times. Yet with sharks made of lava shooting from volcanoes to devour anyone in their way, how could anyone deny it?

CPSIA information can be obtained at www.ICGtesting.com
Printed in the USA
LVOW06s1804060114

368308LV00007B/1148/P